A SPACE BETWEEN

R.S. Haspiel

authorHOUSE®

AuthorHouse™
1663 Liberty Drive
Bloomington, IN 47403
www.authorhouse.com
Phone: 1 (800) 839-8640

Published by AuthorHouse 06/21/2018

ISBN: 978-1-5462-4581-0 (sc)
ISBN: 978-1-5462-4582-7 (hc)
ISBN: 978-1-5462-4580-3 (e)

Library of Congress Control Number: 2018906626

Print information available on the last page.

To Rosemary, Lou and Marie who all had faith in me and knew that one day my stories would be published.

Contents

Jumpgate

Some reckon time by stars
And some by hours;
Some measure days by dreams,
And some by flowers;
My heart alone records
My days and hours.

Madison Julius Cawein
1865-1914

The orange and yellow pastel hues of dusk reflected off the silver orb as it floated towards the figure in the courtyard. It descended slowly then stopped at eye level in front of the shadowed figure. As the orb began to glow the light highlighted the figure of a young woman. She reached out and began to gently caressed the orb. As the sound of helicopters drew closer the orb pulled away and ascended towards a bright star. The young woman's eyes filled with tears as the light from the helicopter bathed her in bright light. She shielded her eyes and wished she had more time. She wished she was not so alone.

CHAPTER 1

Night after night the dreams would come, varied in action and scenery but with the same intensity and central character. A young woman who was well formed like that of a supple willow battled medieval figures with the confidence and agility of a tiger. Evelyn thought this was an indication of what she wanted to be....a strong, attractive woman of action. Even though she had brown hair and her character had black maybe that too was an indication. Maybe she yearned for something different. But why the same dreams night after night? She turned on the tv. Maybe that would help her sleep soundly. She flipped channels in hopes of finding something calming. Ivanhoe, Robin Hood and a talk show on gender benders was not what she had in mind. If the two movies hadn't just started she would have thought these had fueled her dreams. She turned off the tv and picked up her current romance novel and crawled back into bed. Reading of 'Simons throbbing passion' lulled her back to sleep.

Her morning at work was uneventful except for Dan's invitation to dinner which she accepted eagerly. Her tour of the Emergency Room was the usual auto accidents and gang fights. Dan was to pick her up at 7:00 p.m. She figured she had enough time working the 7-3 shift to grocery shop and do her hair.

Dan arrived on time and brought her flowers. Dan was far from her idea of a perfect mate but he was charming, sweet and fairly satisfying in bed. He was working out at the gym and constantly wanted to show her his newly muscled form. As usual their dinner was a swirl of color and taste. They both loved to eat and cook and tonight was Evelyn's turn. They made a list of all the restaurants they ate in and wrote down their

3

favorite food. Then they would attempt to recreate it at home. They had been seeing each other for 4 months and had nearly completed the list.

Evelyn asked Dan if he wanted a night cap and of course he said yes. Dan made himself comfortable on her couch while she ground some coffee. Once the coffee pot was set she sat down next to him as he gently kissed her.

"I can stay the night if you like?" He whispered in her ear as he touched the nape of her neck with his tongue.

She consented as the coffee pot beeped. He undressed her this time as their lovemaking began. But tonight, Evelyn could not focus on Dan's attentions. Her familiar dreams came back to her while Dan took her body. She closed her eyes and envisioned a tattoo of crossed swords and a dragon shield on the arm of a young woman. Over and over the vision of this woman lying across the grass, her face pale and body covered with blood haunted Evelyn. She opened her eyes and gasped for air. Dan was mounted over her satisfied of a job well done. He rolled over and drifted off to sleep. Evelyn wiped her eyes realizing now that they were covered with tears. The phone rang and caused her to bolt upright. She answered hesitantly.

"Eve sweetie, this is Norma. Is it at all possible for you to come in tonight? We're short staffed. Someone fucked up the scheduling again." Evelyn was sure if she fell asleep she would see the vision of the young woman again.

"Yes. I'll be there in half an hour." She didn't wait for a response of gratitude. She looked at her watch....11:30 p.m. She wrote Dan a short note, showered and dressed.

As Evelyn clocked in, the ER was crackling with life. Three accidents, two shootings and a stabbing, and it wasn't even a full moon.

"Nurse Blakley to room 1."

She quickened her pace. She was needed in room one with a motorcycle accident. As she entered the room she began to perform her usual functions responding to the doctor's orders and requests.

The attending nurse seemed agitated. "Damn cops and their high-speed pursuits. Apparently ran into this woman on a motorcycle. Rescue 4 saw the whole thing as they were responding to another call. She's lucky she was wearing this leather suit and her helmet. They had her halfway out of it when the other nurse came in to check with the doctor on another patient."

"She's stable Eve. Let's get her down to X-ray. I'll check on our local fuzz in 3."

As Evelyn filled out the paperwork she looked at the young woman lying beneath the sheets. Something familiar caught her eye. She lifted up the sheet on the right side.

"Evelyn, don't forget your gloves," the young intern reminded Evelyn.

She put on the latex gloves, grabbed some cotton and distilled water. She gently wiped the blood away from the strange bit of color on the woman's right arm. Evelyn stopped as she held her forehead with the back of her gloved hand.

"Good G-d!" she uttered.

"What's wrong Evelyn?"

"The tattoo..."

The young intern looked at the tattoo. "Yeah isn't that something. That's what I call a tattoo. Even my boyfriend doesn't have one like that. It's really different."

Evelyn now forced herself to look at the face of the young woman. She took her chin and gently turned the woman's face towards hers. The woman was still unconscious. Her face was pale. It was the same woman from her dreams.

"X-ray is ready for her."

Evelyn shook herself. She removed her gloves and walked out of the room. She looked at the paperwork when the young nurse came to the main desk.

NAME: Marlena Taggert AGE: 32
ADDRESS: 1278 Montgomery Loop Road
MARITAL STATUS: single
NO NEXT OF KIN NOTED

She saw this woman in her dreams. She knew of the accident as it happened. She needed to talk to someone. She would wait till this morning to see Dr. Jahule. For now, she would attend to her duties in the ER.

Evelyn looked at her watch: 9:00 a.m. She walked down to the main floor to a tiny corridor. The name on the door read: Dr. Sahara Jahule Psychiatrist. She knocked once before entering. Dr. Jahule always reminded Evelyn of an exotic Egyptian queen in a suit and tie.

"Evelyn what brings you here so early in the morning?"

"I worked the 12:00 to 7:00 shift this morning so I'm off for a couple of days."

Dr. Jahule stood and directed Evelyn to a chair. Both women sat down.

"So.....would you like some coffee?"

"Yes, thank you."

Dr. Jahule could see that Evelyn was upset about something. She got to know Evelyn when she was working with some long-term cancer patients whom Evelyn had known and cared for.

"Do you believe in premonitions, doctor?"

Dr. Jahule handed her a cup of coffee as she sat down in front of Evelyn. She smiled slightly at Evelyn's question.

"Well, I think we have senses that we normally don't use in day to day living. Sometimes something happens which causes us to use that undeveloped...sixth sense as it were. Sort of like a protection or warning device. Tell me what happened."

Evelyn unfolded the events of her dreams day by day and night by night. Dr. Jahule sat back in her chair. Evelyn had finished her account.

"Were the tattoos on your body or hers?"

Evelyn sipped her now lukewarm coffee. "It was just one tattoo and it was on HER arm not mine."

"And you say you've never seen her before last night."

Evelyn bowed her head as she answered no.

"I think we should schedule another appointment to discuss your feelings on this. Is that okay?"

Evelyn shook her head as she spoke, "Do you think I'm losing it?"

Dr. Jahule smiled. "Never answer a question with a question. But if by 'IT' you mean your mind, no I do not think so. I'm going to look into a couple of things and I'll look forward to seeing you tomorrow at shall we say..... 2:00?"

Evelyn nodded in agreement. She seemed calmer at telling her story to the doctor.

She walked back up to the first floor. She checked the charts from the mornings emergencies. She paused at the 3rd page......Room 314. She walked to the elevator thinking that maybe this would end the haunting visions she was having during her sleep. She was confronting her dream.

The shades were drawn in the room and the only light was from that of a small night light placed next to the nurses call switch. She walked up to the bed rail and for the first time since she had seen the woman she did not have any image of her other than the one she saw before her. The woman was asleep.

Evelyn looked at her chart at the end of the bed. The extent of her injuries seemed minor compared to what she looked like that night in emergency. A torn ligament in her left ankle and a displaced shoulder bone were the only major injuries indicated. Although there were an unusual number of tests being performed for so little injuries. But Evelyn had never really followed a patient's progress this closely after their visit to the ER. The woman, Marlena, was sedated and would be awakened practically every hour to have tests run.

Evelyn went back to the side of the bed. The young woman's eyes opened slightly. Evelyn held the rails of the bed to steady herself. The woman's deep almost Azure blue eyes met Evelyn's. Maybe the woman would recognize Evelyn and that would help clear some of the mystery. The woman was trying to say something. Evelyn knew the familiar words.....water.

She reached over for the cup of water and looked around for a straw but couldn't find one. She raised the head portion of the bed and lowered the safety rail. She held the cup of water to the woman's lips. Two sips were taken. Her lips mouthed a thank you but her voice was still too weak.

"You're going to be all right. Just rest now."

Once again, the woman fell back to sleep. Evelyn put the bedrail back up, made a notation on the chart and then left the room.

Evelyn's days passed quietly while she kept true to her appointments with Dr. Jahule. With certain revelations made in therapy, she decided to see Dan less. Since their last date was a bit traumatic for her she was not eager to jump into it again. Although that night had not been discussed in great detail Evelyn was slowly realizing that she did have some control over what she did. She was learning to become in tune with her subconscious. Dr. Jahule had her doing breathing exercises in addition to relaxing her body. Every day she spent an hour tuning out the surrounding world and tuning in to whatever came into her mind. It was difficult at first but as she learned how to block out sounds it became easier.

Among her daily duties she would check the main desk chart on the woman called Marlena Taggart. She kept tabs on her through other nurses and physicians but refused to see her. Her dreams at night had become more peaceful in nature and visions of Marlena had all but disappeared. The Easter Holidays were coming closer and as with most holiday's the emergency room was more hectic than usual. Trauma units were backed up and the blood bank was on alert due to the low supplies. She had to pull double shifts and by the time the week was over she realized she had missed the holiday completely. She even missed Marlena Taggart's check-out. She breathed a sigh of relief at having several days off after the holidays. She would go home now, rest and think about where she wanted to go on her mini-vacation.

After her frozen dinner she watched the news and picked up the new spy novel she had just bought. She thought it was about time she broadened her horizons and intellect with something other than a tawdry romance novel. She drifted off to sleep as the terrorists entered some building on tv.

She tossed and turned as she entered a clearing in the woods. Two knights were fighting. She watched as the sparks flew from the swords each time they met each other. Suddenly one knight turned and grabbed Evelyn holding her fast within his grip. He placed his sword across her throat and turned towards the other knight. Evelyn's heart was pounding as she felt the cold steel against her skin. The other knight advanced one step, sword in hand. The sword pressed deeper against her skin till it nicked it and drew blood. The other knight stopped and placed his sword on the ground in front of him. She felt the pressure go as her captor threw her to the ground and lunged for the other knight. His sword found its mark and went clear through the defenseless knight. The knight fell without a sound. Her captor disappeared into the forest brush. She carefully crawled over to the fallen knight. She reached out to feel the cold armor. She reached up to remove the knights helmet but the wounded knight raised his hands and prevented her from doing so. The gloved hands reached up to hold hers. Slowly they released their grip and fell to the sides of the knight. She reached up again hesitating. She had the feeling the knight did not want her to remove the helmet. Perhaps she would find a hideous face behind the mask. She pulled slowly on the helmet. A cascade of raven hair fell from beneath the helmet. As Evelyn stared at the all too familiar face she felt tears rolling off her cheek. Marlena Taggart was back in her dreams.

She bolted upright and quickly pulled the covers away from her body. She stumbled to the bathroom and turned on the lights. She splashed cold water on her face and looked into the vanity mirror at the terrified face staring back at her. She turned slightly as she noticed a small 1-inch scar across a small area of her neck. She stared at it then gently touched it. She didn't remember any scar nor how she got it. It was a dream....it wasn't real. She must have scratched herself whilst she was dreaming. She looked at the clock. It read 6:15 A.M. She showered and then dressed in blue jeans, tank top and sneakers. It was the beginning of her small vacation and she was not about to let some dream turned nightmare spoil it. She grabbed her camera and decided to go to the zoo.

CHAPTER 2

It was a beautifully cool, clear day. She laughed as she took photos of the zoo animals and their early morning antics. She heard some people talking of a natural aviary near some lake somewhere up in the hills. She had always wanted to ride through that area so she hopped in her car and pulled out a map. As she drove she realized that her body was very calm and comfortable. She passed several dirt roads and decided to turn off onto the next one she came to. It was a one lane dirt road that seemed to widen as she drove. There was a sign up ahead. Her brakes screeched to a halt: Montgomery Loop Road. She had seen that name somewhere before but couldn't place it. She drove a bit further along the road. She neared what at first appearance was a roadside shack. As she got closer she saw it was a tiny grocery store. No gas, but then she didn't need any. But food was something she could use. As she got out of the car she looked around at the beautiful color of the trees and sky. She laughed at the cows as they came slowly up to the fence to check her out. The inside of the store was clean compared to the dusty, weathered look outside. She picked up a coke and one of their deli sandwiches. The lady behind the counter was making them fresh and Evelyn thought it was a safe bet with the sandwiches. The woman at the register reminded her of her aunt. Very weary in appearance but very strong willed and hard working.

"Excuse me. Can you tell me what's at the end of this road?" Evelyn counted her change as she waited for an answer.

The woman looked up and took the money Evelyn gave her.

"Well, if you're headin' south you'll be headin' towards the city. An if you're headin' North you'd reach the Taggart place."

"More like a zoo if ya ask me. All those damn animals wanderin' round the place," the woman making sandwiches stated adamantly.

"Oh, don't mind Essie. She just don't like anything she can't identify. Say...you ain't deliverin any of them funny creatures are ya?"

Evelyn paused and then smiled.

"Ah, no mam. I'm just out for a nice drive and some bird watching."

As Evelyn gathered her food and headed for the door the name struck her. The patient information card flashed into her mind: Marlena Taggart, Montgomery Loop Road. She turned back towards the woman at the counter and said, "Taggart. That wouldn't be Marlena Taggart would it?"

"Yeah that's her." The woman went back to making the days sandwiches.

After getting directions from the woman she began her ascend up the dirt road towards a gate marked NO TRESSPASSING. She never thought of calling ahead. She wasn't even sure why she was here except for her curiosity. Checking on a patient outside the hospital was not a necessary duty. If anything, she ran the risk of trouble. So why was she here? She got out of the car and looked at the lock. At that moment behind her pulled a white panel van. A young man stepped out and walked towards Evelyn.

"Here....I have the key. Her groceries took longer than usual."

He unlocked the gate and walked back to the van. Was she expected? Did she look like someone else? She thought of these questions as she got back in her car and drove past the unlocked gate up the road. After several twists and turns she arrived in front of a large two-story stone front house. It resembled something out of an English estate complete with huge stone gargoyles on top of the roof line. She looked around at the forest that now surrounded her and the house. The white panel van pulled up next to her. The young man hopped out and began unloading boxes of groceries.

"She should be in the backyard about now."

Evelyn looked at him and then looked around without saying a word.

"It's through there on the side."

She followed his pointing to the right. There was another gate but this one was made of wood and was unlocked. The stone pathway headed down towards a balcony made of coral rock. As she approached the edge of it she heard sounds from below. She leaned over to see another vision from her dream. There was a woman clad only in shorts and a tank top wielding a sword at a wooden column while several tan colored Llamas looked on. She chuckled silently as they reminded her of the black and white Holstein cows that looked at her inquisitively at the store. Practicing moves and moving the sword with such grace and beauty reminded her of the martial arts class she once sat in on. But this woman's sword took chunks of wood out of the column as it met its mark. Evelyn could see the back of her tank top soaked with sweat. She watched in silence as the woman switched hands and posture not once wiping her brow of sweat. Could this be the same woman she saw lying helpless in that hospital bed? Her thoughts were interrupted by the young grocery boy.

"Excuse me, Ms. Taggart, but your groceries have been delivered. I gave them to Mrs. Potter."

As he padded down the coral steps the woman stopped and turned. She carefully laid her sword down upon a velvet cloth wiping it clean before she wiped her face with the towel that laid next to it. As she signed for her groceries she glanced up at the balcony. She handed the boy back his pen and papers, wrapped up the sword and followed him up the steps. Evelyn noticed that the woman showed no emotion when she looked up at Evelyn. She also noticed that she felt quite content to stay where she was and watch. But as the woman drew closer she knew she would have to say something.

"Hello!"

She was now close enough to see her blue eyes sparkling in the filtered sunlight. Her tanned muscular body showed no signs of the hospital except for the small circular band aid on her arm. The silence seemed longer than usual as the two women looked at each other.

"I...I came to see how you were doing," Evelyn managed to say.

Marlena smiled. "Please come inside."

Her slightly English accent surprised Evelyn. Evelyn turned and headed for the open French door as she heard Marlena behind her.

"Do you mind if I take a shower, Ms. Blakely? I'm really not fit for company at this point."

Evelyn would be glad to have her out of close proximity but not for the reasons Marlena would imagine. It would give her a chance to collect her breath and collect her thoughts.

"No, please go right ahead." Evelyn looked around trying not to seem nervous.

"Thank you! I will not be long. Please make yourself comfortable."

Oh, but if Evelyn could. The woman disappeared into the bedroom. *She seems very comfortable with me, Jesus! She even knew my name.* Evelyn looked around taking everything in. The house was made of red brick and the old brick fireplace was larger than most. She could just imagine trying to get through that loop road in winter. Large wood beams made up the ceiling. Ornate shelves held leather bound editions of books. At closer look they were editions of poetry and novels of fantasy and adventure. The furniture was made of a carved white oak with soft feathered cushions. The aura of the house was warm. As she continued to look around she noticed different swords that adorned the brick walls. Each one was different although they seemed to be of the same relative size. She stopped in front of one and gazed at the craftsmanship. It was the sword she saw in her dreams.

"Can I get you something to drink?" She turned as if in a dream state.

"Just water thank you." Her answer sounded slurred. She grabbed the edge of the chair and sat down slowly trying to assess what was happening to her. She felt someone touch her hand. She was engulfed in blackness. When she came to she was in a room trimmed in deep wood tones. The curtains on the window in front of her had been partially drawn which caused the sunlight to filter in.

"How do you feel now?" the voice came from her left. She turned and saw Marlena smiling at her.

"I'm so sorry. I.... I don't know what happened. Suddenly the room started spinning. You don't even know why I'm here and here I go and faint in your house....."

She started to run on until Marlena touched her hand. It was a warm touch. She looked up and met her eyes, those same unusual yet beautiful Azure blue eyes. They were warm and inviting.

"It's okay. I recognized you from the hospital. Since I already paid my bill I knew you couldn't be here for that." She laughed and Evelyn was caught up in the warmth she felt. She rose slowly and placed her feet firmly on the ground as she stood.

"Do you think standing is a good idea? Perhaps you should rest some more."

Evelyn managed a smile. "I've imposed on you enough for one day. I.." She wobbled a little until she came to rest against a small railing overlooking the courtyard.

"I can't let you drive home like this. I'll send for someone to drive you home or if you like you may stay here. I've called a friend of mine to take a look at you. She works in the same hospital as you."

Evelyn drank the glass of water Marlena offered her. "What's her name?"

Marlena took the empty glass and placed it down on the table.

"Her name is Sahara. That's her first name which is quite unusual but none the less very beautiful. At least I think so." Marlena turned as the doorbell rang. "That's probably her now".

Evelyn was feeling better as her eyes began to focus.

"Dr. Jahule!" She was relieved to see Dr. Jahule and felt safe now that she was here. Marlena left the two women alone.

Dr. Jahule performed several basic tests and came to the conclusion that Evelyn was suffering from a middle ear infection and that first thing tomorrow she should see her own physician.

"I don't think you should drive back home tonight. Take advantage of Marlena's hospitality and great food. She'll see to it that you see your doctor tomorrow okay?" She opened the curtains and let the remaining sunlight in.

"Did you know she was the one I was speaking about when I came to you?" Evelyn propped herself up on her elbows as she spoke.

"No not in the first couple of sessions. You see, I hadn't spoken to her till she left the hospital. I didn't even know she was there until I spoke to her housekeeper."

Evelyn stood up. This time she felt fine.

"How long have you known her?"

Sahara smiled.

"I've known Marlena for 5 years. She was the national fencing champion the year that I met her. My husband was creating a specially weighted rapier for her to use in the competition. He died shortly after she won. I believe she has it somewhere around here." She looked around and spotted a glass case with gold writing on it. "Here it is!"

Both women walked towards the case. The weapon was not very ornate with the exception of the gold hilt.

"I see you are admiring a work of art."

Dr. Jahule turned to see Marlena.

"He would have been pleased to hear you say that." She looked once again at the sword. Evelyn was beginning to understand her host.

"I apparently have a middle ear infection and that is why my balance has been so awful," she spoke as she moved to admire the sword. Marlena chuckled.

"And here I thought you were swooning over me!"

Only two women laughed. Evelyn's eyes faced the floor. Her cheeks felt hot. *If only you knew* she thought to herself. Evelyn reluctantly agreed to stay the night. She would leave with one of the servants for her appointment and be driven back to the estate to get her car. That way Marlena could be assured of her health report. Until then she was free to explore the grounds as long as she had someone with her. She opted for Evelyn's massive library and a seat in front of the fireplace. Marlena asked the doctor to join them for dinner but she declined the invitation say she had to pick up her son from Soccer practice. She remembered what a good cook Marlena was. But she felt that this time was better spent allowing the two women to become better acquainted. The scents of dinner were gradually filling the house and Marlena had not been seen since lunch time. Evelyn put down her book and began to wander about the house. Her nose guided her to the kitchen where she found Marlena putting the finishing touches on not only dinner but dessert.

"This smells glorious. Who else is coming?" She moved closer hoping to get a sample taste.

"No one.... just us." Evelyn looked up at her host.

"What about......" Evelyn turned to look at the housekeeper.

"Mrs. Potter spends her evenings with friends in town."
Evelyn turned to gaze once more upon the luscious food.
"You mean you prepared this for just the two of us?"
"Yes."
Evelyn thought to herself how romantic it was for someone to spend so much time preparing a meal for two people. Marlena removed her apron and guided Evelyn to the dining room. The table had been decorated with fresh cut flowers. And as the two women entered the food was already being laid out by Mrs. Potter. Evelyn could not remember when nor where she had had such a delicious meal. She felt almost giddy at the pleasure the food brought to her. After dinner the two women went to the library. Evelyn sat on the couch in front of the fireplace. Marlena reached above the mantel and held a single red rose. She handed it to Evelyn. Its scent was like none other she had experienced. She knew about roses from her father. He spent a life time trying to create a uniquely scented rose. He never succeeded. She breathed in its soothing scent. How romantic she thought.

"Thank you. It is truly beautiful. I've never seen one quite like it."
"Nor will you ever see it again. It is one of a kind. I grew it myself."
Evelyn chuckled.
"Won't you share your amusement?" Marlena asked as she sat down next to Evelyn.
"Is there anything you can't do?"
Evelyn continued to smell the rose. As she looked into Marlena's eyes she thought she saw tears. Marlena stood up and moved to the window across from the fireplace. Evelyn didn't mean to offend her host and couldn't figure out what it was she had said to cause such a reaction.

"It has been a long day. I will bid you good night."
As Marlena headed for the door Evelyn stopped her.
"No wait! I didn't mean to upset you. Please forgive me. I do so enjoy your company. I've never met anyone so charming and romantic."
As she held Marlena's arm she moved closer.
"I enjoyed our conversation and had a wonderful dinner and I....."
She leaned forward and kissed Marlena gently on the lips. Evelyn looked into her eyes and smiled. Instead of a shocked reaction she received just the opposite. Her kiss was gently returned. Marlena's

tongue parted Evelyn's lips still sweetened by the chocolate dessert from dinner. Evelyn placed one arm around Marlena's waist and the other on her shoulder. She had never felt another woman's body in this way. Marlena was strong. Evelyn felt she could melt in her arms. She felt protected. She realized that her body was responding sexually to Marlena's body. Confusion was beginning to set in. She wanted to feel more of Marlena but Marlena was a woman. She backed up suddenly and held Marlena at arm's length. Gently pushing her away.

"I'm sorry. I don't know what came over me. I think you're right. It's time I turned in. I'll see you in the morning."

Evelyn walked quickly towards the stairs that led to her bedroom. She locked the door behind her. But knew it was not to keep Marlena out but rather to keep Evelyn in. She could feel her body pulsing. Her breathing was erratic. *Calm yourself Eve* she said to herself. She tried to control her breathing. Once her normal breathing regained its pattern she unlocked the door. She was hoping to apologize once more to her host but she could not see her anywhere down the hall. Just as well she thought. I wouldn't make much sense anyway.

CHAPTER 3

Her dreams were filled with visions of Marlena but these visions did not bother her. Now she yearned to know more about her new friend and thinking of her no longer frightened her. The maid knocked on her door to remind her of her morning doctor's appointment. She opened the door to find the maid holding a package wrapped in plain brown paper.

"Compliments of my mistress. What would you like for breakfast miss?"

Evelyn managed to give Mrs. Potter her order of tea and toast as she took the package and stared at it. Carefully she opened it up. Inside were undergarments, jeans and powder blue silk shirt. She smiled as she tried them on. Perfect fit she said to herself. As she headed downstairs she looked at the other rooms down the hall and wondered which one Marlena's was. As she walked downstairs she could smell the tea brewing and the toast. She went directly to the kitchen.

"Good morning miss!"

Evelyn reached over and pulled a freshly baked sticky bun from its tray.

"Good morning Mrs. Potter. And where is my gracious host this fine morning?"

Mrs. Potter poured her some tea.

"She went out early this morning. Said she'd be back before noon."

Mrs. Potter was preparing to serve Evelyn in the main dining room but Evelyn persuaded her to serve it right there in the kitchen. Mrs. Potter was uncomfortable at first but not only did she get served in the kitchen but was joined by Mrs. Potter. They had a nice chat and whenever Evelyn could she asked a question about Marlena. Mrs. Potter had been with her for several years and preferred being employed by Marlena instead of working in the city. But being a loyal servant, she revealed nothing surprising nor new about her employer. Her ride had arrived and she reluctantly drove off with him. He too was a loyal servant who talked even less about Marlena. He managed the grounds and took care of the animals within the compound of the estate. He was due for a vacation and had one more day before he left her services. Her visit to the doctor was brief. He confirmed what Dr. Jahule diagnosed. Her ear infection would also cause her to suffer bouts of nausea for a day or two until the medication took effect. She thanked him and ran into one of the nurses she worked with.

"What are you doing here? Are you all right?"

Evelyn smiled. "I'm fine. I just have an ear infection. No big deal."

"Oh, Dan called. Wanted to know where you were."

Evelyn walked with her part way to the Pharmacy. "I'm staying at a friend for a few days. I should be back to work Monday."

The nurse turned to face Evelyn. "Well since it's only Wednesday I'd say that's a nice little vacation. Your friend must be very interesting."

Evelyn started to laugh.

"I know where this conversation is leading and you can tell Dan anything you like. We broke up two days ago so he is fair game. As for my friend...well. SHE is very interesting." Evelyn kissed her on the cheek and bid her goodbye.

On the way back, Evelyn felt sleepy. The medication was taking affect. When she awoke she was in the driveway of Marlena's home. Marlena was waiting for her in the living room when she opened the door.

"How did it go?" She handed Evelyn a glass of iced tea.

"Fine! I got a shot, some medication and a warning to rest for a couple days." She sat down on the couch as she guzzled half a glass of the tea. Mrs. Potter came in with a pitcher and placed it on the table in front of the two women.

"Well your car isn't going anywhere and neither are you. You can rest here. This way you're not tempted to work or exhort yourself and can do just what the doctor ordered. Do you wish to object?"

Evelyn looked up at this woman whom she wanted to call friend. She knew she was right. She would be tempted to clean the house, wash the car or she would fall asleep and the phone would wake her. She stood up and walked up to Marlena. She looked her in the eye, smiled, kissed her gently on the cheek and said "No". She started to walk towards the stairs.

"Oh, by the way thanks for the clothes. I especially love the shirt. I'll change and give it back to you."

Marlena cleared her throat uncomfortably. "You do not have to return it for it is yours to keep."

Evelyn thanked her again and headed upstairs. She could feel Marlena's nervousness and she felt satisfied in some way. She felt it was about time that the woman who continually made her nervous was shown some of those feelings herself. The more Evelyn thought about it the prouder of herself she became. She opened the door to her room. The bed had been made and fresh cut flowers adorned the room and gave the air a clean scent. She removed her shirt and shoes but left her jeans on. She liked the way they fit. She liked the shirt too but didn't want it to wrinkle. Once her head hit the pillow she was out cold. She was too tired to even get under the pillows.

Marlena tapped lightly on Evelyn's partially open door. She saw her guest already asleep. She walked to the foot of the bed and unfolded the thin wool blanket. She draped it over Evelyn's restful body. Her skin looked so soft and the curves of her partially exposed breast reminded her of a painting she once saw by the painter Paul Rubens. She wanted to stay and watch her but thought better of it.

Evelyn slept most of the day. When she awoke the scent of rain caught her attention. It was the crisp, clean smell one experienced just before it was to rain. She put on a robe she found at the foot of the bed and walked down to find her host. She was about to head for the kitchen when she saw a light coming from one of the rooms off of the living room. She opened the door partially and looked around. It was a large room filled with books from vaulted ceiling to floor.

"Good afternoon." The voice came from behind a chair directly in front of her. She walked up to the back of the chair.

"This is quite an extensive collection of books you have here." Evelyn looked around as she walked to the front of Marlena's view. "People who have this extensive a library tends to be very quiet and tend to hide from public places and people."

Marlena placed her book down on the table.

"Perhaps some people aren't comfortable in public."

Evelyn was intrigued by that response so she continued, "I know there are different people that consider themselves outcasts but there is usually a logical explanation for it."

Marlena stood up agitated. "What would you know of outcasts?"

Evelyn had definitely struck a nerve. "I know that you're not one!"

Marlena lunged towards Evelyn but did not touch her.

"You know nothing about me or where I come from. You know nothing of outcasts. So please do not speak to me of things you do not know."

Evelyn watched as Marlena turned away.

"To be taken from your home as a child and raised with those you do not know. No matter what you do you're not one of them. When you are older the feeling of loneliness never goes away it simply grows. Then when you are reunited with parents they no longer recognize you. You are different somehow. You are no longer part of either group. You are treated as stranger by both." Marlena grasped a glass that was sitting on the mantle. She swallowed the last bit of golden liquid before leaving the room. "You should not speak of things you do not know!"

Marlena walked out of the room. Evelyn tried to figure out what Marlena meant. Maybe she was adopted and Evelyn simply blundered into a sensitive situation. She walked out of the room to find Marlena and to apologize.

As she walked past the window a strange light caught her eye. She looked out into the courtyard to see a small female like figure clad in what seemed to be a shiny metallic bodysuit. The figure seemed to be bald but as Evelyn drew closer could see that the bodysuit extended up to a hood which was over the woman's head. At least she thought she was a woman. Her face held no expression. Her eyes were round and almost twice the size of normal. She thought for a moment and realized that the figure she was watching resembled the pictures she had seen on those alien abduction movies. This woman; this alien was listening to Marlena. They seemed to be talking but Evelyn could not see the alien's lips moving. Nor did Evelyn see anything resembling lips. She watched quietly as the two figures walked as they talked. Then the small alien type creature walked back towards the light and disappeared. Evelyn gasped not believing what she just saw. Marlena turned and noticed Evelyn watching. She walked up the stairs towards Evelyn and through the open door.

"I told you I was an outcast. But I'm sorry for my rude behavior and temper."

Evelyn walked back towards the couch in the living room. She sat down and rubbed her forehead. Marlena sat across from her.

"I don't understand? Was that being an alien? I mean you.... you were communicating with it. How?"

Marlena lowered her head. "I can communicate with 'it' because she is the one that raised me."

Evelyn looked into Marlena's eyes hoping she heard wrong.

"I was abducted when I was 12 from a land known as Etar. My people were a primitive people by Earth standards but we were a peaceful people. I learned later that the peaceful part was due to the fact that we were excellent fighters. I also learned later that they had caused my biological mother's pregnancy. They took me, trained me and taught me the ways of many cultures. They then placed me on here.....on your planet.... Earth. But you see, if my true origin were known I would be an outcast in your people's eyes as well. The 'ALIENS' as you call them do not want me either so I am forced to make an acceptable space for myself here on Earth."

Evelyn became agitated.

"Why did they take you in the first place?" Evelyn was trying to assimilate what she had just heard. It read like a Hollywood movie script. But the person standing in front of her was real. And there were oddities regarding Marlena which could only be explained by her past.

"I am trained to be a leader of my people. To take them into the next century." Marlena recognized the look of fear and confusion on Evelyn's face.

"But what about your own destiny?"

Marlena was quiet. She then spoke very softly, "We were an

experiment that worked. Therefore, to maintain the results the experiment must be properly maintained."

Marlena knew that Evelyn would not understand that the aliens rebuilt fractured worlds that no longer could maintain nor sustain life. In some cases, they had even prevented extinction. But with this came a price and one Marlena knew all too well.

"I'll have Rick take you home if you are uncomfortable here."

Marlena stood up and looked out towards the window. The rain was just starting to come down. She walked to the kitchen and disappeared behind the door.

Evelyn looked around and for the first time felt the loneliness of the room. She realized now that the house had been designed to keep Marlena company.

"I bet she's read every one of those damn books in that room," Evelyn spoke out loud as if to ward off the spirits of loneliness that inhabited the house. She took a deep breath. She hurried to her room and got dressed. She knew now what she had to do.

CHAPTER 4

Marlena was finishing a cup of tea when Evelyn entered.

"Rick will be here in a few minutes."

Evelyn walked over to the cupboard and took out a cup and saucer. She starred at the shape of the saucer momentarily and then poured herself a cup of tea.

"Good but I think you should wear jeans today since it may be a bit chilly with the rain."

Marlena looked up at Evelyn. "What did you say?

Evelyn smiled. "You heard what I said. We are getting out of this house and attempt to have some fun on a rainy day."

Now it was Marlena that had a look of confusion on her face.

"Go on, get dressed. Oh! And sneakers would be advisable." Evelyn did not look up and kept on drinking. She knew that if she could get Marlena out of the house she could sort her thoughts out and get Marlena to trust her. As Evelyn placed her cup in the sink Marlena came in the kitchen.

"Are you sure about this, Evelyn?"

Evelyn turned around at the sound of her name. She loved how Marlena pronounced it.

"Yes, I'm sure. How else are we to become good friends if we don't find out what each other is like? Tell Rick we'll take my car."

Marlena reached up into the cupboard and took out a set of keys. " Perhaps with this rain we should take my truck."

Evelyn thought for a moment then smiled. "Okay....go on.... get dressed." Marlena did as Evelyn instructed.

Evelyn walked outside with the keys. She looked around and noticed a building to her right. She stepped out into the mud as the rain subsided. She opened up the large doors to reveal a four-car garage. She looked at the keys again and read Range Rover. She smiled as she walked over to a Forest green vehicle.

"Well.....if it looks like a Range Rover and smells like a Range Rover it must be!"

Evelyn got in and started up the car. It had seen some work but not enough to classify it as the type of truck one thinks of when someone says truck. She pulled it up to the front of the house.

Marlena walked out in jeans and a slicker.

"I'll drive...remember... you're supposed to be resting."

As the two women drove down the hill, Marlena explained about the grounds and the research several universities were doing regarding the wildlife and habitat areas located there. She also gave Evelyn the history of the small general store and the two elderly women who ran it.

Marlena stopped and picked up a picnic lunch and continued up towards Aviary lake. The two women gazed up at the thousands of birds that now surrounded the huge lake. Several camera blinds had been established for research since no hunting was allowed on Marlena's property. Marlena stopped the car and got out quietly as not to disturb the birds. Evelyn grabbed her binoculars. Flocks of different birds were seen everywhere. To her left she watched as Roseate spoonbills filtered the water with their beaks in the search for food. Herons, storks and ducks were also seen. Each in their own area overlapping peacefully with the raccoons, squirrels, and panthers.

Evelyn stopped her thoughts.....Panther! She turned to Marlena.

"I... I just saw a panther drinking water!"

Marlena smiled. "Well...yes.....I imagine they get thirsty too."

Evelyn gave Marlena a scornful look. Marlena recouped by explaining the research that was taking place in this section with a pair of panthers she hoped will breed.

"How many acres do you have?" Evelyn knew that such large cats had to have plenty of roaming space.

"About 400 acres give or take a few. It's difficult since I have three such lakes that back up to the mountains over there." Marlena pointed to a small mountain range, some of which still had snow caps.

Evelyn looked around as she began to take in the vastness of Marlena's property. She wondered what Marlena did to afford such acreage. As curious as she was, that question would be rude to ask such a gracious host, so Evelyn thought she would simply forget about it for now and enjoy the beauty that surrounded her.

The two women enjoyed the rest of the day hiking and touring the back roads of Marlena's property. They headed back home as the dusk approached. Mrs. Potter had dinner ready with a note on the location of the desserts. Marlena excused herself for a welcomed shower while Evelyn went to arrange drinks for dinner.

After showers and dinner, the two sat quietly in the library as the fires glow lit the room with soft orange hues. Marlena looked up towards Evelyn. She looked like a Rembrandt painting in the firelight. Curled up with blanket and book. Her hair, wet before, was now dried and fell about her face. Evelyn caught her looking.

Marlena smiled. "I was thinking that perhaps tomorrow you should rest.....quietly this time with no movement."

Evelyn placed her book down and looked at Marlena.

"I'm fine really. The medication is working and besides.... this is my vacation. I thought Friday I'd show you what I like to do......museums and the aquarium."

Marlena learned that saying no to Evelyn was becoming increasingly more difficult as time went on. "Alright...if you're certain you're up for it? "

Evelyn realized that what she wanted to do was kneel down next to Marlena and kiss her but realized that that was her dream state.

"Yes...I'm certain."

Both women went back to their reading. Each not daring to look at the other for fear of ruining the peaceful inner warmth they both felt. Evelyn had never felt more calm and comfortable as she did with Marlena but didn't know quite how to express it. Marlena was at peace when Evelyn was with her. Perhaps she didn't know of her past but Marlena felt if Evelyn did know it would not make much of a difference. What she had experienced with Evelyn in the past couple of days had shown her hope and love with no conditions attached and no expectations.

Perhaps one of these days she would let her closer inside. But for now, she was content and happy.

Their day started off with the Museum of Art and continued with the National Aquarium. Evelyn could sense Marlena becoming more comfortable as their adventures continued. Lunch was interesting for both women since neither one had been to a vegetarian restaurant and decided to try it. They laughed as they tried to guess what the equivalent meat dish would be like. Clouds gathered outside as the rain began to wet the street outside. Evelyn decided to finish the day with the Planetarium.

"And the zone we call Alpha Centauri......."

Evelyn looked over at Marlena as the show continued its narration. She thought she caught a glimpse of moisture on Marlena's cheek. Evelyn looked around towards the exit. She stood up and motioned for Marlena to come with her. Marlena wiped her face as they went out the door.

Evelyn turned to Marlena. "I'm sorry. I didn't mean to upset you.... I..."

Marlena stopped her with a wave of her hand. "I know you had no idea. I am not blaming you. I had a wonderful day and enjoyed the company." She reached for Evelyn's hand.

Evelyn moved closer. Marlena's eyes met Evelyn's. The two were about to embrace when the show let out and the doors began to open. The two women walked back towards the car.

Marlena was about to speak when Evelyn spoke, "The day's not over yet. I know this great place for dinner."

Marlena looked down at her jeans and sneakers. "But..."

"Don't worry they don't care how you are dressed as long as you are dressed." Both chuckled as they drove through the flooded streets.

Evelyn spoke very little of her childhood. But as Marlena felt more comfortable she asked questions and Evelyn revealed her abusive parents and struggle for sanity as she was growing up. Evelyn pulled into a small grotto type parking space.

"Well, here we are!"

Marlena was concentrating so on Evelyn's story that she didn't notice her surroundings. It was a small restaurant made of wood and brass. It overlooked the Pacific Ocean at a point where the whales were known to feed. It was early and they were the first ones in the place. Evelyn whispered something in the waiter's ear and he smiled. He then sat them in a section of the room that was separated from the general area and surrounded on three sides by glass. The view was breathtaking. It was as if the room were suspended on the edge of the cliff and all one saw were mountains, forest and sea. Marlena didn't notice Evelyn ordering. All she noticed was the airy feeling of flight.

"Earth to Marlena...come in!"

Marlena turned as if awakened from a dream.

"I am sorry I...."

Evelyn laughed. "You don't have to apologize. I felt the same way when I first discovered this place. I was even more shocked when they not only had a spectacular view but had good food as well."

Both women continued their conversation over wine and dinner.

The company was most enjoyable Evelyn thought to herself. Now the woman sitting across from her seemed less moody and complacent. But what she did notice was that Marlena seemed to avoid direct eye contact. She was very good at it and Evelyn took it as a challenge. There was a small pathway that led from the restaurant to an overlook. The two decided that dinner needed to be walked off before they headed home. As they walked, the mist that surrounded their feet was highlighted by the small safety lights that lined the wooden walkway. They seemed to be the only ones out that evening.

"Marlena?" Evelyn looked straight ahead as she spoke.

"Yes?"

"I had a great time today. How about you?"

Marlena smiled as she answered, "I had a lot of fun. My apologies for being so.... stuffy."

"Apology accepted."

The two women stopped at the overlook. The view was breathtaking as dusk settled in.

"I have a question to ask you."

Marlena stepped back slightly. "Oh no! It sounds serious." She smiled back as she resumed her position next to Evelyn.

"A sense of humor......very good. I like that. But tell me - why do you avoid looking at me?"

Evelyn held her breath after the last word spoken. Marlena looked out towards the ocean and breathed quietly. The silence seemed endless. Evelyn wondered if she had spoiled the moment by being so direct.

Finally, Marlena turned and reached out for Evelyn's hand. She held it gently as she spoke.

"I have avoided looking into your eyes. I do not avoid looking at you. You are a very attractive woman."

Evelyn was aroused by the words Marlena spoke. She realized her whole body reacted to Marlena's compliment. For what seemed like the first time the words: attractive woman: were meant from the heart. Not wanting to lose the moment she persisted.

"And why do you avoid looking into my eyes?"

Marlena turned away from Evelyn. Marlena placed her hands on the railing and grasped them tightly. Evelyn could see it was difficult for Marlena to say. She walked over to her and placed her hands gently on Marlena's back. Without turning around Marlena reached up and touched Evelyn's hands.

"What my eyes see in others is not always the truth. And what I see in your eyes...is...."

Evelyn could take this no longer. She turned Marlena to face her.

"Is what? What do you see?"

Marlena reached up and gently brushed a lock of hair from Evelyn's cheek.

"I see...... what humans call love."

Marlena lowered her head and headed back towards the car. Evelyn followed quietly. *What an odd way to phrase it*, Evelyn thought. "Us humans?" She knew the love Marlena spoke of was more than that of friendship. She had brought this on herself. She was the one who was curious about this woman. Her dreams were filled with her. In the short time they were together she felt she had learned so much about Marlena's surroundings but nothing about Marlena herself. This was the woman she was falling in love with. But now she was not sure what falling in love with a woman meant. What were the boundaries? How far could she venture without getting totally confused in her thoughts and feelings? Simply because you enjoy someone's company doesn't mean you should move in with them. *But it was more than that* Evelyn thought. When

Marlena wasn't around she missed her. When she walked into a room Evelyn's heart rate increased. And when Marlena stood close to her Evelyn remembered trying convince her knees not to give out. The two were silent as they headed home. Suddenly Marlena broke the silence.

"I can drop you off at your house if you prefer and Rick can deliver your car to you tomorrow."

"No, that won't be necessary," Evelyn heard herself say almost immediately.

As the car neared the gate Evelyn took a deep breath. Once at the house Marlena got out of the car slowly. Evelyn got out and waited for her. She stopped her as she continued towards the house.

"I'm not afraid to spend the night with you. Can you say the same?" Evelyn stood firm as she waited for a reply.

Marlena breathed heavily as she answered, "I do not think you have thought this out. You do not know me very well and you are not sure of your feelings and emotions."

Now Evelyn was angry and could control herself no longer.

"You certainly presume an awful lot, don't you? I've told you the way I feel and now you're telling me what I'm REALLY feeling! Well, I thought they were the same. What I haven't heard is how you feel about me. I get the feeling that I'm some sort of amusement for you. To think without feeling is a luxury I was never afforded. Playing it safe was an action that was learned. We never start out hurting those people around us but if we release and let go we ultimately will hurt someone. It is our nature. To some it is unintentional, to others it is a well learned skill. To some we love and to some we are friends. Perhaps the only sadness is not understanding why we love some and befriend others. It's called living! To paint a picture with words is an art form to some and to others a deadly weapon. But to assume that either will not affect someone is a mistake."

Evelyn moved away from the car and towards Marlena as she spoke.

"No, I've never loved nor made love to a woman before but I can't help what I feel inside and what my heart tells me. If you tell me you are not interested then I'll go. But if you tell me as you look into my eyes that you haven't felt the same thing then you're a damned liar!"

Evelyn turned and stormed towards the house. Marlena ran after her. Evelyn reached for the door knob. As she opened it a brilliant white light engulfed the room inside. Evelyn was bathed in it. A thundering sound accompanied the light as Evelyn tried to look up towards the sound.

Marlena screamed from behind her, "Evelyn! No..... get down!"

Evelyn felt someone push her forward onto the floor. It was Marlena. The sound of gunfire sounded throughout the house. Crystal and china shattered and glass flew into a thousand pieces. Marlena pulled Evelyn towards a small protected area out of the way of the flying glass. They could both hear holes being chiseled out of the wood and walls around them. When silence came the dust began to settle. Marlena helped Evelyn up.

"They have found me. We cannot stay here."

Evelyn heard the sounds of the helicopters fade in the distance. Evelyn, confused, followed Marlena as she stood up. Marlena walked carefully throughout the rooms picking up undamaged clothing and packing it into a slightly damaged suitcase. As she placed it at the front door she heard a sound coming from the kitchen. Evelyn ran towards it. Marlena motioned for her to stop.

"No don't go in there!"

Evelyn's images came back but this time the injured woman was not Marlena. Marlena brushed her away and walked to the kitchen. On the floor amidst the shattered glass, pottery and bullet ridden furniture was the blood-spattered body of Mrs. Potter her housekeeper. She knelt down beside her. She turned her gently over and cradled her in her arms.

"I...baked you..a..cake." Mrs. potter smiled up at Marlena and then went limp in Marlena's arms. Evelyn walked in behind her and knelt down next to the woman. She checked for a pulse but she knew she would not find one.

"We should go now. There is nothing more you can do for her."

Evelyn placed her hand over Marlena's. The two women left the kitchen in silence. Marlena threw the suitcase in the backseat of the car and started the car. Evelyn stood at the front passenger door.

"What about your chauffer?"

Marlena looked towards the sky as the sound of helicopters sounded up again.

"Come! We must go! Gilbert will be fine. It was the start of his vacation, remember?"

Evelyn hurriedly entered the car. Marlena drove speedily down the dirt road and realized her dirt trail might be discovered. She took the lake trail back into town since it was still partially muddy from last evenings rains. Marlena continued to drive for what seemed like hours. Evelyn lost track of what direction they were heading. She was still trying to assimilate what had happened. It was as if it was simply a terrifying nightmare.

Finally, the women stopped at a nearby motel and Evelyn checked them in under different names. Evelyn said she would take a shower while Marlena made arrangements for Mrs. Potters' body. Marlena looked at her hands and clothes and realized she still had blood on them. No wonder Evelyn wanted to take a shower. She looked at Evelyn's clothes on the floor. They too were covered in blood. Marlena needed time to think. She did not want to involve Evelyn but as Evelyn pointed out she already had. *She does not know that much about me perhaps I can still keep her involvement at a minimum*, Marlena thought to herself. She wrote a note to Evelyn and told her she was sorry for what she had to do but that there was no way to avoid the inevitable. On top of the note Marlena left a single red rose.

The shower felt soothing as Evelyn let the cool water cascade over her body. Her mind went over the chaos that just happened as if it were clips from a film. Her nurses mind was calm and trying to organize while her regular mind was trying frantically to process. As she began to soap her body flashes of Marlena entered her thoughts. Suddenly an image of Marlena strapped to a chair shot in front of her. She dropped the soap as she leaned forward to grasp the shower tile. Blood poured from Marlena's lip. Evelyn pitched forward and accidentally hit her head on the tile. The image was gone. She hurried out of the shower and toweled off. She quickly put jeans on and an oversized t-shirt that Marlena had in her suitcase. She flew out the door to Marlena's room. As she knocked she noticed her car was absent from where it had last been parked.

"Shit!" Evelyn said under her breath as she opened the door to a clean room. On top of the TV was a rose and a note.

PLEASE TRY AND UNDERSTAND
WHERE I GO YOU MUST NOT FOLLOW
FOR YOUR OWN SAFETY.
LOVE, MARLENA

"Damn you Marlena!"
Evelyn read the note and then noticed the sound of heavy machinery and trucks outside the room. She peered out the window at the military jeeps, trucks and helicopters that were now passing by the motel headed towards Marlena's demolished home.

CHAPTER 5

Evelyn knew she had to find Marlena. But how? She hardly knew the woman and had no idea what direction she was headed. Evelyn laughed to herself as she realized that she had been following the woman in her dreams and now she's complaining that she doesn't know where to find her. She knew that she needed to listen to the dreams now instead of fighting them. Whatever the bond was it seemed to be there for a reason. The last vision she had was of Marlena in the hands of the military so.... why not follow them!

She hitched a ride with a local farmer and walked up towards the military post that was already setting up in a field half a mile down from the grocery store. Confusion was in her favor as trucks, people and equipment were being unloaded and set up. She managed to sneak past the sentries which were just being assigned their posts. She headed towards the Red Cross truck and found a nurse's uniform that she easily fit into. All military personnel were being summoned to a large tent for a briefing. Evelyn blended in with the rest of the crowd and stood towards the back of the tent as a highly decorated military man spoke.

"AT 0:800 HOURS THE SUBJECT WAS SPOTTED AT A BOMBED-OUT STRUCTURE ONE MILE FROM THIS SIGHT."

Evelyn gritted her teeth as she whispered her response, "That bombed out structure was her home, you moron." She said that under her breath.

A computerized voice interrupted the man and he directed their attention to a small screen that had been set up within the tent.

THIS ALIEN MUST BE HANDLED WITH EXTREME CAUTION.

34

*WE ARE NOW READING RADIATION BEYOND THE
TOLERABLE RANGE.
FOR THE MOMENT ONLY MEDICAL PERSONNEL ARE TO
HAVE DIRECT CONTACT.
WE WOULD PREFER TO CAPTURE THIS ALIEN ALIVE BUT
POST MORTEM CREWS ARE STANDING BY JUST IN CASE.
EACH TEAM HAS ITS INDIVIDUAL INSTRUCTIONS
PLEASE SEE TO IT THAT THE SECURITY BORDERS
REMAIN IN EFFECT UNTIL FURTHER ORDERS.
TEAM A WILL MOVE OUT IMMEDIATELY. TEAM B IS
TO FOLLOW.*

Evelyn had seen illegal aliens in trouble with INS before when she worked in the emergency room but never as severe as to warrant the addition of military action of this magnitude! People started to move in all directions. She watched as the soldiers with radiation gear moved towards the house.

"Hey you! Move it. You're with Team B so get with it will ya?" the soldier motioned to her to head in the same direction as the soldiers.

Evelyn realized she'd never be able to get up front but she might be able to create some diversions that might side track them. They were using heat sensitive tracking devices to track Marlena. As they moved through the undergrowth Evelyn set small fires that their heat seeking mechanical wonders were registering as someone lying in the grass.

"She's double backing. Form a circle damn it!" Those were the orders coming through her walkie-talkie she was outfitted with shortly after she emerged from the tent.

Now maybe she could get ahead of the maddening crowd. She caught movement out from the corner of her eye. She had difficulty making out whether it was a soldier or Marlena. She knew she should have taken binoculars with her. Suddenly a gunshot rang past her ear towards the movement.

"Shit!" she spoke out loud as she headed towards the movement. Whatever it was had been hit and was moving slower and more erratic. It seemed like hours before she reached the area. Evelyn stood starring at the crumpled figure before her.

"Damn it Marlena, why didn't you stay with me?"

She didn't move. As soldiers approached, Evelyn did the only thing she could at that moment.

"She's been hit in the left shoulder three centimeters below the clavicle bone."

"What about the radiation level?"

She heard someone call out, "Forget it it's normal! Let's go here. She's unconscious pulse _____over_____ bp ____ and _____. "

She continued to rattle off vital signs as the medical crew came towards her.

They assumed she was one of the med crew that arrived there first. She took command until they reached the secured mobile trailer. Soldiers surrounded the trailer as the medical crew entered. The inside of this trailer had been outfitted with a full emergency room logistics and monitoring system. Screens and monitors showed everything from pulse rate, heartbeat, retina movement to heat transfer levels and oxygen percentages. Evelyn faded towards the back once she saw they were attending to Marlena. She knew if she stepped outside she would run the risk of having to answer questions so she continued to stay with the majority of the med. staff.

"G-d damn it Hughes! I want to know who the first med. tech was that found her. I need to know what they saw. Did she say anything to her?"

The man dressed in a three-piece suit put out his cigarette in the soda can and turned to face the general.

"Look, you pompous asshole, I told you to take things easy. We could have captured her without incident. Now the whole g-d damned countryside knows what's going on here. I'm surprised the fucking reporters haven't gotten here yet! You've got a hundred people out there looking AND shooting at anything that moves and you want me to tell you who the first person near the alien was? Do me a favor, general... stop watching those late-night John Wayne war movies. This is reality and stupidity just doesn't cut it out here for too long... Okay?"

And with that, Hughes, the man in the three-piece suit walked towards the trailer. He walked up the steps and opened the door slowly. He saw Evelyn next to the bed.

"How is she?" he asked quietly.

Evelyn looked at his badge.

"Well, Agent Hughes, she's stable. Her vital signs are good. A few more inches and we would have lost her."

Evelyn placed her head slightly at an angle as not to draw suspicion with direct eyesight.

"Yeah. These damn idiots think they're back on the farm shooting rabbits and acting like it's national security."

Evelyn couldn't help but chuckle at his view.

"So, you were the first on the scene huh?"

Evelyn fell still and silent. Hughes moved closer. Evelyn suddenly felt very nervous.

"I'm sorry...I'm not sure I understand?"

"You were the one who gave clear and concise orders out there in the field. Makes sense that you would want to stay here with your patient.... Nurse...."

Hughes reached over and lifted up her badge. Evelyn was about to stand up but realized how that might look so she held her ground.

"Nurse Edmonds."

Evelyn realized then that she had picked up a uniform with someone's name on it and that it was only a matter of time before someone reported it missing.

"Look I'm a nurse just doing what I was trained and paid to do and that was to monitor her vital signs every half hour on the hour except when the general says otherwise. So, if you don't mind there are plenty of other nurses you can impress and make passes at and not distract me from my duties."

She practically held her breath after that one. She prayed that being a bitch would pay off.

"Jesus! Everybody out here is on a thin wire. Take it easy okay.... I'm not the enemy. I'll check back with you later." He shook his head as he left down the stairs.

Evelyn looked at her badge.

"Jesus!.......Richard Edmonds....... I'm a man! What an idiot. I wonder if he noticed," she spoke out loud as she took a peek out the door.

Hughes motioned to two guards who moved directly in front of the trailer. He then headed for the computer trailer.

"Shit....he did notice." She walked back over to Marlena.

Evelyn looked down at her and wondered what kind of life she had led before her.

"How the hell am I gonna get you out of this?"

She spoke out loud to a silent room. The only sound was that of respirators and heart monitors. In this quiet time Evelyn thought back to the revelations of her feelings for Marlena. She thought about the sad and frightened look as she gazed into Marlena's eyes. Where was this woman's place?

"Humans," she said out loud. *They called you an alien......* she thought.

Suddenly, as if a light had been turned on in a darkened room, Evelyn realized why Marlena warranted such attention. She thought back when she remembered the older woman that was talking to Marlena in the courtyard. She didn't vanish because she was a ghost.

"Oh my G-d!....You're an... alien!" she said as if she were talking to her.

Humans thought of her as an alien.... something to be studied. Evelyn looked up at the heart monitor. The aliens thought of her as human and not accepted by them. All other thoughts fell into the dark recesses of Evelyn's mind. Her main thought was how to protect Marlena. Her calm was broken by the sounds of men shouting and heavy machinery moving.

"Oh great! Here it comes."

She stood up and walked over to the door. As she opened it she saw soldiers firing into the air. A heavy wind created a suction that blew the door closed. She forced it opened it once again and was startled by the creature before her. A female clad in a tight fitting metallic looking one-piece suit. No face was visible through the black helmet. The woman seemed to be breathing from small hoses that fed from a small rectangular box on her back to the helmet. Evelyn moved back towards Marlena. The female seemed to float over to Marlena's bedside. Evelyn stood between the two.

"No! You're not going to take her! She needs to be away from both of you. None of you accept her.... but I do! And I'll not have you harm her."

The female motioned for Evelyn to move and when she didn't Evelyn felt a strong electric shock that seemed to lift her up and push her against the walls of the trailer. Marlena sat stunned on the floor of the trailer. She tried to get up but pain radiated throughout her body. She tried to motioned to the female to move away. Evelyn started to get up again but couldn't move. Her body felt numb. She felt her lip that now felt warm. On her hand she saw blood. Her eyes looked pleadingly at Marlena for answers to what was happening to her. The alien female walked over to Evelyn, knelt down and picked her up in her arms. Marlena stood up and walked over to Evelyn.

"No... it's okay. She won't hurt you again. Just relax. Okay?"

Evelyn nodded as they headed towards the door. She held on tightly to the alien as the door opened. Evelyn felt certain that a barrage of bullets would hit them at that moment. Evelyn saw nothing except a ray of brilliant blue light. She thought she saw movement but there seemed to be a strong wind blowing things, equipment around.

CHAPTER 6

Evelyn blacked out as the images before her began to spin.

"We cannot possibly return you to your people. Ages have passed and only a few with the same bloodline still survive. You would be a stranger to them and far beyond them intellectually. No....I'm sorry but that request is denied."

The alien walked towards a lighted panel and pressed several buttons. A large screen lit the wall in front of Marlena.

"And now you have placed a human into this equation."

Marlena turned to face the alien. " Surely there exists a governing force or code that even your people must abide by! You cannot continue to alter people without some consequence occurring. That woman is my friend. I am close to her. Our thoughts are one. You cannot separate us without some action being created."

A low frequency beep came from the door as both stood and watched. A tall alien woman clad in grey walked towards the two arguing.

"The High Counsel has intervened on your behalf and both you and the Earth woman will be returned to Etar."

"But...." Marlena moved closer to object but the alien woman motioned her to stop.

"The High Counsel has expressed concern about certain influences your knowledge might have on the Earth people. Therefore, the Counsel has determined that remaining with a more primitive people will be safer for all concerned and that while you may influence them it will not present as great a danger for them."

Marlena knew she could read her mind of anger so she said nothing but made a single request.

"May I be permitted to see my mother....I... I mean my parental unit?"

The aliens both looked at one another as if conferring.

"Yes, it shall be permitted."

Both aliens left while Marlena paced about the room. She walked to the light panel and entered a code. The screen flashed a picture of Evelyn pacing about a similar room.

"Evelyn...can you hear me?"

Evelyn looked about the room. "Marlena? Where are you?"

Marlena moved closer to the screen.

"That's not important now. Please don't be frightened. I shall be with you soon. I need to speak with my mother first."

A low frequency beep was heard again. Marlena turned towards the door panel. A tall female alien walked in and placed her arms around Marlena. Evelyn could now see the image on the wall that resembled Marlena and the alien she had first seen her with.

"Mother......what have I done to affect them so? I have lived quietly for 75 years upon Earth with no signs of influence from me. Why do they now feel threatened?"

The woman alien looked towards the screen where Evelyn was watching. She adjusted a small switch on her armband and a piercing sound came through both rooms. She adjusted the volume as she spoke.

"The Counsel feels as you say.... threatened because you now have another life form you have become involved with. You must care and protect the Earthling."

Evelyn heard that loud and clear. She thought she should have been shocked but since it was said as a perfectly normal statement she decided not to object.

Marlena turned to face her mother as she spoke, "And they are afraid that I would choose Evelyn over the High Counsel to be loyal to?"

The alien woman stood back so that she could face both of them.

"Yes, my daughter. And is that not the way it should be? Give the Counsel time. Both of you need time together to explore your new surroundings and feelings for one another. You will protect each other well and will learn a lot from each other. I will be in contact with you in the usual manner."

The woman moved closer towards Evelyn's screen and addressed her directly.

"I felt how fearful you were of me yet you protected my daughter. It is with that same feeling that I place my daughter with you. Please see to it that she keeps up her sword practice. She will need it on Etar."

The only expression Evelyn saw was that of tears welling up in the alien woman's large opal shaped eyes. Evelyn turned away from both the alien and Marlena. She needed time to assess what was going on…. what was just said. Thoughts and questions raced into her mind. She couldn't focus. Would she not see Earth again? Etar was not a planet name she was familiar with. This was a bad dream. She must have fallen asleep in front of the tv. Would both of them be going to this planet Etar? Planet……travel…… She looked around at her room. Was she on a ship?

Evelyn sat down on the floor and covered her face. *This is all a bad, bad dream. The door must have knocked me unconscious and this is a dream. When I open my eyes, I'll be back on Earth…. just like Toto!* These thoughts were slightly comforting as she closed her eyes. She opened them slowly. She was still in the same sterile white room.

"That's it! I'm going mad! I'm hallucinating. I've been committed. That's it……Dan must have…."

"I am not familiar with that word 'hallucinating?'"

Evelyn scooted around to see Marlena standing before her on the screen in a light blue jumpsuit.

"Please tell me this is a dream!" Evelyn said as she stood up.

"I almost wish it were but it is not. Both worlds created me, guided my growth and encouraged me yet neither world will accept me. Now you are caught up in the loop." Marlena walked over to view the screen. "I'm sorry Evelyn. I never meant to involve you in this. I…."

Evelyn placed her finger gently over the screen that showed Marlena's mouth.

"Shhh. I know that. I'm an adult and…."

Marlena wanted desperately to hold her hand.

"Yes, but you could not know where it would lead you. Or how far you would be from your home. You have not known me for long. You're with a stranger who has disrupted your life forever."

Evelyn stepped away angrily.

"I don't need you to remind me of that. I know now that things will never be the same for me. But G-d help me …. I love you. I've fallen in love with you and I need you in my life. I don't want your pity."

Evelyn was losing it. The only thing she seemed to know with any certainty was that she loved Marlena. Tears welled up in her eyes and she could no longer stand. She slid down against the wall, held her knees and sobbed.

Marlena turned and walked away from the screen. Evelyn looked up as the door slid open. Marlena walked in and knelt down beside her. She pressed several buttons on her wrist bracelet.

"Evelyn…. please come with me."

She held out her hands for Evelyn as she stood up.

"I don't ………"

Marlena leaned into her as she softly spoke, "It will be alright. Please come with me."

Marlena coaxed Evelyn up and held onto her as they walked towards the door. As the door opened Evelyn could see for the first time the internal structure of the ship she was obviously on. The corridors all faced a central hub like that of a wheel. When Evelyn looked back she could see the walls give way to huge windows that showed a star pattern. The planet she called Earth grew more distant as she focused on it. Marlena led her to another door which parted into an elevator. The ship and its corridors seemed to be devoid of any markings or symbols yet Marlena seemed to know where she was going. As the elevator stopped Evelyn felt slightly queasy. She realized that the elevator was not just going down but seemed to move left and then right. She gripped Marlena's hand tightly as she leaned forward.

"It's okay. Don't try to resist it. The nausea will pass as your body becomes accustomed to the low gravity."

Evelyn blinked as if trying to understand a complicated equation.

"But I'm not floating I'm walking."

Marlena chuckled at Eve's comment.

"Well that is partially correct. Look at your suit. The cuffs are designed with tiny weights and your shoes have small suction plates at the bottom."

Eve picked up her foot to look and instantly lost her balance. Marlena caught her and held her firmly.

"Here.........we have arrived."

Evelyn looked up to see another door with no markings on it.

"How do you know what is here? There are no markings or numbers."

The other woman smiled patiently as she spoke, "I do it by sound location and visual light guides. Your eyes weren't developed to sense the spectrum of light that is used here. Mine were. Come!"

Once through the door the whites gave way to shades of green and tan, yellow and orange. The room seemed to open out into a garden that led into a forest. Evelyn felt the pressure that once held her feet to the ground ease slightly. The smells were that of scented flowers and misty grasses. As Evelyn walked further she saw a pale shade of blue up ahead.

"Is all this real?" she asked as she headed for the blue area.

"Yes. These are all samples my people brought from your planet. We took cuttings and grew them. The animals were more sensitive so we have holographic animals on the ships and raise the animals on planet Aldebron."

Evelyn reached the patch of blue. It was water that reflected a crystal-clear vision of the surrounding foliage. She knelt down at the water's edge and took in the expanse of tree line, sky and Marlena.

"This is positively beautiful!"

Marlena knelt down beside her. "Then that means you like it here?"

Evelyn looked over and kissed Marlena on the cheek.

"I love it! It's relaxing and soothing."

"Then you would not mind being here with me?"

Evelyn let her hand float just below the water as she took in a deep breath.

"Are you asking me to stay here or be with you?"

Marlena stood up and moved back.

"I ......I suppose .... both."

A sudden breath of wind came up and the tops of the tall pines rustled along with it. Evelyn stood up and walked up to Marlena. She raised her hands and felt Marlena's face. She caressed it gently as she looked into her eyes.

"Don't you understand? You have truly bewitched me. I have fallen

44

hopelessly in love with you. As long as you are by my side I guess I can adapt to anything and any place."

Marlena closed her eyes as she felt Evelyn's touch and the gentleness of her voice. Marlena opened her eyes once more as she spoke.

"Evelyn......Etar is not unlike that period of time you call the Middle Ages. The people are primitive and the weather is severe. I would be allowed a place like that of the one you saw on Earth with little or no contact from the outside."

Evelyn looked Marlena in the eye. She watched as their eyes met. She then leaned over and kissed Marlena. The kiss was passionate and Marlena, for once, felt light headed.

"Does that answer your question?"

Marlena smiled and wrapped her arms around Evelyn. She never wanted this feeling to end and she knew that in time the Counsel would come around and place her and Evelyn back on Earth. As they walked down the corridor Evelyn turned to Marlena

"Are you really 75 years old? You don't look a day over 30!"

Pleasant voices filled the corridor as the two women walked down the corridor. For now, this would be their home and Evelyn would share with Marlena whatever situation would arise. For now, they were both happy at the thought of a new adventure together.

The End

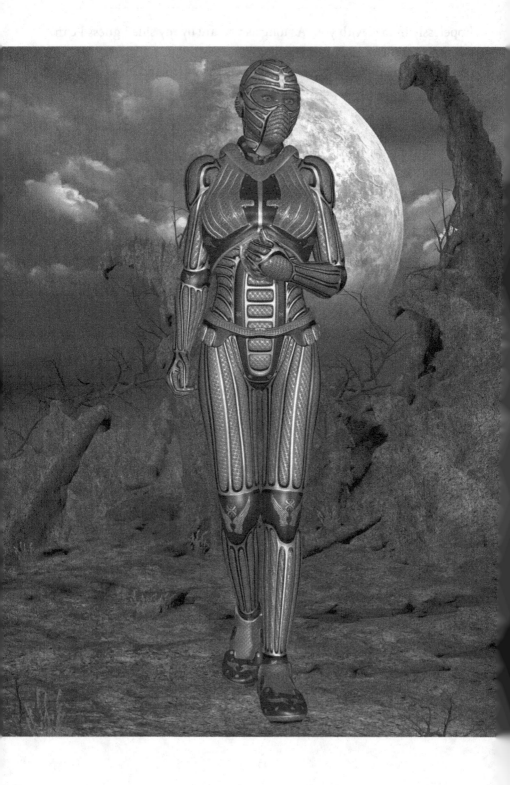

Arkania

Dr. Marissa Andrews smiled as the last piece of luggage was loaded onto the sea plane. Her travel plans were almost complete. She had no idea that her grant for Marine research would come through so soon. The current economic state of her country along with the talk of war had put several peaceful projects on hold. She tried to think ahead of all the items she would need.

The tiny island was found halfway between Australia and California some 20 years ago and had developed some interesting flora and fauna, which Marissa had discovered by accident, while tracking some wild dolphins. The ownership of the island was still in the legal system; however, both parties agreed that in the meantime it would be left an uninhabited island, used for research purposes only.

Marissa knew that this status would change as soon as the legal ownership had been decided. The island was a scientist's dream; full of exotic wildlife and cascading fresh water. Once she was deposited on the island, her only source of contact with the outside world would come in the form of a sea plane once a month and an emergency beacon weather balloon. As she nestled herself in the cockpit, the pilot smiled and gunned the engine. The plane lumbered over the marina like an overweight sea gull.

"Gee lady! What the hell you got in those crates? If I didn't know better I'd swear you got lead in them."

The pilot struggled with the steering controls until he leveled off. Marissa thought she owed him an explanation.

"I'm doing some research on Markham Island and since there are no hotels or diners within swimming distance I'm sort of stuck. A girl can get kind of hungry out there."

He looked at her with a puzzled look.

"You mean all that cargo is nothin but food!"

She laughed and realized that he was serious.

"No. Some of it is food; the rest is equipment and temporary housing. The Zodiac inflatable is being delivered with next month's shipment, along with some oxygen pumps and a generator."

"Well looks like you're all set to settle in. But I'll tell ya it's gonna take us 4 hours to unload all that stuff."

"Good then you should make it home in time for supper," she said sarcastically.

"Yeah I guess you're right."

With that bit of charming conversation over with Marissa decided to get some rest. She closed her eyes as the horizon stretched out before her. The hum of the plane seemed to quiet her nerves.

She dreamt that she was going through a revolving door as bits and pieces of her past came rushing through. Her beginning years in college seemed so distant. Professors she admired and even had a crush on became pleasant memories. The traumatic years when discovery and exposure seemed to take priority now were looked upon as learning experiences.

Her updated images came through as she spoke with her mother. She was happy that her daughter was successful but was afraid that her solitary behavior would end all hopes of marriage and family. Marissa was elated that this position of research was given to her, but her mother had great difficulty in accepting it. Marissa tried to explain to her mother that this was how she became so successful and that she functioned better alone. Marissa tossed a little and realized that the key through all these images was responsibility. Marissa had no one to be responsible for except herself and that when other people got involved relationships became complicated. Therefore, her life became simple because she involved no one. This solitary job was what she was made for, no one to worry about and no one to be responsible for.

The sound of the engines increased and her body noticed a difference in altitude. She opened her eyes to see the ocean coming closer to the nose of the plane.

"Well welcome back! You were sleeping so soundly I didn't have the heart to wake you. At least you had a good long rest. From the looks of the cargo you're gonna have your hands full when we eventually get the stuff unloaded."

As he eased the controls back, she could feel the pontoons of the plane hit the water. The plane glided towards the open area of the beach. A specially designed anchor was dropped and there on the beach were two men dressed in wet suits.

"No wonder you weren't worried about unloading all that stuff. You got help."

Marissa smiled and waved at the two young men.

"Don't worry they're helping us unload and then they're going back with you. So, you won't have a lonely ride back."

"Thanks"

With four people unloading the plane the time seemed to pass quickly. A military issue aluminum frame shed was erected prior to Melissa's arrival, so that sensitive equipment could be housed and not exposed to the elements. Food as well, as some dive gear, was stored on the 12-foot boat that the young men arrived in. Sundown was rapidly approaching and most of the boxes were off shore and safely tucked away within the shed. One of the men handed Melissa the keys to the boat, shook her hand and wished her luck with her new position. She watched as the anchor was lifted and the men climbed into the plane. The engine started, the plane turned and headed for the horizon. The pilot made one pass, waved, and then took off towards home. Marissa was now faced with the tasks ahead of her: storing the remaining boxes, making dinner and preparing a room to sleep in. She decided to unload boxes tomorrow, when she would have full light. The sound of the ocean and the birds settling down for the evening were taken in by Marissa. She smiled as the sun sank further down into the ocean and the last of the boxes were stacked in the shed. She cracked open a case of peanut butter and withdrew a jar. Searching her knapsack, she found the Tupperware container of crackers and proceeded to make herself dinner. *At this rate I'll look great by the end of the year,* she mused. As she ate she continued to unpack her sleeping bag, lantern, fuel and log book. The night was beginning to look pretty clear and so she thought that her first night should be spent outside. She picked on an empty crate and decided that the height was perfect. She struggled and managed to get it a yard from shore and placed her sleeping bag up on top. Thinking that the height of 10 feet would be perfect, she turned off the lantern and settled in for the night. The light of the half moon was very romantic coupled with the sounds of the sea. She drifted off into a very comfortable sleep.

A gloved hand parted the coconut palms and a black helmeted figure watched as Marissa adjusted her pillow. The moonlight highlighted Marissa's hair and face. The figure moved towards Marissa slowly. Suddenly, a small yellow light flashed on the figures left arm band. The figure stopped and seemed to study the light. It then moved silently back towards the heavily forested area where it came from.

Marissa felt the warmth of the sun on her face and realized it was time to get up. Her body was used to the strange sleeping positions she had developed and was only slightly aching. The ocean was calm and the tide was low. Birds could be heard in the distance and the wind was starting to blow. Marissa collected some dead wood, dug a small pit in the sand, and added some crumpled receipts to her Girl Scout stove. Once the fire was lit she rummaged through the boxes and pulled out her trusty coffee pot. The dents and scratches added character to its already worn metal. Pouring only enough freshwater for one cup she sat down and watched the sunrise on the horizon.

The days seemed to go smoothly as Marissa went about her task of organizing her equipment. The shelter that was built for her was larger than she thought for not only was there room for the equipment but space for a tiny yet efficient kitchen. She realized that her cot was perhaps the only piece of equipment that she would not use. She had grown accustomed to sleeping outdoors even in the cooler months. She was glad that her girlfriend had insisted that she take the old horse blanket her brother gave her. She sat down at her crate which she saved for her desk and began to fill in her journal.

NOW THAT I HAVE SETTLED THE EQUIPMENT IN, I CAN NOW BEGIN MY LONG-AWAITED EXPLORATION OF MARKHAM ISLAND. THERE IS MUCH TO DO BUT I MUST BE CAUTIOUS OF MY ENTHUSIASM. I'M SURE THERE ARE SPECIES

UNIQUE TO THIS ISLAND AND I WOULD NOT
WISH TO MISS THEM DUE TO MY EXCITMENT.

Marissa thought that was enough for the morning and so she gathered her binoculars, backpack and canteen and made her way up the beach towards the stand of coconut palms. As she hiked through the sand and weeds she looked at her watch and made a marker of rocks so that the trail she made could be used again and without worrying about the destruction to the beach line.

The mosquitoes were surprisingly low and Marissa noticed the lack of them in some areas where the dampness and moisture should have provided an excellent habitat. The habitat she was entering was like that of a rain forest. Short trees were growing beneath tall trees. Some plants had long vines which grew in the moist ground and had leaves growing high up towards the light. Most of the animals lived high in the trees. The forest seemed quiet now but Marissa knew that toward evening everything would come alive. Ants, beetles, termites and other insects were numerous and supplied other animals with food. She heard crickets and tree frogs singing. Suddenly, Marissa felt that she was being watched. It then occurred to her that if this was indeed a true rain forest that it might also include nocturnal carnivorous cats which would hunt for deer and the monkeys that now chattered above her. She knew that the dart gun she packed would be a bit weak but should be enough for a curious wild boar. She knew once nighttime came the only light to guide her would be the one in her own mind. She then set her watch alarm and proceeded forward. She still could not shake the feeling of being watched. Again, she looked around but saw nothing hostile. As the sunlight filtered through the leafy canopy another type of biome seemed to be forming. This one was densely vegetated and tangled with vines. Not quite a rainforest but a jungle.

Marissa sat down and began to write down the species of plants that grew in front of her. It was as if a scientist had selected the plants and provided them with the perfect environment within which to grow. No sign of leaf blight or other natural diseases were recorded. The leaves rustled with a sudden gust of wind. The hairs on Marissa's back seemed to stand on edge. As Marissa knelt forward to part the dense leaves a low muted growl came from behind her. She reached down into her backpack to grab her gun but as she felt its handle she also felt something rip at her flesh. She rolled over to find a jaguar about to make another swipe. A rush of air passed her right hand and at that instant a small dart lodged itself in the neck of the big cat. A perfect shot her though but who shot it? As she lifted the body of the cat off her own another rush of air was felt but this time she was the recipient. She tried to reach for the dart but as she saw her hand move she felt the effects of the dart.

Marissa felt the cold sensation like that of a probe touching her skin. Her mind was in a fog. She could feel someone or something tending to her wounds from the cat. She tried to move but was held securely to a table of some sort. From the corner of her eye she could make out another figure. This figure was wiping her wounds and applying some sort of cream. The figures became faint and once again Melissa blacked out.

She awakened to the ocean breeze and rustle of palm trees. *Could she have dreamed her encounter?* She felt her arm and back shoulder. The pain was faint but the bandages were intact.

Well, I suppose I could have fixed myself up, she thought.

She then felt her shoulder again. She could barely reach down to the edge of the bandage.

That settles that! Couldn't have possibly done my own bandaging back here. Thought the paperwork said no native cultures were on this island.

Marissa rose slowly. The room was in focus. So far so good. She noticed that fresh fruit had been picked and placed in the bowl she had outside her tent. She knew she had to locate her guardian angels and thank them for their assistance. She also wanted to know what they were doing on the island. She wondered why she could not remember their faces but thought under the circumstances that were perfectly normal.

The day was cool and breezy as Marissa walked along the beach. She hoped to find some clue or pathway to where she was taken yesterday. Navigating through the lush tropical undergrowth would be a bit difficult in her present condition. The branches would cut and tear at her bandages and her energy level would be rapidly depleted. She decided instead to continue her shoreline research.

As the days went on Marissa continued her research and daily beach walks. She ventured in to the brush only as far as the ocean sounded then she would return and make her notes. Her radio transmitter was finally put together but the solar cells seemed to be damaged. She placed the cells near the sunniest part of the beach. She could then receive but could not transmit. Her station guardians warned her of fragment showers and choppy waters due to the missile testing the Navy was doing some 2,000 miles away. She chuckled when she realized that if she hadn't put the damn radio together that she could have had a more major problem than just cat scars. The seas began to pick up and Melissa secured every loose item including her fruit.

Suddenly she heard a horrific crash that caused the ground beneath her feet to vibrate. At first, she thought a plane had crashed. She quickly gathered her medical bag and started off in the direction of the sound. Then she heard a sound that was chilling yet indescribable. She slowed her pace wondering what on earth the scream came from; animal or human. Her nose began to sense the direction, the smell of burning plant material and something else. She walked as quietly and cautiously as she could towards the smell. The sound of crackling fire caught her eye. Approximately 200 yards in front of her was a huge rocket. At least she thought it was a rocket. She was not familiar with the black color or the markings. A movement in front of her caused her to freeze. There, kneeling underneath a twisted piece of metal was a figure dressed in a black what appeared to be space suit. Two tubes ran from the back of the helmet to the suit. The figure was gently digging at the ground. Marissa moved very slowly towards the figure. The figure then caught hold of something and began pulling. As Marissa moved around to the side she could see what the figure had been pulling. When Marissa moved closer her foot caught hold of a twig and the sound caught the attention of the black suited figure. It turned quickly and when it did Marissa saw it grasp and hold onto an identically suited figure. Blood seemed to cover the body as well as the figure which held it.

"Please......I want to help you," Marissa said softly as not to frighten the figure in front of her.

The figure cowered against the metal and held the body tightly. Marissa moved forward again. As she did she noticed that the body being held was that of a female. She knelt down a few inches away from the frightened figure.

"I won't hurt you. I want to help."

The figure did not let go. When Marissa placed her hand on the body a red light flashed from the figures helmet. Marissa became still. She felt that the light was not a friendly response. She looked at the body and saw it was partially pinned under the wreckage. With the amount of blood, she saw she had a feeling that the victim was already dead. Marissa looked in the direction of the flashing helmet and gauged where she thought the eyes of this person might be.

"We need to get her out of here. Then I can help you care for her. Okay?"

Marissa waited for a response. She knew that this was some sort of secret military mission and that she needed to get help. The light stopped flashing and the figure slid her arm around the underneath side of the body. Marissa could feel the coldness of the body. When the body was removed to a suitable distance away from the burning wreckage she could see that the bottom half of the body had been burned and one leg was virtually torn in half. When she looked up she realized that the figure was also a female. Could this have been her mother or sister? How odd for a military mission. Which one cared for Marissa when she had her accident? Was this the same creature that cared for her? The figure smoothed out the suit which Marissa now saw was some type of uniform. The figure then began to rock the body back and forth as if waking it gently from its sleep. Marissa began to feel for the faceless people in front of her. She felt for a pulse, nothing. Marissa reached up towards the neck area. Her hand was gently pushed away. The figure adjusted the body in her lap and then reached behind the helmet. A hushed sound like that of a hydraulic brake was heard. The figure then twisted the helmet slightly and slowly lifted the helmet off the body. Silken hair tumbled down and around a beautifully tanned face. The woman was probably in her early 30's. Marissa judged by the body type of the other figure that this was not her sister but a colleague.

"Your buddy is dead."

Marissa felt so cold. What could she say to the woman? The bond was very strong as she gathered from the figures actions.

54

The woman reached down and lifted up the hand of the dead woman. She removed the glove from the right hand and took a golden ring gently off of the dead woman's finger. Marissa didn't think it strange at first but then saw the other figure remove her glove and place the ring next to its identical twin. Marissa got up and went over to a nearby tree. She placed her medical bag down and sat down leaning against the tree.

She watched the woman for what seemed to be hours, trying to figure out what country she might be from. She stayed quiet holding back questions that kept bothering her. She hoped if she remained there quietly she would not interfere yet let the figure know she was there to help. The burning wreckage began to burn itself out. And the smoldering scent filled the air with burning wood and smoke. Soon Marissa fell asleep. The woman looked over and emitted a pale blue light which covered Marissa. It continued scanning for several minutes and then withdrew the light. The woman picked up the lifeless body of her friend and walked through the woods to the beach. She laid the body in the sand and then stood up. She removed a small blue package from her pocket and unfolded it the length of the body. Marissa woke up groggy and looked around for the woman. If she had not seen the wreckage she would have thought it a dream. She saw a glow coming from the beach. It was almost dusk and the glow was fairly pronounced. She went through the woods and got to the beach in time to see the most beautiful yet strangest sight she had ever seen. The woman had encased the body in some sort of blue cloth that fit tightly around it. Marissa looked out into the ocean and saw in the distance movement in the form of splashing. As she watched in awe two dolphins swam up to the shoreline. A small singular whale waited just off shore. None of these animals were beaching. They just seemed to be waiting. The woman then carried the covered body to the shoreline and laid it in the water. She then stretched out her left hand. A small thin light came from her ring finger. It covered the whole body and caused it to glow. The light then stopped and the body drifted out to sea still glowing. Melissa then watched as the dolphins escorted it precious cargo out towards the whale. With several quick movements the body went under the water. Both women followed the glow until it disappeared.

Marissa went towards the woman and stopped when she noticed

the flashing red light on the woman's suit. The woman turned and looked at Marissa. It was the first time Marissa had seen her face clearly. She resembled a Polynesian woman but with softer features. Marissa wondered how she ever got a tan if all she wore was that space suit. The evening sea breeze blew her hair back and for an instant Marissa thought she caught a glimpse of a tear.

Marissa continued walking towards the woman the red light stopped flashing. Marissa smiled.

"I'm sorry about your friend," Marissa said as clearly as she possibly could.

The woman smiled and then looked down at the sand. She then began to walk away from Marissa.

"Wait!" she called.

The red light began to flash. Marissa continued towards her. The woman put out her hand as if to stop Marissa. Marissa slowed. The woman then placed her hand at her side.

"I must go back and remove some specimens from the wreckage." Her voice was deep, clear and silky, hearing it made Marissa feel warm inside.

"Won't your military be sending a search and rescue for you and your ship?" She smiled as she realized to what lengths men would go to for that sultry voice.

"No. We …. I am not part of a military mission. I must get back to the specimens."

"Perhaps I can help you. It's getting very dark and you'll need some light." Marissa waited for a response.

The woman walked towards Marissa. For the first time Marissa felt a bit of fear creeping inside and she became very stiff.

"My name is Ryla. My title is... Scientist."

She held out her hand in an offer of greeting. Marissa was relieved and gently held her hand. *If she wasn't with a military group then where was she from?*

"My name is Dr. Marissa Benninger."

The woman looked puzzled.

"Why are you on this island alone?"

Marissa realized the confusion.

"I'm a doctor of science. I'm doing my thesis on the evolution of certain species on this island."

Ryla then smiled again. The two women walked back through the maze of trees to the direction of the glowing wreckage. Marissa grabbed her kit from the ground and searched for the flashlight she kept inside.

She shined the light around and came upon Ryla's helmet. She examined the inside. There were several pressure pads located under the silk or nylon lining. As she pressed each one she noticed a different function being performed on or through the shaded visor. A hand reached over her shoulder and took the helmet out of Marissa's hands.

"Forgive me for startling you. I need my helmet back for a while. Your air takes some getting used to."

She placed the helmet on and began walking around as if she were looking for something. *Must have infrared vision*, Marissa thought, *but what about the comment about the air?* The woman worked for what seemed like hours unloading thickly packed containers. The heat had damaged some but the majority of specimens were not only clear of burns but still living. Finally, the last container was removed. Marissa looked around at the muted blackness of the area.

"You can stay with me tonight if you wish." Marissa watched as the woman removed her helmet.

"I am not familiar with the word WISH."

The woman then sat down beside Marissa. Marissa laughed and placed her hand on the woman's arm. The red light flashed.

"I'm sorry. I meant if you need a place to stay you can stay with me. Since you said that your rescue party wasn't coming."

Ryla turned towards the containers. "I have to release the specimens they..."

Marissa stood up and looked at all the containers.

"Can the specimens live till tomorrow?" she asked softly.

"Yes. They were prepared for the long journey."

Marissa was tired and was curious about the 'long journey' but decided that tomorrow would be just as good a time to clear up her questions.

"Leave them here and we can release them tomorrow morning. I will help you, okay?"

The woman removed five long sticks from her belt and got up. She then placed the stick equal distances from one another in a semi-circle around the containers. When she walked back towards Marissa the sticks began to give off a reddish glow.

"It will protect them until tomorrow." And with that she walked toward Marissa's camp.

Marissa was impressed by this woman's dedication to her specimens of fish, plants and small insects. She wondered how Ryla could walk so assuredly through the pitch-black night. Not even the moon provided light tonight. The clouds were thick and uncooperative.

Once back at her campsite Marissa prepared the other cot and took out several blankets from one of her many boxes. She showed Ryla the makeshift tent with the bathroom and freshwater supply. The two women went to sleep as soon as the lantern was extinguished.

The sounds of morning awakened Marissa. She sat up and looked about the room. At first, she thought she had dreamed last night's events but the neatly arranged cot told her otherwise. She sat up and dressed. She went into the bathroom to brush her teeth and saw a crystal shard the size of a tablespoon. She picked it up and it began to glow. An image of Ryla faced her in the mirror.

"Thank you for your kindness shown to one not of your own species. With my ship gone there is little I can do to repay you. However, if you need assistance in your research for the duration of two full moon cycles I will be......pleased........to help you. Thank you again."

The crystal faded with the loss of the image and turned to a white powder in Marissa's hands. She remembered the woman's difficulty with the word 'wish'. Her phrasing was unusual but Marissa understood it. She began to smile. *Must be a foreign country doing research on the island the same as her. After all she did say long journey.*

But then Marissa turned and looked towards the powder that was once a crystal and the image it played. She shook her head. *I must be dreaming. Better get some of that green tea.* She finished brushing her teeth, grabbed her thermos and went in the direction of Ryla's plane.

She reached the site sooner than she thought but saw no sign of her visitor. She looked in the direction of the strange red glowing sticks of last night. All that was left was the familiar white powder. She called out

Ryla's name in several directions but no answer was heard. Perhaps she went on another ship. But the message said two full moons. How was she to get in touch with this woman? She checked the shoreline to see if she might be releasing one of her specimens. No sign not even footprints. Maybe her rescue party did arrive. Maybe to avoid embarrassment they simply whisked Ryla away. Marissa realized she needed to get some research of her own done. She headed back in the direction of her campsite. She logged in her soil samples from the other day and grabbed her scuba equipment to drag out onto the beach. The sky was clear and the sea was calm. Once in the water Marissa was amazed at the clarity of the water. She checked her gauges and proceeded out towards the direction of the reef. One by one she collected plankton samples and placed them in her underwater crate resembling small milk bottles. A shadow from above caught her attention as she turned towards it. She watched carefully as a 10 ft. Hammerhead shark swam past her. As she followed its movement she was not prepared for its buddy who swam into her knocking her back into the coral head behind her. It was as if it didn't see her. She was 20 ft. down and was beginning to feel light headed. She tried to swim towards the surface but was too weak. Blinded by a strong light she lost consciousness. As her head cleared she could feel the water draining off her body as she was being pulled ashore. Her equipment was lifted off her and her body dragged further up onto the sand. Marissa tried to look up at the figure for identification but the morning sun was too strong.

"Ryla?" Marissa cried out.

The figure bent down and shielded Marissa's face from the sun. It was then that Marissa could see her friends face.

"I looked.... for...you. But..."

"Lay still. You are bleeding but I cannot determine the location. I'm going to move you to your campsite."

Ryla placed her arms gently around Marissa and lifted her up off the sand. Marissa could feel no pain only a warm sensation from her back. Marissa had never been carried by a man let alone a woman and was amazed at how nice and comfortable it felt. Once inside Ryla placed her down on a couple of crates.

"Your protective suit will need to come off."

She moved to the front of Marissa and slowly unzipped the vest of her wetsuit. Blood diluted with seawater was evident everywhere. As the suit was removed Marissa began to feel a pain that seemed to race through her entire body.

"I'll have to remove your......"

She seemed to be searching for the right word.

"It's called a bathing suit."

Marissa tried to reach behind her back to release the catch but felt the pain again. Ryla placed her arms around Marissa and released the clasp. She then pulled the straps gently off Marissa's shoulders. Marissa became slightly embarrassed as her nipples grew hard. Ryla slid the bottom half of her suit off and tossed them to the side. She started to pat Marissa's body with a towel to remove the blood and seawater. She then noticed several puncture wounds located above her stomach. She placed a clean towel on the cot and instructed Marissa to lie down. Ryla removed several tubes from her utility belt and put them on the cot.

"These medicines may cause you some pain."

Marissa felt exposed and weak. She was never totally nude not even for her doctor, let alone another woman! As if Ryla was reading her mind, she covered Marissa partly with a blanket. The cream was applied gently but the wound was painful. It began to throb and ache. The second cream was cool and cut the throbbing down considerably. The third cream was applied and the aroma caused Marissa to feel sleepy.

"It's okay. You can sleep if you want. I will stay with you so that......."

The words drifted off as Marissa did.

Days went by as the strange woman stood vigil over Marissa. She cooled her when she was hot and warmed her when she was cold. Marissa regained her strength somewhere around the seventh day. She awoke to seagulls and ocean breezes.

"Good afternoon!" Ryla came from behind her with small jars in both hands. "Your algae specimens needed additional nutrients so I released them into that small cove over there."

Marissa realized that Ryla must have brought her out to the beach. As if Ryla could read her mind.

"My research indicated that your body required some additional solar healing. If you are too warm I can..."

"No. I'm just fine. You've done so much for me already. Where are you from? I mean…. I've never seen a plane quite like the one in the wreckage and you said your specimens were packed for a long journey."

Ryla hesitated as she watched Marissa.

"I am from Arkania……the…. planet Arkania."

Silence filled the air. Even the sea gulls could no longer be heard by Marissa. *She must be having an inner ear problem* she thought to herself.

"My hearing must have been affected. I mean…. I know I didn't go down more than 5' but…I thought you said planet."

Ryla sat down in front of her as she placed her hand over Marissa's.

"I did…. say planet."

"If that's true how do you know our language and about our environment and what are you doing here collecting samples?"

Ryla placed the bottles down and turned to face the ocean.

"My people have been studying your planet and its people for centuries. We have gathered samples from your animal and plant kingdom and have observed your history. We have read your great books and our computers have a full collection of……dictionaries. That is the proper name?"

Marissa laughed. "Yes, that is correct. But why haven't you made contact with us before now?"

Ryla turned and looked out toward the ocean. She almost seemed ashamed.

"Our code does not permit any human contact. It is punishable by termination. We must protect our species as well as others and this code insures this."

"But what you are saying is that by your saving my life you have gone against your code and will be terminated!"

"I tried to keep my distance…I…..committed several errors. I was not thinking properly."

Marissa didn't mean to make her new friend uncomfortable. If anything, she found herself wanting to protect her.

"My life mate and I were to be the first to present evidence why contact should be made with your species. We were considered outcasts by the counsel. The Federation of Scientists supported our research on this island. Our planet, like yours, was not prepared for the extinction of certain species of plants. When your planet was researched it was noted that we had similar Flora and Fauna. Reintroducing species to both planets would have proved beneficial to both people. For a while we bioengineered certain species from its DNA but placing the two strains together made the plants and animals hardier. But now federation will either forget us......me or terminate me."

Marissa could see the pain in Ryla's eyes.

"What is your life partner like? There was this guy I knew back at the university that I thought would be my partner for life but he turned out to be a selfish insensitive fool."

Ryla managed a smile.

"My life partner is dead. Leka died in the wreckage. Thank you for helping me that night. I forgot my directives temporarily."

"She was your .... partner!" Marissa tried not to sound surprised.

"Yes. I believe your term is mate or husband/wife."

Marissa began to laugh. "I'm sorry I've never met a lesbian before let alone one from another planet."

Marissa couldn't control what she was saying. She could hear herself being stupid but couldn't control what was coming out of her mouth.

"I apologize. I don't know what is happening. I....."

"Please don't worry. It is my aura which is relaxing your inner thoughts. I must put my helmet back on."

"I don't understand. Your aura is causing me to say stupid things?"

Ryla smiled.

"Your inner senses are relaxed and you feel no inhibitions or negative controls on your statements."

"Are you trying to say that I say what I'm thinking?"

"Yes. It generally passes after you've been in close contact with us."

Ryla got up and looked out towards the horizon. The lights on both her helmet and wrist lit up. Marissa looked out in the same direction but could see nothing.

"What is it?"

"Radioactive particles in the air are increasing."

"Radioactive part....G-D no!"

Marissa awkwardly stood up trying to adjust to her senses. It seemed like years since she was on her feet.

"Help me to the hut please."

Ryla placed her arm around Marissa and helped her up the beach. Luckily her hut was not as far away as she had thought.

"Can you give me a measurement?"

Ryla touched her helmet. "60-140 kV range and increasing."

This was being translated to a low powered radiation source like that of a radiotherapy unit in a hospital.

"Any idea of what is causing it?" Marissa asked Ryla as she tried to reach someone on her emergency radio. Not even a newscast or weather station could be found.

Suddenly Ryla looked up.

"Come! We must hurry!"

She grabbed Marissa's arm and realized that Marissa was still a bit wobbly.

"Come. We don't have much time."

Ryla picked up Marissa and carried her to the far side of the island. As she placed Marissa gently down on the sand two other black suited figures emerged from the trees and helped guide Marissa to a strange light in the clearing. Marissa was dazed. Actions were happening too quickly for her to assimilate. The light was brighter than ordinary daylight. The light seemed to be pulling her upward. She started to panic but was held securely by the two figures. She then realized she was being escorted into some sort of spaceship.

"Please come with us."

She turned to find a youthful looking alien with very pale skin smiling at her. Before she could open her mouth, her question was answered.

"Commander R....Ryla will be with you momentarily. Your other questions will be answered then."

"Thank you" was all Marissa could say as she watched the large screen in front of her.

It was a view of her planet Earth from space. Numbers below the screen were accelerating and lights which looked like matches being lit were shown directly on the screen. There was little noise in this room but movement was all around.

"Sensors reading small cylindrical objects heading for quadrants

0...6 NW. Unidentified object has just breached the outer atmosphere. Sensors indicate 3 such objects now orbiting Earth's atmosphere."

Marissa's eyes began to water as she realized what she was watching. Her world was rapidly coming to an end.

"Perhaps you should sit down."

The voice was strong yet soft to her ear.

"I am known as the Guardian."

Marissa sat slowly down next to the monitors as lights flashed faster and faster on the screen.

Ryla watched the monitors as the information changed rapidly. The Guardian saw Ryla and walked towards her.

"Does she know what is happening to her world?"

Ryla gazed at Marissa.

"Yes, I believe she does. Although I'm not sure she knows how quickly things are going down there."

"Perhaps you should have counsel with her."

"I would like to Guardian but I have already been banished from the chambers for bringing her here. I just now have been allowed entry again."

The Guardian came closer.

"My child, you have given many honors to your people. Your conquests as scientist and pilot speak for themselves. Some say the chambers would not exist if it had not been for you. This woman is about to lose not only her family but her race as she knows it. She has a universal right to know the truth."

Ryla knew that the counsel could not say anything against her once she had the Guardians blessing. She bid the Guardian a respectful thank you and went off to find Marissa. Meanwhile, the counsel held a meeting to determine the events of the planet Earth. There were still Arkanian researchers on the planet and getting them out would require time which they did not have. Ryla realized that had it not been for the ships beacon that went on automatically after the crash she would not have been rescued from the island. Even with that they took a week to respond. She wondered if they were going to seek punishment for her soon or wait till the current crisis was over. Would they blame Earth's current crisis on her and her fellow scientist's beliefs?

Earth knew its situation was desperate. The events that were set in motion by their great leaders were affecting every continent, country and people. Several shuttles were being prepared for launch. Children were being loaded onto them daily. It was still unclear as to whether they were going out into space to wait or attempt a settlement on the moon. Knowing Earth's technology, the latter was not yet possible. The Arkanians were able to track and predict meteor showers and impact. The earth people had not. The counsel was bound by Universal law to see to the safety of any planet children. So, as a result they watched very closely. If Earth's intentions were to truly destroy itself and set the shuttle children adrift then the Arkanians would be forced to retrieve them.

The human forms of both people would make the encounter a little easier but problems still remained. Arkanian pilots would have to be gathered and ships would have to be launched. The only ships available were fighter squadrons. Clearance from the Council and the Guardian would have to be given. Placement of the children would be the next consideration and the adults that were sure to accompany them. Thus, the Arkanian ship was busy preparing documentation and clearance. Ryla and certain other members had mixed emotions regarding these current activities. On one hand it would have been simpler to make the Arkanian presence known to the people of Earth. But knowing Earth's propensity for violence they would have managed to drag the Arkanian people into their cause and the outbreak of war would be more devastating if one could possibly imagine.

The Arkanians were not always a peaceful people. They began as warriors mastering the art of killing not only individuals but planets as well. Through the centuries interbreeding of a more peaceful, docile species caused the current peaceful race of Arkanians. Laws were created and no interference of planets or people would be tolerated. Research and scientific studies were the only exception to this rule. Fine tuning these guidelines sometimes made it impossible to rationalize some their experiments.

Ryla's communication relay beeper (C.R.B.) went off as she walked to the nearest communications bay.

COMMANDER

ERICKSON LEVEL 4 DOCK 17

...EMERGENCY

Quickly she entered the elevator and pushed Dock 17. As the elevator door opened she could see security standing with weapons drawn. There in a corner stood Marissa with a laser aimed at an Arkanian physician and her hand on the lever of a pod separation module. The warning sign above clearly read danger for inhabitants of the pod.

"No!"

Ryla ran past the crew and the guards that had collected by the door. She placed herself between Marissa and the guards.

"Marissa, please don't do this. There are other ways of handling this. Please!"

"No! I don't belong here and you know it. I want to be down there with my people."

Ryla turned to face the screen and closed her eyes.

"Then you will surely be terminated by your people. Look at you. You're behaving like those men down on your planet. They will destroy their entire race to prove who is mightier. Neither side will win. Both has his hand on the button. We have ways of dealing with your request. We still have people on your planet that we must get out. Please!"

Ryla moved closer.

She knew that Marissa was not prone to violence and would not take an innocent life.... hers. Ryla looked deeply into Marissa's eyes as they made contact. Marissa turned to face the large window that opened to a view of the moon. She dropped the weapon. Ryla motioned to Security that she would handle the matter. Ryla moved towards Marissa and put her arms around her.

She whispered gently, "I was a prisoner on your planet when my ship was destroyed. I know that feeling of loneliness. I've arranged for you to be placed in front of a continuous news monitor. There will be a hearing on your request and status tomorrow. Okay?"

Marissa reached up and held Ryla's hand glad that she was facing the vision of the moon instead of Ryla.

Night fell as the war on Earth continued. Each crew member had their own predictions. The reasons for the outbreak of war didn't seem to change much throughout earth's history. Oil, weapon stock piles, hostages, religious beliefs all seemed minor points to destroy ones' world for. Ryla dreamt of simpler, peaceful times on her own planet where she herself was an outcast until she became involved with Arkanian military. Aliens of superior intelligence were thought to be a threat and not given the same privileges as other citizens. But Arkania seemed to be a planet that practiced what it preached:

PEACE AND HARMONY FOR ALL.

A simple phrase but true. She worked her way up slowly. Proving herself not only to her superiors but to the people of Arkania as well. With her science studies she came up with several different methods of treating space bacteria. This in turn led to new discoveries in child bearing in space and the side effects that a low gravity environment could cause. Her more popular successes unfortunately were always with the military. She earned a name for herself and is now consulted before action is taken, before treaties are made and before crews are sent on potentially dangerous research expeditions.

The buzzer went off and Ryla went back to her official mode. While gathering papers for Marissa's request to be returned to Earth she wondered if she would be able to present a strong case for her friend. She called down to Marissa and left a message for her to be ready by 14:00 hours. She then took out her chamber wardrobe which consisted of a teal blue robe lined in black velvet.

Ryla tuned into the situation on Earth while she dressed. War was now considered full scale and it seemed that no country was left out no matter how hard they tried.

Every country was a battleground with direct hits recorded on everyone's side.

Ryla reported to the chambers on time. The counsel gathered within the chambers as Ryla prepared her transmission tape. The chamber was designed in nautical woods and deep tones of brass lined viewing ports. The three-member council took their positions and the Guardian began the hearing. Marissa was seated by the guards in the center of the chamber. Ryla presented her transmission tape and listened as Marissa's background and credits were shown to the counsel. As the transmission ended the Guardian stood and faced Ryla.

"It seems that all the leaders of Earth have made this hearing invalid."

At the command of the Guardian a screen was lowered at the front of the chambers. A transmission was viewed of Earth North America. A flash of light at various points on the screen created heat reading sensors to move off the scale. All verbal transmissions were dead.

PLANET EARTH TOTAL ANNIHILATION.

SURVIVOR FACTOR 1ST STAGE 2%

As the computer ended the flashes of light continued. Long after the people were gone the computers still carried on the war.

"No! It's a lie! Noooo!"

Marissa stood up and stared at the screen. She then fell to her knees. Ryla lowered her head. She walked over to Marissa. She removed her cape and placed it over Marissa's shoulders.

"The Physician will escort Dr. Benninger to her quarters."

The Guardian then looked at Ryla.

"Commander Erickson, your presence is required in private chambers".

Ryla firmly but gently lifted Marissa up and guided her towards the medical officer.

"Yes, My Guardian."

The private chambers held the counsel, Ryla, the guardian and another officer.

"Commander Erickson, 3 shuttles of Earth children were launched shortly before 5:00 sectons this morning. Five of our Research Technicians are also on board. Under Universal Law Section 2004:10 we must prepare to remove the children as well as our people. You have 72 hours to organize your pilots and secure your flight plan. Placement for the children has yet to be determined. Perhaps you're......friend Dr. Benninger can be of assistance?"

Ryla was pleased with their use of Marissa and her involvement. The sooner she was working the better. No time for shock.

"Yes, counsel I'm sure that would be very beneficial. She is a dedicated scientist and I'm sure will understand the Earth children's requirements... Is the necessary paper work in order?"

The Guardian handed Ryla a 3.5 computer disk.

"The paperwork has already been processed."

The counsel was dismissed and Ryla knew she would have to work fast to get the necessary pilots and ships for her mission. She wondered whether there would be any human resistance once the shuttle linked with her ships. The adults could be military personnel or political staff. There was no communication from the Arkanian research technicians onboard the shuttles so she had no way of knowing what was going on. The only thing she knew was what the sensors had told her. *Would the Arkanian technicians be spread out between the three ships or would the all be on one?* Ryla could only hope that things would be simple. She sat down at her master computer. She went through her ships files. Five speeders would be used to rendezvous with the shuttles. These ships were quick and easy to maneuver. They were suited to short distance travel and protected special dignitaries between ships. Particle beaming would be too unstable and therefore docking procedures or space suits would have to be used. The speeders would have to be equipped with survival equipment and several space suits in case anything went wrong. Weapons were standard to all ships including research vessels. Next was her crew. Most were women since research found that they were less of a threat and use force less often than their male counter parts? They gain compliance without excessive force and are better at defusing potentially violent confrontations. They also possess better communication skills and respond more effectively to incidents of violence against women and children. For this job they would be perfect. They also would have a more calming effect over the children. Her crew of 14 was picked. She sat in front of the computer rubbed her eyes. She was glad that her eyes could go back to focusing on the matters at hand. She entered her code on the Communications link.

"Sick Bay Level 4."

"This is Commander Erickson. I'm checking on the condition of the human female called Marissa."

"Yes, commander she's in stable condition. There was some difficulty in getting her to accept a stabilizer treatment. She's awake but not very responsive."

"May I visit her?"

"One moment."

Ryla realized how helpless she felt. She wanted her new human friend to talk to her. She missed their discussions on the beach and their sharing of ecological views. A handful of her people had destroyed innocent women, children, men, and wildlife.

"Commander!"

"Yes, I'm sorry"

"You may visit her on Level 2."

"Thank you."

"Commander."

"Yes."

"I was sorry to hear of Leka's death. If there is anything I can do please let me know."

"Thank you, nurse...."

Ryla searched the bottom screen for her name.

"Nurse Kano. Please keep an eye on the human female."

Ryla switched to the satellite camera that now positioned itself over the area not far from where they were rescued. Severe winds, seas and slow death were present all along the area once known as the east coast. Temperatures ranged from 104 degrees during the day to 20 degrees at night. Ryla let the screen fade. She got up and headed towards Level 2.

As the doors to her room parted she noticed Marissa standing at the window. The Earth moon reminded Ryla of the Arkanian stellar moon; very bright and romantic.

"Hello."

Marissa turned slowly to face the voice. Her eyes were heavy and her color was practically ashen. But Ryla noticed Marissa looking at her and producing a small smile. She held out her bandaged arms towards Ryla. She had read about this form of greeting with certain humans. Ryla came closer. Marissa wrapped her arms around her. Ryla could feel her body against Marissa's.

"You're cold. You need to get back in bed under the blankets."

She backed up and looked at Ryla.

"No. What I need is for this nightmare to be over and for me to wake up."

Ryla gave a frustrated sigh then spoke.

"Marissa, I have to talk to you but unfortunately there is no 'right' time."

She waited for a response. Marissa rubbed her face and eyes, turned and sat down on the edge of the bed.

"You'll have to forgive me. Your medications do some pretty funny things to humans. This stuff would be the rage back in my home town. Go on. I'm listening."

"We....I need your help. There were survivors. They are on a shuttle around Earth's orbit. I need you to talk with them and help comfort them somehow. Marissa .... they're children. We're not sure how many or if there are any adults or soldiers with them. We are required by our law and the Universal code to rescue these humans yet we know little about them."

Marissa started to chuckle.

"Well then what the hell were you guys doing watching us that long and not takin notes?"

Ryla managed a smile.

"We studied Flora, Fauna, and wildlife creatures. Your people were not on this list!"

Marissa wiped a tear away from her eye.

"I'm sorry. I'll help you just as soon as they get me off of this stuff."

"Consider it done!"

"Thanks. I hated drugs when I was a kid."

Ryla motioned to a screen in the corner.

"No. No more pictures please!"

Ryla moved in front of her.

"These are not pictures. They're configurations and statistics on the shuttles and their orbits."

Marissa looked up at her.

"I don't know anything about those things."

Ryla poured her a glass of water.

"I know. But if you're going to help, I need you to be familiar with some things. I know it's not much time but we've only got two days before the shuttles change position."

Marissa swallowed the water hard as if it were liquor.

"Okay, I'll freshen up and get to work."

Ryla smiled knowing she had succeeded in getting Melissa's mind tuned to a different mode.

"I'll meet you on the observation deck at 14:00......sorry. I mean in about 4 hours from now. You'll find a fresh change of clothing in the closet. It should fit."

Marissa nodded as she stood and began to undress. Ryla felt a strange curiosity come over her. She wanted to observe Marissa more closely. She shook her head as if to realign her thoughts and walked out the door.

Ryla stopped at the Communications Bay and checked the position of the shuttles. The Guardian stood behind her as she read the list of numbers.

"How is the Earth woman doing?"

The Guardian watched the screen as the satellite bounced signals to various parts of the planet Earth. Ryla turned to face him.

"She is doing well. She has agreed to help with the rescue of the children and their acclimatization periods."

The Guardian motioned for Ryla to follow.

"The council has agreed to accept the earth woman with our people. Since her title is that of doctor, she can be of great use to our people; with proper re-education signatures."

Ryla knew this was a great honor which was rarely given to Earth people or Terrans since they were thought of as too warlike to be educated. Ryla also knew it would provide the perfect opportunity to show Marissa the Arkanian planet and people. *But would she agree to this honor?* Ryla wasn't sure yet how Marissa felt about anything.

"I think she will need to be informed properly upon her return from the shuttle mission."

"Yes Guardian." And with that both figures separated.

The pilots were gathering on the Observation Deck as Ryla walked in. All six pilots stood and saluted. As they sat down a young red-headed woman walked up to Ryla.

"Commander?"

"Yes, Captain Hedren?"

"Is it true that these children are survivors of Earth?"

"Yes. I'll begin the briefing shortly."

Ryla gathered her notes she had left earlier by the window. Marissa appeared behind a tall dark-haired pilot. The room fell silent. Curiosity seemed to be present on both sides as eyes met from around the room. Ryla cleared her throat.

"Please be seated.... Marissa......"

Ryla motioned to the seat next to hers.

"I hope you all read your disks. This particular mission involves 3 Earth ships with an undetermined number of Earth children on board. Our sensors have been unable to get a stable reading. Three of our researchers are also thought to be onboard. The Communications Bay has been refitting their equipment to enable us to communicate directly with these ships. The link should be complete as we speak."

Ryla pressed a small button to her right.

COMMUNICATIONS LINK WITH EARTH SHUTTLES ALPHA, BETA, OMEGA ARE COMPLETE COMMANDER. AWAITING FURTHER ORDERS

Ryla marked down the time on her folder.

"Acknowledged. The window for our synchronous orbit is in 03:00 hours. This is Dr. Marissa Andrews from the planet Earth. She has agreed to help us with this mission."

Ryla pointed to Marissa and motioned for her to stand.

"I'm not sure how much I can help you but I'm willing to assist with any information I can give you."

As she sat down she noticed Ryla slipping a note in front of her:

You're doing fine. Don't worry.

She smiled as she sat back down.

"At this time, we are expecting no resistance to our presence. All necessary safety precautions are being taken to ensure no casualties. If there is resistance by the humans the weapon they will most likely use is called a g-u-n. If the humans use them they will penetrate the type of suits you are wearing. Neutralize all weapons immediately upon sight."

Ryla made eye contact with each pilot as they nodded their orders.

"I will be the first to enter shuttle #1-Alpha and access their computer for immediate link. It is at this time that you will know which method to use upon entering the shuttles #2-Beta and #3-Omega. Your ships will be overloaded as it is so proceed at 1.4 speed upon departure back to the station. Any questions?"

She looked around the room as most of the pilots watched Marissa.

"Commander?" An older woman at the table raised her hand. "We all wish to express our prayers to you over your recent loss of your life-partner and as such will wear the Golden Triangle for our mission."

Ryla bowed her head.

"That isn't necessary I...."

"We insist Commander Erickson."

Ryla placed her chart down.

"Very well. As requested."

A communications message sounded.

2:99 HOURS MARK. ALL PILOTS TO THEIR STATIONS

Ryla gathered up her things and motioned for Marissa to follow. She could see the faces of her pilots clearly. Each one wanted to pay their respects but there wasn't time. The symbol of the Golden Triangle dates back to the time when loved ones killed in battle were remembered by their credits or medals. When several of the credits were worn together they formed a triangle. When peace time came the triangles were worn with a small heart in the center.

The hallways were busy with personnel heading for their stations. All ships were loaded except for Ryla's. Marissa was helped into the ship and given basic overall instructions on what to touch and what not to touch. She looked at her helmet and thought of all those times when she was a little girl; stealing pots and pans from her mom and pretending she was an astronaut. If only her mom had lived long enough to see her. She then thought about if she had lived. Which would have been less painful: to die from cancer or to die from nuclear radiation? Tears can to her eyes. She faced the instrument panel, gave a hard swallow and placed the helmet over her head. She sensed movement. Ryla was on board. She fastened herself in and began her pre-flight check.

"How are you feeling?" Ryla asked Marissa as she continued checking.

"Okay. It's a new experience yet an old one."

"Yes, I know. I sensed your thoughts regarding your parent. The helmet tends to magnify your brain waves. Sometimes pilots don't communicate verbally. They think what they want to say and it is heard by the other pilot."

Marissa thought how embarrassing that could get.

74

"Don't worry. I'll try not to sense your private thoughts."

Marissa knew there was something odd when she first encountered Ryla but she couldn't put her finger on it. She could feel the sudden vibration of engines. Ryla began repeating numbers as the ship moved slowly in line with the others.

"Marissa you'll need to hold your breath as we take off. If not, one tends to get sick due to the G-force okay?"

Marissa signaled back.

"Good you're getting the hang of it as you humans say. Now watch the small meter at the right-hand corner of your screen. When it shows double 00 we shoot out of here like a beam of light."

"Got it," she signaled.

One by one each of the ships took off and began to form an arrowhead pattern as they headed for their rendezvous point. The computers did trajectory calculations as Ryla received an emergency signal. The space station sensors picked up a meteor shower which was headed towards the path of shuttle Alpha. Some of the particles passed through the Van Allen belt. Due to the disruption of the troposphere and stratosphere by the nuclear radiation the particles were not burning up as they would normally and were creating craters in the earth. The shuttle Alpha had now been detected at 1000 km which was the normal satellite range. Radiation levels were remaining constant. Ryla's ship was on target. The speeders reached their rendezvous points within minutes of one another. The shuttles were in sight of ships 2 and 3.

"Captain Seerve awaiting countdown entry on shuttle Beta."

"Acknowledged"

"Captain Hedren awaiting countdown entry on shuttle Omega."

"Acknowledged"

Ryla saw the shuttle Alpha drifting.

"Computer atmospheric sensors on audio."

Ryla began her approach.

SHUTTLE ALPHA ENTERING 700 KM, 600 KM, 500 KM, 400 KM, 300 KM, 200 KM, WARNING! MESOPAUSE AT 80 KM

Ryla locked on the shuttles main hatch on the left side of the shuttle.

"We can only hold this position for 20 minutes. Any longer and we go down with her!"

Ryla unfastened herself and moved to the hatch. She removed a large tool from the space next to the door. She banged twice on the hatch before she turned to unlock it. A vacuum seal sounded and suddenly the hatch was opened. Directly in front of her was the stairs. Ryla signaled Marissa. The two women entered the shuttle. Only the auxiliary lights were on. Marissa looked around but saw nothing but the mid-deck and the toilet. Ryla slowly moved up the stairs to the flight deck. As she lifted herself up the last step she noticed movement to her right. Three small children in space suits were floating in front of the control panel.

"Marissa, check the sleep stations on the mid-deck."

There Marissa found two more small children strapped to their beds. Marissa released them and began to talk to them.

"Marissa, I sense more children but I don't know where to look. We don't have much time."

"Load the children onto the ship. I'll search the shuttle."

Ryla communicated the situation to ships 2 and 3. They would begin unloading immediately. No adults yet had been found on shuttle Alpha. But the signal was still to proceed with caution. Marissa checked the air lock module that controlled the cargo bay. She peered inside. As she gasped Ryla picked up her fear pattern.

"Marissa what's wrong!"

Ryla quickly strapped the last child in as she moved to find Marissa.

"Stay where you are it's all right. I found the adults, three are dead. They're floating in the cargo bay. I think they were shot. I don't see any......wait! I'm going in."

"Marissa, we don't have time there's 5 min...."

"I'll be there! Just get ready to leave."

Ryla fell silent trying to link with Marissa. She could see her maneuver through the airlock to the cargo bay. She could see the floating bodies. Two females one male. Blood formed tiny pearls that floated about like ping pong balls. The fourth adult was clutching a child in the corner next to the RMS (REMOTE MANIPULATOR SYSTEM) shoulder joint of the robotic arm. Ryla could feel Marissa smiling as she pulled them both towards her.

"I'm on my way."

Ryla breathed a momentary sigh of relief.

"All sensors reading no other human life forms on board the Alpha. We're clear."

Ryla waited between the main hatch and the airlock to assist Marissa. Ryla pressed a tiny green button on her helmet. This signaled the other ships and gave the boarding command. Once everyone was in Ryla released the gravitational mechanism that held her ship to the shuttle. Ryla amended her order regarding speed due to the unknown condition of her passengers. Two children were awake and crying the other four seemed to be in a daze. Marissa checked their oxygen supply pressure gauge. It seemed fine. She checked the adult female and found that her cooling tube was damaged. Through her pressurized helmet she could see the woman's eyes closing.

"We're losing her."

"Hang on we're almost there."

The other ships had signaled successful retrieval of 7 adults and 8 children. Two of the adults had been identified as the research personnel left on earth before the war. Due to the speed at which Ryla had pushed her ship the outer temperature was 2700 F.   They would have to be cooled down before their doors could be opened. As the ship entered the docking bay all personnel were in protective head gear. Blue foam was released from holding tanks on either side of the bay. Only a slight bump signaled the ships landing. Immediately Ryla began to shed her space suit and help release the children from their seats. The doors swung open and were immediately filled with several helmeted figures.

"The adult female needs emergency medical attention."

She was quickly moved onto a floating stretcher and moved to the infirmary. The children one by one were taken by a crew member specially assigned and taken to the medical bay for checkups. Since most of the children were in an almost dream like state their recovery might take a while. Marissa removed her helmet. In all the excitement Marissa didn't realize that she had burned her arm on the ship. Small bits of her suit had fused into the wound.

"You need to take care of that now."

"No! The doctors are busy with the children. I'll live. It just smells terrible."

Ryla gave her a look of impatience.

"Well since you don't mind pain come with me."

Ryla grabbed her by the shoulder and placed her into the elevator.

"Medical level"

"Look I told you they......"

"I know. I heard you. So, since you do not want them to bother with it I will."

Ryla escorted Marissa into an end room. She turned on the lights and punched several buttons on a silver panel in front of her. From behind white plasticized panels came a sink, surgical instruments, and several fluorescent liquids. She took a scissors out and cut the suit around Marissa's wounded arm.

"Okay now you can remove your space suit."

Gently she was helped off with her suit.

"I seem to remember you doing this before."

"I told you my title was Scientist but my secondary is physician."

The protective undergarments now provided little warmth for the cool air now felt on her skin. Ryla handed her a short-sleeved robe.

"How many titles do you have?"

"Several"

She then gave Marissa a glass of fluorescent pink liquid to drink.

"It tastes like strawberries and cream."

"Is that good?"

"Yes, it's delightful."

Ryla then took tweezers and began to delicately remove the bits and pieces of the suit from her wound. As she pulled, parts of skin were removed but Marissa felt nothing.

"This pink stuff tastes pretty good." Ryla chuckled.

"Wait till you get to the blue...stuff."

Patiently Ryla removed all the pieces.

"Okay now take this blue liquid."

Marissa did as she was told. Her arm was bandaged as Marissa finished the blue liquid.

"Well, thank you doc. That's not a bad job. Did you ever think of changing your profession? What is your profession anyway?"

Marissa suddenly felt worried. She didn't seem to be able to control what she said. She started to hop down from the table she was propped on and fell forward.

"I'm sorry. I think it's time I went to my room. I......."

Ryla placed an arm around her. She then lifted Marissa up into her arms and started to carry her towards the door.

"What...are... you doing?"

"Shhh. I don't think it's wise of you to walk on your own up to your quarters. So, I'm carrying you. Don't worry. I won't drop you."

"You have...to understand. I've never been carried by a woman before. Is this a...."

"Just be quiet. You'll soon be in your bed and you can rest. We'll talk later if you wish. Alright?"

By this time Marissa had fallen asleep with the combination of drugs and warmth from her friend. She nodded as several pilots met her in the hall. Quietly the red-headed pilot Seerve walked over to her and summoned the elevator.

"Need help Commander?"

"No thank you I can manage."

Ryla stepped in and tapped in Marissa's room and deck number. As she entered her friend's room she wondered what the procedure on Earth was for partnership and if Marissa would accept her. She laid her down and pressed the visual communications code s that she would not be disturbed. She herself was tired but needed to do some research on this matter. A final report would be given on the children in 7 hours so she had plenty on time to bathe and report.

Days passed as Marissa recovered and began working with the Earth children. She found this rewarding but yet she missed talking with her friend Ryla. She guessed that she was busy with other matters and so she did not bother her. Ryla sat down in front of the library computer and typed in Earth circa 2002. The computer gave her various categories but none seemed to apply to what she was searching for. Human Relationships, Family Relationships, Family Unit, all listed family groups with no indication of female intimacy. She tried Singles,

Sexual Relationships, and Marriage but still she could not locate the information. Perhaps her good friend Verlin could help. She had been assigned to Earth's information core for several light years and might give her the key word she needed to locate the information.

"Mastering Officer may I help y....Greetings Ryla."

"Hello Verlin. My apologies for not communicating with you sooner but I..."

"Yes, I heard. You had things to do. Once again, you're in council news. I'm sorry to hear about your loss. She was..."

"Thank you. I need some assistance with Earth relationships."

Verlin sensed Ryla's sadness.

"How can I help you?"

"If one of our people wanted to take a human as a life partner what would be Earth law regarding that?"

Verlin paused then cleared her throat. She could sense something but wasn't sure what it was.

"Maybe I should come up and talk to you about it."

"Well, I did not want to take up your time."

"Nonsense! Besides, I miss your company. I'll be up shortly."

The communication screen went blank. Ryla felt this would not be as easy as she thought. She poured through screens of information hoping to pick up additional information. A hand gently touched her shoulder.

"Hi! It's good to see you again."

Ryla stood up to embrace her friend.

"Let's use one of the conference rooms."

Ryla smiled as she followed her friend. As Verlin closed the door she poured herself a glass of water.

"Want one?"

Ryla nodded favorably.

"I suppose you've already given this a great deal of thought."

"Yes, and let me spare you any further embarrassment by saying that I have already put a request for hearing with the council. I simply want to do the correct thing when I ask Marissa. I would not wish to offend her or do anything improper."

"Marissa. Is that the human that helped with the Earth mission and the children?"

"Yes"

Verlin sat directly across from Ryla.

"Listen, my friend. I do not wish to cause you any further stress so I will speak directly. In Earth's history, relationships such as life partners did not exist openly. They were forbidden by most civilizations. The punishment for such humans who dared to express their relationships varied from alienation to death."

Ryla listened to her friends' truths.

"There are some terms which you can look up in the computer such as Homosexuality, Lesbian, and Gay." As she spoke she entered them into the computer.

"They have cross-reference material but I'm not sure how accurate it is."

The screen blinked with page after page of information.

"Most of this information indicates that some humans were open about their homosexuality and some were more private. Some viewed their orientation as biological and others as a preference."

"What was the word you used ho...? mosex.."

"Homosexual. This is the word they used to separate themselves. We don't have an equivalent term. Here read this."

Ryla moved closer to the screen:

HOMOSEXUALITY IS A PREFERENCE FOR THE AFFILIATION AND SEXUAL ACTIVITY WITH A PERSON OF THE SAME SEX.

"Most humans who were not of this...type were very offended or hand negative feelings if you were to ask them if they were one. Is Marissa....a... homosexual?"

"I'm not sure. According to what I have read so far I do not think so."

"Well, then you may want to wait until you can talk to her about it."

"According to this I do not see a 'right' way."

EMERGENCY BEACON: SECTOR 12

The monitor quickly switched to the communications area. Ryla signaled her location.

"Commander Erickson we have a hostage situation on Deck 12. A human male Earth survivor has killed one Arkanian guard and wounded two others. Several research staff and medical personnel are also on that level. Awaiting your presence on Deck 11. "

"Let's go. I'll need your information on human behavior."

"Right"

Both women made their way down to Deck 11. Amid the crowd of guards and pilots Ryla found the Guardian.

"The Council will not stand for such behavior on the part of these humans. The survivor will have to be terminated immediately!"

Monitors showed both the human and his hostage.

"I understand Guardian but perhaps we can give the human what he wants.....to go back to Earth."

"I find that there is no difference between a swift death and a slow one."

"Yes, I agree but the humans think differently than us."

As Ryla spoke these words she realized that the issue of Marissa was just that. If she thought differently then there would be no resolution. She would not feel as Ryla did and her feelings would not matter.

"We cannot beam the human down. He is holding Dr. Maynar. They will both perish."

"I'll take care of it."

Ryla walked to the elevator.

"Ryla wait!"

Verlin caught the arm of her friend.

"Remember what human history has shown us. The humans are basically a violent race. This human will not hesitate to kill you. He is not a friend as was your Marissa."

Ryla looked at her friend and smiled. She kissed her on the cheek and stepped into the elevator.

As the elevator opened to Deck 12 Ryla noticed the hallway was clear. The male human stood at the end of the last doorway. He held Dr. Maynar around the waist with one hand and with the other held a laser scalpel at her neck.

"What is your name?" Ryla asked.

"Fuck my name. You people can't hold us here."

"Who is us?"

"US! The shuttle and her crew."

A young man stood up from behind the group of people at the doorway.

"He wants to go back not the rest of us. We want to live not...."

"Shut up you weasel! You always were spineless!"

Ryla moved closer slowly.

"Your choice is to die here or be beamed back to your planet. Look around you. This is reality. What has happened on your planet is reality. We had nothing to do with your war. We can not interfere."

Ryla noticed the young man moving closer to Dr. Maynar.

"You have killed one of our people and as such you must die. It is our law."

Ryla could sense the man's confusion. Tears ran down his face as he realized what she had said. He gripped the laser tight. She knew all too well what he was about to do. But she also knew she was still too far to reach him before he killed his hostage. She blinked and as she did the young man came from behind and grabbed his friends hand with the laser. The doctor shook herself free. At that moment Ryla jumped towards the two men. A swift punch to the man's chin upward knocked him out. The young man fell back holding his hand. In the struggle the laser had severed several nerves in his hand. The heat from the laser prevented bleeding but the numbness and pain were still there.

"Here let me take care of him."

Dr. Maynar took the young man back into the room. Ryla stood up.

"Communications: Security to Deck 12 on the double."

As the rest of the personnel came out of the room they gazed at the man as security banded him. He was immediately particle beamed to an area pre-programmed on Earth's location. Ryla felt drained. She was no longer sure of her emotions. She needed to rest. She would go to where she would find peace and quiet for her thoughts.

Marissa was working with some of the children when she was told of the excitement on Deck 12. She stopped one of the crew personnel and asked what happened. She walked to the elevator and entered Level 12.

"Guardian!" Marissa called. "Can you tell me where Marissa is?"

The Guardian motioned for Marissa to walk with him.

"She has left message not to be disturbed."

Marissa rubbed her eyes.

"Guardian, I must speak with someone. I have questions but I don't know how to ask them or even if I'm asking the right ones. I..."

"Guardian the council wishes your presence on Deck 2."

"I'm on my way."

"What is the nature of your questions?"

Marissa sighed.

"Some of them are questions about your people and their laws. Others I'm not sure of."

"Well, perhaps I can leave you with someone who can answer some of your questions. Master Officer Aldridtre is in charge of input information of various civilizations. He should be able to help you."

"You summoned me Guardian?"

"Yes, this is......"

"Marissa"

"You have met before?"

"No but I have heard of her from the Commander."

"Well them I leave you in good hands as you humans say."

"Thank you"

Marissa was not sure of the officers' reaction to what she was about to ask until she watched him with the other personnel. She then was relieved that Officer Aldridtre was somewhat feminine, almost gay in behavior since some of the questions she had to ask were sensitive.

"Officer Aldridtre..."

"Please call me Verlin"

She breathed a sigh of relief that this man seemed as friendly as Ryla.

"Verlin, I'm not sure how to ask these questions."

"Well usually the best way is to be direct."

"Right. Your culture seems to be very accepting of different people."

"Yes, we have many different people that make up the Arkanians. Come let me show you on the computer."

The two talked as they walked back up to Deck 15 where Verlin and Ryla had their conversation.

"So, your life-partners are exactly that."

"Yes, they share their lives for as long as both live. When one dies the other is free of their vow and may seek solace or another partnership."

"And life-partners can be men or women?"

"Yes, of course."

As Marissa sat down she looked at the computer. She then looked up at Verlin.

"You people really do read minds."

Verlin looked at her puzzled. She then realized that the computer was never cleared before the emergency message.

"How do you feel about that?"

"This is on human social behaviors?"

"Yes"

"It seems fairly accurate. I mean from what I've been told."

Verlin decide to risk a sensitive question.

"Marissa if an Arkanian took an interest in you how would you feel?"

"What kind of interest and would I know them?"

"Well, let's say you knew them and they asked you to be their life partner?"

Marissa rose up out of her chair.

"See that's what I was talking about but how do you think you as an Arkanian would feel? See I'm not sure if...but maybe I was reading her wrong and I...."

She sat down holding her head. Verlin walked over to her and sat down directly in front of her.

"You humans can truly be quite amusing at times. I as an Arkanian, if I chose a man, would not be shocked and would probably want to show you my world before I agreed to any vows. I would want you to know what you could expect and what your laws were. Now answer my question. If Ryla asked you what would you say?"

"I would say yes. I... wait a.... you said...Ryla?"

Verlin smiled.

"That is who we are talking about isn't it?"

Marissa bowed her head in embarrassment.

"Oh, Verlin I wish I knew how to talk to her. I've had so much happen to me. I'm not sure if what I'm asking or doing is the right thing."

"I cannot answer that but I think Ryla can."

"Does she really like me?"

"I'm not sure if 'like' is the correct description. Love is what she has been expressing and I think it is love that she is feeling. But I think it is her you should be saying this to."

"Well, I would but the Guardian said she has requested to be alone. I've been working with the children and haven't spent much time talking with her lately."

"I might be able to help you with her location." Verlin said softly.

Verlin and Marissa rode to the 23 level of the station. Verlin took out a card and placed it in the slot that was next to one of the many doors off of the hallway. The doors drew open to expose two more doors with windows.

RAINFOREST AREA CURRENTLY OCCUPIED

Verlin punched in a code and the doors opened. The smell was one of outdoors and woods.

"This is beautiful."

"There are several pods like this and several simulating the ocean. It has been found practical to have these for long voyages. We have taken some of your species of plants from Earth and transplanted them in here with great success."

"And you think Ryla is in here?"

"No. I know she is in here. This is where she comes to think and relax. I'll leave you now."

"No wait! Thank you for all you've done."

Verlin smiled.

"All I want is for my friend to be content."

With that Verlin closed the doors and walked back to the elevator.

Marissa looked around at the beauty and splendor that had once been on Earth. Perhaps one day the planet can be re-seeded with all the natural things that once existed there. The sound of splashing water drew Marissa's attention to the waterfall in the distance. She marveled at how everything including the insects had been given a habitat. She also guessed that a proper balance of these creatures kept the rest of the forest balanced. As she drew closer she saw a nude body swimming among the section of shore. The partial solar light reflecting on the shimmering water resembled a painting. Marissa stood on the shore taking in all the sights. The sudden splash of water brought her back to reality. Both women starred at each other. Marissa looked around for a towel but couldn't find one.

"Is there something about my body which displeases you?" Ryla floated as she spoke.

"Uhm no. I just thought you might be cold when you got out." Marissa backed up a little to catch her breath.

"The solar sun is still out and providing warmth. I do not think the temperature would be cold."

Ryla then sensed her friend's shyness.

"On your planet if I were a human female would I cover my body with a..... towel?"

"Well, if you were getting out of the water, yes."

Ryla began to understand that this must be the custom and that was why Marissa felt so uncomfortable.

"Forgive me; my robe is behind that rock."

As Ryla pointed Marissa quickly walked to the rock and found the lilac blue robe. When she turned around she noticed Ryla there dripping wet.

"Oh! Uhm Here!"

She lifted up the robe and held it open blocking Ryla's body from her sight.

"I did not.... mean...to...make you...uncomfortable. Not many people know where to find me."

Marissa placed some distance between her and her friend.

"I'm sorry I didn't mean to disturb you. I needed to talk to you but it could wait."

"Please! Don't go. I am not familiar with your customs. I do not mean to offend you. I am not sure what ones' proper behavior is with a human female."

"Well, for starters you can stop referring to me as a human female. I know what I am. I'm a person who's......forgotten how to communicate."

She turned and began to walk towards the pathway exit. Ryla walked around and stood in front of her.

"Please sit down."

She grabbed Marissa's hand and led her to a small grass clearing. Marissa did as she was told.

"Marissa......We are both.... new to each other. This place is different from what you are use to and I believe you have done quite well in adjusting. But I am not......I... I do not understand how you...." Ryla paused searching for the proper word. "feel...about me. I know there has been a friendship between us and I as an officer have respected that but I sense within myself certain......feelings."

Ryla looked everywhere except at Marissa. Marissa started to giggle.

"Have I said something humorous?"

Marissa moved over to Ryla and hugged her tightly as she whispered in her ear.

"We may be of different planets but we are basically the same. Are you trying to tell me that you love me?"

Ryla returned the embrace.

"Yes."

Marissa looked into Ryla's eyes once more.

"Well, I love you and...I... would like...to be. your......life-partner."

Ryla bowed her head. Tears began to well up inside her. She could hold them back no longer. Marissa saw them fall for the first time. She reached up and began to wipe them away.

"I'm sure there will be many things for me to learn about your people and you. You'll have to be patient with me. Does your society allow for this?"

Ryla smiled.

"Yes. I have already asked the council for clearance."

Melissa moved back.

"What if the council doesn't allow it?"

Reality was starting to come back to both women.

"I can be demoted and placed back on my home planet with you."

"Demoted! Why would they lower your rank? After all you have done for them and your people."

"Because it is our law."

A green light flashed on Ryla's bracelet.

"Yes Guardian!"

THE COUNCIL IS MEETING ON DECK 5. YOUR PRESENCE IS REQUIRED ALONG WITH THE HUMAN FEMALE.

"Acknowledged!"

"We must go. I'll get my clothes."

"They are already here."

Another voice came from behind.

"Verlin"

"At your service Commander."

"I knew you would need these since the council has summoned all crew personnel and visitors."

"What?"

"Whatever they have to say is very important."

"The disposition of the humans and the children?" Ryla asked.

"Yes. They requested all computer records and observations."

For the first time since Marissa had seen Ryla she noticed she looked worried.

"Could this pertain to us as well?" Marissa asked.

Ryla turned to face her.

"Yes, I believe so."

The three women headed for level 5. All were silent as they walked through the halls. Marissa had not been in the chambers since the day her world collapsed one month ago.

"The council usually does not require all personnel to be present. I wonder what else this is about."

The Council chamber had been expanded to resemble a great hall. Each of the council members dressed in formal attire. Monitors were running for transmission back to Arkania.

"Come and sit with me Marissa!"

As she looked around she found one of the children she had been working with smiling up at her.

"Yes! Since we have to sit up front denoting our rank."

Ryla smiled and walked up to the front with Verlin. A strange chill came over Ryla. She did not feel good about this meeting. The hall fell silent as the council walked in and sat at their respective seats. Council member Allman spoke:

WE, THE GREAT COUNCIL OF ARKANIA HAVE MADE A
DECISION REGARDING THE DISPOSITION OF THE
SURVIVORS FROM THE PLANET EARTH. DUE TO THE
RECENT OUTBREAKS OF VIOLENCE ON THIS STATION IT

HAS BE DECIDED REMOVE THE HUMANS TO THE COLONY OF

PHAETON. THERE THEY WILL BE RE-EDUCATED FOR FUTURE

INTRODUCTION TO OUR PLANET ARKANIA. WE CAN NOT

PERMIT THE HUMANS TO REMAIN ON BOARD THIS STATION

FOR THE DURATION OF OUR TRAVEL. THEREFORE, THEY WILL

BE MOVED TOMORROW MORNING. TRANSPORTATION TIME 9:00 A.M.

COMMANDER ERICKSON WILL BE CHARGE OF THE SHUTTLES

AND THEIR PILOTS. DR. BENNIGER WILL BE

RESPONSIBLE FOR THE ADULT HUMANS AND CHILDREN.

Ryla looked in the direction of her pilots. They were not pleased at this new information since many of them had already formed attachments to the children. The rest of the people seemed surprised. Marissa glanced over at Ryla. Ryla smiled and turned back to face the council.

IN ADDRESSING ANOTHER MATTER REGARDING THE REQUEST

OF A LIFE PARTNERSHIP BETWEEN THE HUMAN FEMALE

PHYSICIAN NAMED MARISSA BENNIGER, THE REQUEST HAS

BEEN POSTPONED UNTIL HER RE-EDUCATION HAS BEEN COMPLETED.

Marissa wasn't sure whether this was good news or bad news. She watched Ryla but could see no indication of emotions.

THE COUNCIL HAS TAKEN INTO ACCOUNT THE EXCHANGE OF

KNOWLEDGE DR. BENNIGER CAN PROVIDE TO OUR PEOPLE

AND THE GENETIC OFFSPRING THAT WOULD RESULT FROM

THIS PARTNERSHIP.

Now Marissa was totally confused. She leaned and held onto the small child's hand for comfort.

"What are they talking about? Are we going somewhere?"

The child's questions were echoes of Marissa's own.

THE COUNCIL HAS COMPLETED THIS TRANSMISSION. ARRIVAL ON PHAETON WILL BE IN TWO MOONS.

The council members rose and walked out slowly. As the last member left the pilots raced down to Ryla and crowded around her.

"Please! You'll have your assignments by nightfall. I think I understand your requests."

She quickly moved through the crowd to find Marissa. She had been standing at the entrance to the hall with the small child in tow.

"We need to talk."

Ryla led the way as she spoke.

"Verlin will take care of the child. Alright?"

Marissa nodded her head as she gave the child to Verlin. The two women entered the elevator silently.

"Deck 7 Room 200" Marissa watched the numbers rise as they came to Ryla's room.

"Will this be okay?"

Again, Marissa stepped out and nodded.

"Marissa, I know there are some things I need to explain to you but I'm not sure where I should start?"

Marissa turned and looked at Ryla.

"How about insemination for starters! Offspring! They were talking as though you and I were going to have a baby. I mean a real big stomach and everything baby!"

Ryla poured a clear liquid into two glasses and handed one to Marissa.

"If you choose re-education one of the things you will learn about our people is that if you choose a life-partnership with a female and you yourself are female then the two eggs are fused and the sperm comes from the Guardian. So, you see, the offsp.... the child's traits are from both females."

Marissa drank the liquid slowly.

"Fascinating! Doesn't the Guardian have a claim to the children?"

"No! The Guardian has no claims or attachments to the children other than we are all his children. In our society the children are raised to accept all groupings of parents including a single one although those are rare. We do not have a division of what is male and what is female."

Ryla sat down in front of her.

"Do you understand?"

Marissa chuckled.

"Sort of. An almost perfect society. But your society doesn't allow for humans does it?"

"Of course, it does. Re-education is what we call getting to know your environment. It teaches you about our laws, beliefs, society, foods, and even our enemies. This way when you enter Arkania you will know what to expect. There is no test, just a meeting with the council. Your entry can not be refused unless you are shown to present a danger to the other population. Once you enter Arkania you are no longer referred to as a human or from earth. You are an Arkanian."

Marissa got up and filled both Ryla's glass and hers.

"Are you originally from Arkania?"

"No. I am from a planet many light-years away called Altareon. It is mainly a water planet with small islands. Our planet was attacked by Menites. The Arkanians rescued several of us and placed us in their re-education program. I was afraid at first. I thought they were going to.... what you call brain wash...me. But it is not like that. They give you temporary homes to live in and they teach you the various languages of the Arkanian planet. Then they give you samples of the food and show you how the planet structure works."

Marissa sat quietly as she listened to every word Ryla spoke.

"They have permitted me to travel with you so I can stay with you while you are learning. Unless you would not permit it."

"You mean I can have you there with me? "

"Yes of course!"

Marissa felt as though a great weight had been lifted from her.

"Why can't we travel on the space station?"

"Probably due to the speed at which the station travels. Phaeton is in the opposite direction of its scheduled path. Also, I am sure that the council felt that the remaining four adults might show the same desire to return to their fated planet. This way they are able to make a more responsible, logical choice."

"You mean after all this that if they wanted to return they could?"

"Yes. If I want to return to Altareon I can at any time during my travel. I simply put in a request."

Marissa was taking this new information in as she yawned.

"I still have ship assignments to make out, since the pilots want to accompany the children. I think they have grown attached to them."

"It's not difficult. The children look upon them as heroes or I guess heroines."

She yawned again.

"Should I explain the re-education program to the adults and some of the older children? I think it will make it easier for some. They're frightened that they'll be brainwashed. At least I think that's what they're afraid of."

"Well, if you feel up to it."

"Sure. They don't mind my yawning only I do."

"Thank you."

Ryla spoke softly and gently brushed Marissa's lips with hers. Marissa felt energized.

"With a thank you like that I'll be back!"

And with that she headed towards the elevator.

Ryla worked most of that evening on shuttle loadings and schedules. It would take one Earth month to reach Phaeton and therefore both children and crew would have to spend some time in suspension. The shuttles were three times the size of Earth's shuttles but still would be crowded for the children and adults. Each child's profile, as known, was entered into the computer and logged into the shuttles computer memory. Nourishment and health care also had to be entered since they would be placed in suspended animation until their arrival at Phaetons orbit.

Finally, the last pieces of information were fed into the computer regarding tracking and seasonal meteor showers. Her communication link flashed as she rubbed her eyes.

"Yes?"

"Hi. It's Marissa. I've told them about the council's orders and explained what you basically told me. They seem okay but I'm sure they're still a little scared."

"Well, I will explain more to them tomorrow. I have asked the council for an extended departure time which they have agreed upon. This way I can explain about their trip."

"Is it possible I could meet you in your room?"

Ryla could not tell the tone of Marissa's voice.

"Yes!"

The screen went blank and Ryla began to pick up a few things she had left around her room. She then sat back down at her desk and rubbed her eyes once more. Her door signal sounded.

"Enter!"

Ryla turned to face Marissa.

"Is there something wrong?"

Marissa pulled up a chair and sat across from Ryla.

"I wanted to know if it is...permitted for me to stay with you tonight. I... Don't want to be alone tonight."

Ryla could now sense her fear and an emotion she was learning to identify with...loneliness.

"Yes, it is permitted."

With this she leaned over and took Marissa's hand and pulled her towards her. She hugged her for what seemed like hours. Then the two women got ready for bed. Marissa curled up tight next to Ryla and slept that way most of the night.

The morning appeared as a flash of color. Both adults and children were moving back and forth between the loading bay and the shuttles getting ready for their long journey. Ryla called her crew together to assist the others in loading the children. While on this space station Ryla knew that the children had made certain attachments to space ship personnel and that time must be given for their goodbyes. While checking the shuttle's cargo a message came direct from the council.

"Marissa!"

She walked over to her friend and handed her the cargo listing.

"Can you finish checking this list? I am to report to the council at once."

Marissa looked her in the eye.

"Is there something wrong?"

"I doubt it. Everything has been done according to the rules."

Marissa looked worried.

"Maybe it's about us last night. Maybe they......"

"Hush. I am certain that this has nothing to do with last night."

Ryla kissed Marissa on the forehead and walked towards the elevator. Marissa went back to checking the cargo feeling embarrassed over her fears of last night.

Ryla walked through the council doors to see the Guardian speaking very loudly to the council head. As Ryla moved closer the Guardian stood quiet.

"Commander Ryla reporting as ordered."

Ryla watched the Guardian as she spoke.

"Please sit commander," the council ordered.

"We have received notice that the Traloians have put a claim in for the Earth children. They are citing treaty laws of dispersal as their right to the children. They...."

Ryla stood up agitated.

"Please council! Surely you cannot allow the Traloians to take the children. Their planet is a harsh one and they show no affection for their own children. These Earth children would not survive their environment. We...."

The Guardian raised his hand.

"Calm yourself Commander. There are certain laws which have to be followed. If the children reach Phaeton then the Traloians can make no claim on them since they are under Arkanian protection."

Ryla faced the Guardian.

"And if they don't reach Phaeton?"

The Guardian glared at the council as he spoke.

"If you are intercepted on the way to Phaeton then the Traloians have full rights to the children and adults of Earth. We cannot engage in protection under the Arkanian law for people who have not yet be re-educated. The Traloians would not harm you or your crew since you are Arkanian. "

Ryla turned back to face the council.

"When was this message received?"

"Early this morning."

Ryla clenched her fists in anger.

"Am I permitted to leave?"

"Commander you are a representative of the Arkanian people. You must not engage the Traloians in any hostile actions. Your duty is to protect the children and get them safely to Phaeton. Is that clear?!"

"Yes. May I be dismissed for early departure?"

With a sigh the council agreed. Ryla could see the Guardian trying to follow but Ryla knew she had no time to waste in heading for Phaeton. She entered the elevator and tried to calm herself before her crew and Marissa saw her. As she stepped off the elevator she noticed the bay was clear. All ships had been loaded and were ready for departure. She ran to her ship and closed the air lock behind her. She took her helmet and her place at the controls. Marissa was seated behind her and could sense something was not right.

"The Guardian said we had to be loaded for early departure so here we are."

Marissa expected a response but none came. Ryla began to read off the coordinates and boosted the engines up to full power. Her crew merely looked at each other in silence as she led the four shuttles toward open space.

"Commander Erickson would you like me to take over?"

Ryla did not move as she spoke.

"No! I want round the clock surveillance on the perimeter of all four shuttles. I also want a report of any radar contact within 2 parsecs of us. I will explain later."

Her crew had been with Ryla off and on throughout research missions. They knew that sometimes she was thinking of things so fast that she did not have time to explain them and set them up. She would set them up first and then give them a detailed plan. They trusted her. Ryla clicked on the communication channel for all shuttles. The captain of each shuttle was ordered aboard hers.

"Navigator. Pull map sector 112.8 on screen."

As was ordered, the navigator entered the requested map sector in the computer and placed it on the front viewing screen for all to see.

"The council was informed that the Traloians have placed claim on the orphaned children from Earth. If they reach our ships before we reach Phaeton they will take the survivors."

Marissa realized what Ryla was saying and rose to object as did several of Ryla's officers. She raised a hand and motioned for them to be seated.

"I know! I know! I have no intention of handing any of the survivors over to the Traloians. But since their ships travel faster than our shuttles we are forced to do one of several things. We can not engage in formal battle since they are under our Universal Protection Treaty but we can delay our meeting. Navigator what is our present logged course?"

"Map Sector 112.7 Saturn N, Uranus S. Map Sector 112.8 Traloia S, Menoia N to Phaeton W commander."

Ryla stood studying the maps.

"Reroute the following course but do not log. I repeat: do not log. Map Sector 112.7 Jupiter N, Saturn S, Neptune S, Pluto S. Map Sector 112.8 Menoia S, Phaeton SW. Track Traloian ships and give me an intercept warning. If they are tracking us by tele signal we can mask our travel behind those planets. If identified we will split up and make our way to our scheduled destination. This way we have violated none of the sanctioned treaties."

Ryla looked around the small room at each of the helmeted officers. She knew they were angered and frustrated at these new events. Housing them in ships which had neither speed nor weapons was bad enough but telling them they had to honor their planets treaty and not fight was like tying their hands behind their backs.

"Very well. Until further notice we are under full alert. I want to know everything that comes into our sector even if it is a meteor. Is that clear?"

"Yes, commander!"

The call was simultaneous. All officers reported to their ships and informed their crew. Ryla left the central command and went to her quarters. She flipped on her computer and studied chart after chart of stars, planets, and asteroid belts. She rubbed her eyes as she refigured each plotted course. The door intercom beeped as she yawned.

"Yes."

"It's Marissa. I need to talk to you."

Ryla pushed the button to her door.

"Please come in."

Marissa could see the toll this new problem had taken on her friend's face. She walked over and hugged her. Ryla began to relax in the warmth of Marissa's arms.

"No!" Ryla pushed herself away from Marissa. "I....We cannot afford to do this. We have to remain alert...."

Marissa walked over to her and held her once more.

"Your crew is quite capable of handling things at the moment. You need some rest or you won't be good to the crew, children or me. Now come on."

Marissa walked Ryla over to her bunk and unzipped her suit half way.

"You do not understand. We cannot afford to enter our sleep chambers if we have to watch the monitors and if we do not sleep we will be very old by the time we reach Phaeton. These shuttles simply aren't fast enough. We...."

Marissa began to rub Ryla's neck. She could feel the tense muscles start to relax.

"You need to relax so that you can continue to think clearly. I'll be right here."

Soon Ryla drifted off to sleep under the watchful eyes of her companion.

Weeks passed as the crew carried on their various functions and research that they did on each trip. The ships were just passing Saturn's rings when a small warning light on the instrument panel flashed. Navigator Zimmer watched her screen as two small blips appeared.

"What do you make of this?" she said as Communications Officer Azure looked on.

Engineer Lacky pushed several buttons and flashed several ship configurations across the screen until the computer matched one.

CLASS B FREIGHTERS SUBCLASS NEMON

"Well are we betting traders or smugglers?"

Ryla spoke from behind as their startled faces regained their composure.

Navigator Zimmer said, "This far into Sector 112.7 I'd say their smugglers."

Ryla smiled. She realized that Marissa was right. The sleep she had received had renewed her brain and her body.

"Let's hope their smugglers. Perhaps they have something we need."
"Yeah like a turbo booster."
The engineer said under her breath. Ryla turned to face her.

"Actually, you're on the right track."
And with that she hailed the two ships and particle beamed aboard the first ship. The shuttle crews waited patiently, constantly checking their monitors. Marissa entered the Command Deck.
"What's going on?"
Communications Officer Azure said, "The commander is talking with the smugglers on those ships. We haven't heard what the plan is yet."
Marissa finished snapping her gloves on and positioning her helmet as was regulations for the Command Deck. In cases of emergency all crew would already have their life support functional. It was only in the outer decks that formality and practicality gave way to comfort.
"Engineer Lacky! Please beam aboard the following screen items. Will transport shortly."
The crew watched the screen as several engine parts appeared.
"What the hell is she doing?"
"Building another ship is what it looks like," Navigator Zimmer replied.
Marissa looked over the list also and began to smile.
"I'm not sure how she's doing it but I think she's boosting ours!"
The crew turned and looked at the engineer.
"Is that possible?" they asked.
"Well, it is not fighter capacity but it certainly will speed up things."
She walked over to the computer and began time calculations.
"Near as I can make it if those pieces fit we are talking about a 1 moon trip as opposed to a two-moon trip. As long as the Traloians don't know what we have we may have a decent lead."
The navigator looked at her charts again.
"Damn it! I wish they had Satellite Sensor Stations in this sector. I'll be bouncing signals forever out here trying to get a fix on those Traloian ships."
As Ryla beamed back, the navigator shouted: "I've got it! The Traloian

ships position is...... Heading for.... the.... Arkanian Space station? I don't get it? Don't they know we are already near Neptune S.?"

Ryla turned towards the screen.

"You've forgotten our early departure time."

The communications officer spoke: "The space station seems to be giving them the impression that we are still there! A message from the Guardian is being sent commander. It is on a coded signal. I'll need a moment to translate."

Marissa caught Ryla rubbing her jaw as if she were in pain.

"Put it on the screen Kyle."

THE COUNCIL HAS AGREED TO DISCUSS THE DOCUMENTATION

OF THE TRALOIANS TREATY RIGHTS TO THE CHILDREN WITH

THE TRALOIANS DIRECTLY. YOUR LOGGED FLIGHT PLAN WILL THEN BE TURNED OVER TO THEM AS PROMISED. SAFE JOURNEY COMMANDER ERICKSON.

"We might just pull this off after all! Thank you, Guardian."

"Any reply commander?"

"No! He's buying us some time let us make use of it. Inform all ships as to their new instructions. We will run on generated power until the new crystal fuel units can be installed."

The engineer got up.

"I'll get right on it."

Ryla turned.

"Meredith!"

"Yes commander?"

Ryla smiled.

"Be careful."

Meredith winked and disappeared through the corridor.

For the next few hours Marissa watched as the crew fed in the new coordinates to the computers and additions were made to the ships engines. On the screens before her were images of planets she had only seen on television or in drawings. They were heading towards Pluto and she was seeing it all. Somehow all of what she learned on Earth seemed insignificant at this point. She looked over at the Communications Officer.

"Kyle."

"Yes, Marissa?"

"Do you travel through space like this all the time?"

Marissa knew her question sounded a bit stupid but she had already said it. Kyle smiled.

"Well, if you mean this hap hazard...... no. Our missions are usually very well planned. Actually Sector 112.7 is one of the more peaceful sectors. Now Sector 112.8 is usually traffic heavy. All those populated planets with flight technology and you're bound to get in someone's way."

Marissa looked at Sector 112.8.

"You mean all of those planets have people on them?"

Marissa was truly amazed. Kyle laughed.

"I said populated. Some have mostly androids, malkanoids, aliens or humans. It depends on size of planet, atmosphere and stuff like that."

Kyle reached over and flipped a switch in front of Marissa.

"Here! Just press this button and the computer will give you the facts on each of the planets in Sector 112.8 Anything else you wish to know just ask me. Okay?"

Marissa placed a friendly hand on Kyle's shoulder as she nodded her instructions. She sat down in the chair and began her reading. The first planet, Traloia, was a planet populated by a mixture of Malkanoids and Androids. As close as she could figure Malkanoids were man-like creatures who stood upright and lived in cave like structures. They had a civilized society that was created by the androids who also inhabited the planet. Their animalistic behavior made them well suited to their rugged terrain. She could see now why Ryla and the crew were so adamant about getting the children to Phaeton. It was a few hours later that the crew began to take their positions on the Command deck. Marissa was on the last planet within the 112.8 system: Altareon. She remembered Ryla speaking only briefly of her home planet. Mostly water she said. Altareon was 90% water. The land masses were but islands rising from under sea volcanoes. Most of the small population (4%) lived underwater in self-contained domes. The rest of the population lived on Arkania and shuttled back and forth between the planets. Marissa realized that when she first met Ryla she had been collecting sea life in small jars. She was transporting them to her own planet. She wanted to learn more about Ryla's planet but the time had come to try the new equipment. Days were going by slowly as each section of the new equipment was tested. Now the time had come.

All shuttle crews prepared their ships for the hopeful burst of constant speed. Captain Kahbrill signaled that the Argo would take the backdoor when engaged. Marissa remembered meeting Captain Kahbrill and thinking how formidable she looked especially in a black space suit. Marissa was beginning to feel more comfortable with her new helmet and remembered the warning Ryla gave her about magnifying ones' thoughts. She figured everyone was so busy that they wouldn't have time to pay attention to her thoughts.

"Engage all systems."

The sudden roar of engines was what she expected to hear but instead only heard a high-pitched whine. She watched the front view window and noticed the star patterns passing by at increased speed. The crew was silent. Everyone was watching their monitors and instrument panels. Marissa needed to break the deafening silence.

"I hope this means it's working."

Ryla smiled while the rest of the crew laughed. The tension that was once felt was gone now. Each of the shuttles made their way past Pluto and on into Sector 112.8.

As they entered Menoia's orbit a communications signal came through.

"Commander the Traloians have just left the Arkanian space station and are on a direct intercept course to Phaeton."

Ryla breathed quietly.

"Acknowledged"

She then entered a message to Phaeton stating they would be arriving late due to the meteor shower in their sector.

"I want another meeting with all shuttle captains at 02:00 hours. We need to make one more adjustment."

Ryla got up and walked out into the corridor.

The meeting was held in Ryla's quarters for time was a factor.

"We need to move the children from shuttles Atos and Argo to shuttles Nekton and Sarza. Only two shuttles will be landing on Phaeton with children. The other two will be setting up decoy ion fuel trails. I'm hoping the Traloians won't be as tactically well versed as we are. If they do board us they will only find crew members.

"This time there were no objections or questions. Everyone knew their mission was coming down to the wire. Marissa supervised the disconnection of the children on the two ships. Ryla stayed aboard the Argo to plot their course decoys.

"Commander all is well with the children. All reconnections went as planned. Other than a few headaches in the adult section all should be fine for the remainder of the trip."

"Dr. Andrews......"

"Yes commander?"

"Thank you! The crew awaits your return as soon as you are able."

Marissa had each child's profile from Earth's computers phased in with the ships monitoring systems. Each child's blood type, oxygen level, and general medical history would now be taken over by the ships computers and alert the crew if a malfunction or problem arose. Marissa finished programming the last set of instructions into the computer before particle beaming aboard the Argos.

Once aboard, Marissa realized that the crew appeared to be as energetic as they were on the space station. She walked over to the navigator.

"Do you mind if I ask you a personal question?" Marissa said softly.

Zimmer looked up and smiled.

"Of course not, Dr. Andrews."

"Where do you all get the energy? I mean other that a few bags under the eyes the whole crew appears to work as though they were fully rested."

Zimmer chuckled.

"You should see us in battle. Most of us are deep space pilots. We have been doing this for quite some time. We do get tired but the rest time required is less."

Marissa looked up at the screens in front of her.

"So, what you're saying is that you've been doing this for a long time and that's why you don't get tired."

"Yes doctor. I suppose that is what I just said."

A blue light began to flash throughout the ship as the computerized voice gave warning of an impending meteor shower.

The bridge of the small shuttle was alive with activity as Marissa made her way towards the navigator. Ryla turned to catch Marissa's arm.

"I need to speak with you. Now!"

Ryla walked out into the hallway and waited for Marissa to follow.

"What is it?" Marissa asked puzzled.

"This is where you exit."

Marissa was about to object when Ryla placed her finger gently on Marissa's lips.

"Before you misinterpret my actions let me explain. You must not be onboard my ship if we engage the Traloians. They will take you and there is nothing I can do if this happens. You will go now onboard the Nekton and remain with the children when they reach Phaeton. If all goes well and our decoy plan succeeds we will meet you back on Phaeton."

Marissa understood but still felt awkward.

"Very well. I don't like it but I understand."

As she spoke she reached over and kissed Ryla gently on the lips. A crew member walked by and saluted Ryla and smiled at Marissa. Marissa withdrew and lowered her head. Ryla looked down at her.

"Do not worry. My crew is very perceptive. Most of them already know about my new life-partner. Come! I will walk you to the transport bay."

Once Marissa was safely onboard the Nekton Ryla gave orders for the countdown to begin.

"Commander!"

"Yes Zimmer?"

"The children will be safe will they not?"

The commander smiled at her navigator of five Earth years.

"If we do our mission as planned they will."

And with than she laid her hand on Navigator Nora Zimmer's shoulder and gave the order to 'execute' as the countdown ended.

The Nekton and Sarza began their separation and made a hard-right turn towards Pluto. The Atos and Argo made a left and headed towards

Traloia. Ryla's plan was now committed and there was no turning back. The meteor shower area would mask Traloians satellite station sensors and therefore hide the two Arkanian ships until they reached the outer edge of the planet Menoia.

As expected the Traloians opened up a hailing frequency with the Atos and Argo. Commander Erickson waited. She ordered up the films that the crew had taken earlier of the children. She had her communications officer run the tape of the children's voices as she responded to the Traloian call.

"Greetings Commander Erickson. I hope your journey has gone well. Our ship the Lectic is enroute from the Arkanian space station and will link with you within 1 Earth day. We have been advised that all human children and adults shall be turned over to us as per the treaty. Shall you be needing assistance?"

The commander again waited.

"We have been advised of the treaty request and will comply with the best of our ability."

"Good journey to you commander we look forward to meeting you. Communications ended."

Only silence was heard as the communication ended.

"Engineer Lackey how are those thrusters holding up?"

"They are at a full 90% Commander."

"Well you are about to find a problem with them. We will have to reduce them by 65%. Understood!"

"Yes commander."

Ryla looked over the navigator's shoulder as she plotted the Sarza and Nekton's course. Communicating with them directly was too dangerous since now the Traloians would be monitoring everything that enters their sensors.

Hours passed as the crew prepared their next move.

"Commander! I have two Traloian ships leaving the planet and heading on an intercept course with two unidentified ships near satellite station #2."

Ryla looked at the map and then at the estimated time of arrival for the Nekton and Sarza. The communications officer looked at the map.

"They could not possibly have enough time to reach Phaeton. They would only be halfway between Menoia and the S.S. Izon. They did not have enough time!"

Ryla turned around to face the young officer.

"Return to your station Officer Azure!"

Ryla reached over the officer's shoulder as she sat down and signaled the Argo. Suddenly a red light lowered from the bridge and a siren sounded throughout the ship.

"I have just sent an emergency signal to our sister ship the Argo. We will need emergency assistance from all ships in the area. Our containment area of the ship has been breached and we must evacuate all personnel from this ship. Please send that message to the Traloians. Under treaty they will have to respond to us before their intercept course. It will buy Marissa some time."

The crew began setting the necessary charges throughout the shuttle.

"Commander! The Traloians are on their way. "

Ryla engaged the main sequence relay for the charges. All crew were at their stations and were braced for impact. The explosion rocked the entire ship. All of the crew had their helmets on and waited as the smoke cleared and the computer rerouted the oxygen and controlled the remaining air locks. Only one injury was reported.

Ryla and her crew waited what seemed like hours for the Traloian ship to come to their aid. As the Traloian ship docked Ryla escorted her crew to the transport bay. Engineer Lacky finished placing the last charge alongside the main reactors.

"The last charge is in place Commander." Ryla nodded as they were transported.

Once onboard the Traloian ship, they were screened and their tattoos checked.

"Captain they are all Arkanian!"

A Melkanoid pushed through the crowd. He sniffed the air and looked at each of the Arkanians.

"Children not here!"

He grabbed each crew member and began to shake them.

"Where children!"

Ryla stepped forward.

"We are Arkanian and under treaty law you must behave in a manner befitting a treaty member."

Ryla knew this was not going to work but had to say it anyway. An android stepped forward and spoke directly to Ryla.

"Commander Erickson we are not clear what type of plan you are engaging but let us assure you it will not succeed. I have been instructed to hold you and your crew as enemies until we reach Traloia at which time you and your crew will be interrogated. Unless you care to save time and effort and tell us where you have hidden the children."

The Melkanoid pushed aside the android and gave orders for the Argo to be boarded and the disabled Atos to be scanned. As he spoke an explosion caused the Traloian ship to jolt throwing the Melkanoid into a nearby column. He growled as he got up.

Nora whispered to Ryla: "I thought they have no emotions?"

Ryla smiled.

"Evidently our records need to be updated."

"SILENCE!"

The Melkanoid starred at Ryla.

"Take them away."

Ryla and her crew were separated, bound with leather straps and placed in small cells secured with shock sensors. Ryla knew it would be some time before word of their treatment would circulate. She slid down in a corner and decided to get some sleep.

Meanwhile, the Nekton and Sarza landed safely on Planet Phaeton. Marissa joined the children as she was led to a great hall.

"Greetings Antarians and Earthlings! We the people of Phaeton are here to make your re-education as comfortable as possible. Each adult and child will be assigned an instructor and counselor. They will be assigning you homes and jobs during you stay on our planet. We ask that you please hold your questions until later after your medical examinations."

The voice seemed to come from everywhere and was heard in the native language of each human. A tall young woman and a middle-aged woman motioned to Marissa.

"Hello Dr. Andrews we will be your teachers for one full moon phase. We will be glad to answer any questions you have after your physical."

Marissa nodded and followed her teachers. She felt a sense of loneliness come over her. She missed Ryla and hoped she would return safely.

The physical was one of the most pleasant Marissa had if such a word could be used. It was an array of lights and small sounds which passed through her body and the only probe used was the one Marissa picked up and played with. She was then shown to a two-bedroom structure and was given clean clothes and a manual entitled ARKANIA. She located a communications port within one of the rooms and punched in numbers she remembered from Ryla's brief training. A woman appeared on the view screen.

"We see you have learned well your communication codes Dr. Andrews. What can I assist you with?"

Marissa took a deep breath.

"I need some information on Commander Ryla Erickson of the Arkanian shuttle Atos."

The woman looked away at another monitor.

"I do not have much current information doctor. The Atos has been destroyed. Cause yet unknown. The commander and her crew have been taken to Menoia under armed escort. Her sister ship the Argo is due to arrive on Phaeton in 1 of your Earth hours. They are headed towards Phaeton's moon base as we speak. Additional information will be provided then."

Marissa rubbed her forehead.

"May I be permitted to speak with the crew of the Argo when they arrive?"

Again, the woman looked at the other screen.

"Yes. I have been told you have security 12 clearance. After they are debriefed that will admit you to the docking port. You can arrive there by taking the sub transport to junction C."

"Thank you."

Marissa was amazed at the total appearance of trust and honesty she was shown. Not at all like that of earth. She called up a map and located the sub transport stations. She gathered that sub was short for subterranean transport much like subway trains back home. She took her manual and figured she could study on the way to the station.

The transport ship escorted Argo and its crew to the main corridor of Moon Base Alpha. Phaeton has two moons and can load and unload cargo in a matter of hours instead of days. But this time cargo was unloaded in a matter of minutes. Captain Kahbrill and her crew requested a debriefing clearance emergency.

"Captain shall we wait for Dr. Andrews? She is on her way as we speak."

"Yes, that will be fine."

Marissa was rushed up to the central corridor where all official personnel had gathered.

"Dr. Andrews we are glad to see you again. I take it the children are well?"

As Marissa had recalled Captain Kahbrill was an awesome presence and Marissa was glad she was on the same side.

"Yes, captain the children are fine and adjusting quite well to their surroundings. Captain what has happened to Ryla......Commander Erickson and her crew?"

The hall fell silent.

"That is what we are here to discuss. The Traloians are holding Commander Erickson and her crew prisoners and have instituted interrogation proceedings. I have informed the Guardian and counsel on Star base Arkania of this. We are awaiting the Guardians command."

The captain then sat down and the hall was once more filled with noise. Marissa walked to a large window opposite the monitor and hall. She lowered her head. The captain's first officer stood behind her and placed her hand on her shoulder. Marissa turned and the young woman could see tears streaming down her face.

"My name is Shelly......Shelly Becker. I wanted to.... see if you were okay."

Marissa looked at the young officer and spoke.

"Back on Earth when someone violated a treaty it took months or years to resolve it and in the meantime families and cities were destroyed. I have a feeling your treaty is no different. I need Ryla.... the commander to return safe. I've been reading about the Traloians and fear for her life."

Marissa could no longer hold her composure. The young officer took her in her arms and held her securely.

"I know of what you speak for my home planet was Earth. I chose not to return for many reasons. I suppose all treaties are the same but what makes the difference is the reaction to them. The one thing you will learn about being an Arkanian is their sense of fairness and their reaction to treaty violation. Their judgment is swift and most often deadly for the planet that breaks it. That is why Arkania is so strong. They...."

"Excuse me but your presence is requested. The Guardian and counsel have sent us a message."

This officer was younger than most of the people Marissa had seen. He apologized again for interrupting. All three headed towards the large monitor to their left.

IN DIRECT VIOLATION OF THE UNITED UNIVERSAL
FEDERATION TREATY NUMBER 493.2 OF THE
UNIVERSAL CODE THE TRALOIANS HAVE IMPRISIONED
SIX ARKANIANS. THIS WILL NOT BE TOLERATED BY
THE COUNSEL NOR THE ARKANIAN PEOPLE. RETURN OF
ALL ARKANIAN CREW FROM TRALOIA IS DEMANDED
WITHIN
4 SENTONS OF THIS MESSAGE. IMMEDIATE DUST OFF OF
WARSHIPS KENTAR, LASTUS, AND NEMON WILL BE
EXECUTED
FROM MOONBASE GAMMA.
THIS IS OUR FINAL COMMAND REGARDING THIS MATTER

Marissa was looking up the meaning of sentons when Captain Kahbrill and her crew cheered the Guardians decision. Shelly turned to Marissa.

"See I told you it would be swift."

Marissa smiled.

"How long is a senton? I mean in earth terms."

The two women walked back towards the Phaeton transport ships.

"Well each senton is a half hour so the counsel has given them 2 hours to comply."

"Yes, but what if they don't?"

Shelly held the door as they stepped in the transport.

"We land on Traloia and go get them then the warships destroy all their transportation systems as a sort of punishment. Anyone who resists or fires back gets terminated."

Marissa closed her book.

"You make it sound so simple."

"That is because it is!"

A male officer came from behind them.

"One decision that everyone sticks to. Your commander knows what will happen. She was prepared long before they made her and her crew prisoners."

And with that he exited the transport.

"Can I escort you back to your quarters on Phaeton?"

Marissa was beginning to feel at ease with this young officer.

"Well I'm still not too sure how to navigate through the system yet."

"Then consider me your guide on Phaeton."

Upon entering Phaeton's atmosphere Marissa peered out the window. Phaeton resembled the type of futuristic drawings she had seen on the covers of Isaac Asimov books. Towers and monorails could be seen for miles. As they began to dock she saw how vast in size the population was. As the crew disembarked she gathered her belongings and headed back to her apartment. She tuned in her monitor to the information station, took her manual and began to read up on Arkania. She was getting use to eating and studying in front of the monitors waiting to hear some news of Ryla and her crew. Weeks passed as she wondered if she would ever be able to adjust to her new environment without the help of Ryla. Her daily visits to the two she called teachers were always conducted in a pleasant and friendly manner but Marissa missed Ryla. She had many unanswered questions regarding her status. She requested a work assignment for the space cruisers that were in repair docks. She needed to keep busy. The work was manual but she learned a lot and enjoyed it. She wondered how long it would be before she would see her friend. The planned attack was to have been swift but still no word.

Back on Traloia the Arkanian prisoners had arrived and been placed in their cells with their hands electronically bound for several weeks. Each had been separated and stripped of all their Arkanian clothing. They were given clothing that resembled brown Earth rags. A high-pitched whine was played in each cell and the temperature was adjusted to warm. Dehydration seemed to be their first form of punishment along with attempting to drive them crazy with the high frequency whine. As Ryla attempted to knock out the speaker that played the offending sound she felt a strange vibration from the floor. She knelt down and determined that it was Arkanian ships landing. She needed to get her crew to a safe area. She pounded on the wall for attention since the area where the door was had been wired with a shock sensor. An Android guard appeared.

"I will tell you where the children are if I can see all of my crew one last time before I am punished according to Traloian law."

This sounded like a logical request and so the android granted it. The Arkanians were moved into one huge room.

"Two clicks and counting."

An android called. The Arkanians gathered in a circle. Each one touched the right back of their neck where their implanted locators were and activated them. They all started to feel the vibration through their feet.

"Back against the walls!" cried the navigator.

With a blast of dust and gravel a huge spiral rod came up through the middle of the floor. It slowed its twisting movement. When it stopped, the blades transformed into steps. The Arkanians ran for the steps. Ryla made sure each member of her crew got on first. As she stepped towards the tunnel a huge clawed hand grasped her shoulder.

"You no live!"

The Melkanoid grabbed Ryla and threw her to the ground. She wished she had her space suit on as the small pebbles and rocks etched into her skin as she was thrown to the floor. Ryla found a sizable rock and waited for the Melkanoid to come closer. Before she could take aim the Melkanoid went down with a thud. Standing behind him was Verlin with a small stunner in his hand.

"Your ride is ready Commander."

Verlin smiled as he helped Ryla aboard. The ship went back underground from where it came and through the tunnel it had excavated. Once on board the warship Kantar she sent an "all clear" message to the other ships. The Arkanian space station was also notified and the Traloian counsel was then released to go back to their planet. Since all Traloian transports had been destroyed as per the Arkanian order, only the Traloian counsel ship would be left for transport. The Arkanians deemed this acceptable and would require all trade negotiations that involved Traloia to be cleared with the Arkanians for one full era. Dependency was to be their punishment for the kidnapping and torture of their people.

Marissa read the news alert as she looked up from reading her manual. She had completed all the reading and had two more sessions with her teachers before she was released from her re-education status. A special message was sent on a coded channel directly to Marissa.

WILL WAIT FOR YOU AT CENTRAL COMMAND.

TIME: 0:900 DAY: TOMORROW

PACK BAG AND DRESS WARMLY.

RYLA

Marissa smiled as she raced around the room packing the clothes she was given. She was not sure if she could wait till tomorrow to see Ryla. A knock at the door stopped her momentarily. She walked to the door and opened it slowly. Captain Kahbrill stood before her with a heavy coat in one hand and an envelope in the other.

"Hello. I was told to make a special delivery to you."

She handed Marissa the envelope as she stepped in. Marissa walked to the center of the room and opened the envelope.

Dear Marissa,

*I have received special permission to take you to my home
planet Altareon. This will not
Affect your re-education time for I have been told you
have been doing and exemplary job. I
Am pleased to see that you have been doing well. Kabrill
has offered to transport you
Earlier if you are able. Hope your feelings and thoughts
have not changed regarding us.*

*See you soon
Love, Ryla*

Marissa looked up at Captain Kahbrill. It was as if she had been given oxygen. Her fears had been put to rest as she read the note once more. How she longed to see Ryla.

"My bag is on the bed in that room. It's ready to go and so will I as soon as I find something warm to wear."

Captain Kahbrill moved closer to Marissa. She instinctively took a step back for she always thought Kabrill a very imposing woman.

"Please permit me," she said as she held out the coat.

"Consider it a joining gift."

Marissa thought a moment and then smiled.

"Thank you, Captain."

It was then she remembered that the word joining was used like engagement was on earth. The coat was an engagement gift from Captain Kahbrill. It was warm and more comfortable than she expected a coat of that weight to be. The two walked out the door together.

Their ride to Central Command was a pleasant one, both women engaging in friendly conversation. Marissa got the impression that Captain Kahbrill and Ryla had known each other well and might even have flown together during their early days of training. Upon Marissa's arrival she was given a small computer card with a digitized photo of her on the back. She was to use it to gain entry back on Phaeton. She waited in a small room made of a material similar to Plexiglas. The two moons of Phaeton could be clearly seen from one of the windows. She thought how lovely a backdrop it would make for a movie.

"Would it be a love story?"

A familiar voice said from behind her. She turned and the light of the moons reflected off of a thinner slightly grey haired Ryla. Marissa ran to the woman she missed and longed for. She held her so tightly she thought she would injure her. She looked into her eyes and saw her old friend and new partner. Her heart was pounding so madly she thought she would have to sit down.

"Do you still wish to accompany me to my home planet?"

Marissa was about to answer but instead reached up and kissed Ryla on the lips. It was an intense and passionate kiss and one that would answer all questions and doubts that Ryla had. The two women walked arm and arm towards the awaiting ship and the beginning of a new life together was about to unfold before them.

The End

Moonstone

The jeweled stone lit the way as the figure entered the tunnel. The animal skins he wore gave little protection against the icy cave. Soon he would make the discovery of the new world. A world of sunlight and blue sky; a world of green valleys and lush trees. This image drove him further along the walls of the cave to the small patch of light at what appeared to be the end. Sunlight he thought. His fur wrapped feet shredded against the small sharp rocks he stepped over. But still he hurried towards the light. Finally, the small patch of light gave way to a bright blinding light. His eyes attempted to adjust. He had made it! But as his eyes began to adjust and focus he looked out across a barren, mountainous wasteland. He stepped out into the sunlight and walked away from the cover of the cave. He walked down a small deer path and then sat down amidst the gravel and rocks. There he sat and gazed up at the blue sky.

CHAPTER 1

The mist was heavy as Dr. Vyla made her way to the car. She had put in a long day at the institute. Due to the recent discovery of ancient skeletal remains dating some 400 years ago everyone was putting in a little overtime. The site was virtually littered with small fragments of pottery and a shiny substance which appeared at first glance to be metal. This discovery alone would have caused a sensation but the accidental find of an intact skeleton by one of her assistants was the real news. He had a flat tire on this desert road and got out to repair it when he realized he needed something to brace the jack with. It was dawn when he started looking around for a rock and found much more. He said the teeth were what he spotted first.

Dr. Vyla laughed as she got into her car. Any normal person would have screamed or shrieked at the discovery of a human jaw on the side of the road but not her crew. She knew she was considered weird by her family for studying old bones but Jeff her assistant was simply beside himself at his discovery. When the police were finished with their investigation and ruled the skull older than their jurisdiction, Dr. Lydia Vyla and her crew were contacted. She remembers Jeff walking around the institute like he had just lost a puppy and questioning why the police were taking so long for their findings. She shifted gears in her battered old MG as she looked out the window at the valley below.

The mist still clung in the air and muted the lights of the city as her car climbed further up into the mountainous desert. The entire skeleton was found that morning somewhat intact, due to the claylike material surrounding it, and carefully air lifted to the Carstair Archeological Institute of Nevada. She and her crew of five began immediately working to treat the remains so that the exposure to the air would not make them more fragile. Molds were cast and measurements taken and fed into a laptop computer. Tomorrow they would have their work cut out for them. Lydia arranged for two more crews to be formed from the local college and they would begin unearthing the rest of the site. Until then she would return home to her irate cat and hungry dog. Her home overlooked most of the desert and was in direct line with the small observatory being built just west of her.

As she opened the door she was greeted by a scent of fresh flowers. Mary, her maid had set out fresh cut flowers and three bowls of food for her furry companions. Oscar, the dog loved cat food as well as her own so she would get a little extra. Max her cat was the opposite and loved dog food. Lydia spotted the note on the refrigerator as she walked into the kitchen.

Saw your new discovery on the 10:00 p.m.
news and thought the "kids" would need
to be fed. Congratulations!
Mary

She smiled as she looked around at the contented household. Even her fish had been fed. She remembered when she hired Mary 5 years ago and how she never expected Mary to last 1 hour let alone 5 years. They were both head strong women who were well educated. But due to a financial misfortune on the part of Mary's broker she had lost everything in investments, lawsuits and personal life. She was forced to seek menial work since she was classified as "over qualified". Lydia poured herself a glass of iced tea as she thought of their first encounter.

Lydia knew she had mellowed over the years since she recalls herself being arrogant, haughty and full of herself at the time. It's a wonder they ever spoke to one another. The verbal arguments became common place until one evening in December. Lydia had come home from a not-so successful financial meeting at the institute. Her projects were being cancelled due to lack of funding and she could no longer afford to fund them herself. She was anticipating her usual disgruntled meeting with Mary when she walked up the steps of her home. But something was wrong. Her cat was on the lower roof of her kitchen. She hated being outside especially in the snow. Lydia opened the door quietly and slowly. She heard muted cries coming from the back room. Calmly she opened her purse and removed a can of mace her father had given her. He gave her a gun but she refused to use and kept it in her study. Now she had second thoughts. Even the house smelled different. She tip toed over to the phone. Quietly she picked up the receiver. No dial tone was heard. She hugged the wall with her back as she headed slowly for the rooms where she last heard the sounds. As she rounded the corner she saw a half-naked body on the floor. She tilted her head forward and could see it was a terrified Mary and that her attacker was in the bathroom. How she wished she had listened to her police officer father when he would give her lectures on safety and self-defense. Mary's eyes were practically closed shut due to the swelling. She had been beaten and raped. As that realization seated itself in Lydia's mind her hand tightened around the can of mace. She crouched down to peer between the frame of the bathroom door and the door itself. He seemed to be armed only with a knife. That explained the rips and tears on Mary's clothes. She stood up and took aim just outside the door. The man finished washing his face and hands and took two steps to the door frame. Lydia held her breath. He zipped up the zipper of his trousers and started to walk back into the bedroom. Lydia fired the mace directly into his face. He fell back clasping his face and screaming. He waved his hands out looking for his attacker but only wound up knocking toiletries off shelves. He then began to curse and ask how this could have been done to him. Lydia turned to check on Mary. Mary had managed to crawl down the hall. Lydia knelt down and touched her. She defended with fists. Lydia spoke softly to her.

"It's okay Mary it's me Lydia. We need to get to my car. Okay?"

Mary then permitted Lydia to help her stand. They managed to get to Lydia's car. Once inside she locked the doors and took out her cellular phone to call the police. The two women waited in the car for the police. Lydia's hand never left Mary's. It was a link that from that moment on would only grow stronger. As the police searched the house and led the attacker out in handcuffs Lydia's feelings were changed. She stuck by Mary throughout the police questioning, hospital and courtroom trial.

Mary in turn allowed Lydia to help and as a result a friendship grew. The house was certainly big enough for the two women but Mary still wanted her independence. It was shortly after that when Lydia presented Mary with a present - Oscar, a German Shepard puppy that would be Mary's guardian and companion.

Lydia poured herself another glass of tea as she took off her shoes and sat on the couch in front of the tv. Max jumped up and took her usual place on the armrest purring as she was stroked. Perhaps Lydia would ask Mary again tomorrow about moving in. Maybe this time she'll say yes.

CHAPTER 2

The amulet glowed as the four warriors carried the litter with their wounded guardian through the cave. The mist and fog were thick as they walked towards the projected light of the stone. The amulet would allow them to pass as it had in past centuries. From one world to another these warriors would enter in hopes of saving the one they called the Guardian. While she was not as old as the Wise Ones she was a guardian of their people. Her raven hair and sparkling blue eyes made her seem almost mystical. But her talents for words and her strength of fighting made her the chosen one.....the Guardian.

They, the Navox, had lived in peace for centuries and now for the first time would face total extinction at the hand of their new enemies the Jahude. The Guardian had trained them to fight and learn the rules of the ruthless. Their race had a chance but only if the Guardian continued to live. For without their leader the Wise Ones would not help the Maihab people. And no one would fight without seeing the Guardian. This strange group was almost there. The cave was long and the journey a perilous one for they would be the enemy in other worlds. Each warrior knew the risk. Each one pledged their allegiance to the Guardian and to their people.

The fog was settling around the newly set up tents. Supplies were unloaded and security was set up around the perimeter. Lydia was glad she decided to wear jeans since she liked to organize and check equipment as it was being off loaded and wearing a skirt was never conducive to that type of work. Two other skeletal remains had been found by Lydia's crew and the recent discovery of a cave was being closely guarded. Food and gasoline for the generators were trucked in daily to this remote stretch of mountain road. All other personnel and computers were moved permanently to this spot. Lydia walked the area several times before setting up measurements and excavation crews. Areas two feet wide were worked on by shifts that would rotate. Excavation went on 24 hours a day, round the clock. Lydia knew that her funds would soon run out and that publicity was the only way. But that would open the project up and take it beyond her control. So, in the mean time she wanted the satisfaction of discovery for herself. The infrared photos she ordered would be taken tomorrow by military jet. That was one favor she considered collected.

Lydia walked out along the perimeter she had mapped out for photographing. She stopped at the large boulder that seemed to be awkwardly placed against this side of the hill. Although the boulder was several feet taller than she was it still looked to her as if someone had just placed it there. She placed her hand on the huge rock and brushed away some of the sediment that collected on the ridges. She moved closer to the rock and realized that the ridges were not natural. It seemed to be a marking of some kind. She quickly took out her map and marked the sector with a red flag. She folded back the map and tried to move the boulder with her weight. It did not move. She felt the rock over its face but nothing looked familiar. She started her walk back towards camp and quickened her pace the more she thought about the boulder. She would separate the crews and have one work on the newly found skeleton and the other on the boulder.

Once back at camp she made a list and gave everyone a specific duty. She needed to work quickly and efficiently if she was going to get the boulder uncovered.

"This will be perfect!" she spoke out loud as her secretary entered.

"What will be perfect?"

Karla sat down on a crate and opened up her notebook. Lydia threw her the stack of mail as she spoke.

"Those reporters can focus on the skeleton while I work on that rock. That way they won't get in my way and Carstairs will still have their positive publicity. It's great. It'll work I know it will."

She then reached behind her desk and checked her backpack.

"Do me a favor" she said as she took out the folded map. "When those students from team B arrive send them to this location and tell them to bring brushes and the documentation kit. "

She put on her lab coat and marked the location on Karla's map and circled the area to be covered.

"I'm going out there to work for a little while see you at lunch." And with that Lydia was off on foot to her boulder discovery.

She stopped and took photographs of the perimeter being sure to mark the numbers on her map. She stopped and watched a lizard displaying its colors. Lydia was glad to be out of her office at the institute. She felt she always belonged outdoors. She watched as the college students began arriving with picks, shovels, and small paint brushes. Jeff was directing group A and showing them where the first skull had been located. As she made her way further up the trail a mist could be seen forming. She wondered what set of circumstances had led these once living people to this site.

The amulet hummed as its wearer neared the stone.

"It glows but the stone does not move Coryla? What do we do now? The Guardian grows weaker!"

The bearded warrior looked back towards the young warrior with blonde hair.

"We move it with our hands!"

And with that the four warriors gently put down the one they called the Guardian and stood in front of the stone.

"PUSH!"

All six of the figures pushed the stone forward until it began to move. A mist filtered in. A small opening was made when a rush of fresh air hit their nostrils.

"We are almost there! Hurry."

Coryla, the young blonde woman directed them forward. The four warriors went back and picked up their delicate charge.

Lydia scanned each step she took on her way toward the boulder. She regretted not staying on task when she looked at the sun as it was beginning to set on the horizon. She knew her campsite lights would help guide her back but she still wanted to get one look at the boulder.

She took out her flashlight and scanned the ground. Her day-dreaming had cost her.

"Someone approaches!"

The figures took refuge behind the brush. Lydia could barely make out the stone and its location.

"Wait a minute," she said out loud. *The stones moved,* she thought.

Quietly the bearded warrior stepped from behind the brush. He reached out and grabbed Lydia. Her flashlight fell from her hands. She started to scream as he placed his hands across her mouth. The others then appeared from behind the brush. Lydia stopped struggling for a moment as she saw the group.

Coryla spoke first.

"You are the one they call doctor. You will heal the Guardian. Come!"

Lydia was lifted as she walked with her captors. She glanced down when they stopped. The vision she saw was of incredible beauty. The raven-haired woman was clad in well-fitting leather tunic with small triangles of metal. Her pants were of a softer leather with lace straps around her boots. A necklace or amulet she wore glowed a pale blue as she knelt down to touch this vision. She was still warm to the touch but did not move. She placed her fingertips on the young woman's eyelids and opened them partially. She drew in a short breath as the brilliant blue eyes met hers. Surprised, Lydia drew back and rested against Coryla's legs.

"You will cure her now!"

Lydia closed her eyes, took a long deep breath and then opened them. The figure was still there. This was no dream.

"I can't help her here. I'm not that type of doctor. I....."

"SILENCE," the young woman shouted.

All warriors drew their swords. Lydia closed her eyes. *This can't be happening,* she thought.

"Look guys I'm not really into pranks and this one certainly is a hum-dinger but I do like your costumes. They're so..."

The bearded warrior and Coryla grabbed Lydia, pulled her up and lead her towards the boulder. The others picked up the Guardian and carried her past the three and headed back into the tunnel. Lydia tried to struggle but their grip was like a vise. The woman at one point seemed stronger than the man. Suddenly the tunnel went dark. The stone moved back on its own to cover their tracks. Both amulets glowed to light the way. Lydia now felt fear and kicked and shoved. The blonde woman reached up and knocked out Lydia with the butt end of her sword.

"We must hurry to avoid capture. The Jahude know we are coming. I can feel it."

CHAPTER 3

Images were muted as Lydia's eyes began to open. She made out a glowing fire and several figures gathered around a body that laid on a litter made of tree branches and leather. Since she could not see very far Lydia reasoned that it was night time. She rose slowly as not to attract attention. She started to crawl towards the darkness when she felt the brush of cloth above her.

"I trust you slept well doctor?"

Lydia turned to see the young woman who hit her standing above her in a silken blue cape.

"What do you people want from me?"

She stood up now to face the woman.

"Please, let us talk in there."

The woman pointed to a tent now coming into focus towards Lydia's right. Her eyes were beginning to adjust to the surroundings. She realized she was in some sort of clearing with a cave. She looked around for the entrance to the cave but found nothing but brush. The effects of the blow could now be felt as Lydia stood up. Her jaw was sore and her head ached. She sat down inside the tent but leaned back down on her elbows.

The inside of the tent was lined with furs and soft leather. Golden threads and braids adorned several blankets and the markings were familiar in style.

"I apologize for the manner in which you were brought here but our people were never known for their subtleties. I am Coryla of Pangorne. The woman you are to heal is known as the Guardian. She has kept our people in peace for centuries. The Jahude have now threatened that peace and our very existence with war. The Guardian was wounded in an ambush. We have crossed into your dimension of time so that we may heal her and therefore ensure peace. You will be returned when you have completed your part."

The young woman uttered some call and in came the litter with the body of the woman she saw before. She was covered with the skins of what looked to bear or wolf.

"Look, you don't understand. I can't help her. I'm not who you think I am."

The woman flashed her sword.

"You are the one we seek. You wear the coat of the healer. The Guardian taught us this. If you do not help her you will be put to death."

"But you can't kill me I...."

"You will be put to death not by us but at the hands of the Jahude."

And with that the woman walked out of the tent. Lydia noticed the two guards just outside. She walked to the rear of the tent and lifted up a small corner. Three more were at the rear. She realized that two of the warriors were women. She heard someone call "Alera" and one of the warriors left her post. Lydia walked over to the woman's body and knelt down beside her. She covered her face in her hands and began to cry. A hand touched hers. Lydia, frightened, fell backwards. Lydia swallowed and kneeled once again beside the woman. The woman looked up at Lydia and smiled. Lydia leaned towards the woman.

"I don't know how to help you. I'm not the kind of doctor you need. Do you understand?"

The woman nodded slightly and began to speak.

"I....know who you are...... Dr. Lydia Vyla....but..you...are..all I have at..the..moment. I have...been...shot with an...arrow...head..and it must be..removed.. The burns are not important."

Lydia stood up and looked at the woman. She could see the slight burns on the woman's neck beneath the fur covers. She looked around. She felt the tent and she felt the ground. Was this her reality? She reasoned that for the moment it was. Lydia knelt down next to the injured woman. She gently pulled back the covers to reveal the woman's blood-soaked leather tunic and burned leather arm bands. She closed her eyes and opened them once more hoping the vision would change. When it did not she stood and walked to the entrance of the tent. She poked her head out the tent. Alera saw her and came running towards her.

"Alright, I'll need some cloth and antiseptic."

The woman walked into the tent with her and showed her a bag of soft clean clothes that were made from weaved fibers, animals skins and wool.

"I fear I do not know your meaning of an..ti..s.s.ep.tick."

Lydia looked at her.

"May I look around outside?"

The young woman looked around.

"Yes come!"

Lydia looked around outside and found what looked like the ancestor of her modern-day Aloe plant. She continued to look around and found Calendula and Comfrey growing around some rocks. She picked several bunches.

"Here, this will do but now I'll need some fresh water."

"Shall we boil it?"

Lydia smiled for she realized that these people were not stupid or uneducated. They were simply different.

After gathering the necessary herbs and plants she began to work on the woman called the Guardian. She placed the tools she had gathered in a small wooden bowl and poured the boiling water from the crude metal pot Coryla had given her. As she looked down she realized that the woman's skin was as tanned as hers. She pulled the furs further back to reveal the woman's waist and an ornately carved golden dagger that was attached to it. The woman's tunic was fastened by a series of leather ties which Lydia began to untie. As she pulled them back the woman's left breast was exposed. She looked at it for a moment marveling on how perfect it was in shape and form. She cleared away some of the blood with a damp cloth. Lydia then enlarged the wound to remove the arrow head. She used small tweezers she had left in her pocket and a probe-type instrument that she used for scraping around fossils. To her surprise the woman did not cry out in pain. The herbs she used to numb the area must have worked either that or the woman had an incredible threshold to pain. She placed the bloodied arrow head in a small wooden bowl filled with fresh water. She used the clean cloth to absorb the blood.

Coryla brought in a small pouch which contained a small sharp bone with a tiny hole pierced through it. Lydia looked around for some type of thread but realized that the only thing that was small enough yet strong was the nylon that her lab coat had been sewn with. Carefully she unraveled her bottom hem and took the thread and put it in the bowl with the homemade antiseptic. She then mended the woman's wound using a hem stitch for easier removal. She was beginning to think that this whole procedure might just work after all. The young woman watched Lydia as she worked on the Guardian.

"What magic do you possess?"

Lydia looked up at her and smiled.

"No magic, just simple chemistry and med school."

"M.mmed.Skchoool?"

Lydia laughed at her pronunciation.

"See these burns here? They are what we call second-degree burns that damage the lower layer of skin or dermis and can cause swelling and blistering. Those I've treated with Calendula and the Comfrey has what's called allantoin, a wound healing agent. Actually, you have quite a pharmacy growing out there!"

Lydia continued to explain what she was doing as the young woman looked on.

"Back home we would treat severe burns with Aconite or Arnica. But my mom had the strangest remedy for burns. You see there is this little Spanish beetle whose bite causes this burning pain. Well, my momma used that on us to relieve that very symptom."

Lydia continued to talk until the sewing was done. She then continued to treat the burns with the cloth she had left. The woman slept throughout the night. In the morning Lydia was given a wooden bowl filled with oats and grains. She was then given a pouch with milk. She smelled the milk. It had a strange yet familiar odor.

"My g-d! It's goats milk."

She poured the milk into the oat like cereal. The sweetness of the oats set off the slightly bitter taste of the goats' milk. She was then asked to join the group in a smaller tent. Once inside she saw different leaves next to a strangely shaped metal pot of boiling water. She was handed a stone cup from which the others placed a series of different leaves and dried berries. The water was then added to it. They stirred the mixture with a stick resembling cinnamon. They gave her back the cup and waited for her to sample the mixture. She smelled it first. To her surprise it smelled wonderful. It was a mixture of raspberry fruits, orange peels and nuts. She took a small sip and then another. It was like a brand of tea she had had once before. Before she realized it, she had drunk the entire cup. She looked around at the others. They laughed and then placed the same leaves and ingredients in the larger pot. They sat around and drank the wonderful blend of tea till the sun was straight above in the sky.

Lydia looked at her watch: 12:00 noon time. She stood up and went to check on her patient. As she reached for the flap of the tent to open it she was met by a woman clad in leather. With the exception of an ornately carved dagger she seemed rather peaceful looking compared to the others. As the woman smiled she realized it was her patient. She stood back.

"Now I know I'm good but surely I'm not that good. If I were I'd change my profession!"

She laughed a nervous laugh. The woman's deep blue eyes focused on Lydia.

"You are quite a good healer but once the arrowhead was removed my body healed quickly. Your stitching was very well done thank you."

The woman was slightly taller than Lydia and had that darkened tan that dreams were made of. As Lydia was marveling over the woman's' recovery the others came walking out of their tents. Once the Guardian was seen they came running over and bowed before her. As she acknowledged them another placed a velvety cape over her shoulders.

"You will escort this woman back to her place of origin. She has fulfilled her agreement and is no longer needed."

As soon as she finished the warriors began packing up their belongings and tearing down the tents.

Lydia was amazed at their speed and neatness, leaving the area as natural as it had been before.

"Wait! I don't even know who you are and where we are. Your people were not very informative," Lydia spoke as she followed the young woman.

"I am called the Guardian although my real name is Azure. I

am a Goetiat...a traveler. Where we are is of no importance to you. It is dimensional and would take too long to explain. I have been in your dimension for a while and was very interested in some of your discoveries. But the majority of your people were too violent and self-centered for any direct contact so I was called to another dimension."

She motioned to her to follow as she entered the tent.

"Your people are still in the learning and developmental stage and my contact could seriously alter your natural development. That is why I moved you to my environment."

Lydia watched as the woman continued to dress.

"So, what will happen to these people now that you are back?"

Azure turned to face Lydia.

"I will attempt to regain the peace that once existed here. A peace that all but the Jahude want. In your dimension not, all people want peace. There are too many who want different things for themselves and not for others. It is most complicated."

Lydia watched as the woman sharpened the ornate dagger she pulled out of her sheath on a small stone.

"And what if you don't succeed with the...Ja..Jahude? What will happen then? Will you just move on to another dimension?"

Lydia stood firm as she looked into Azure's eyes.

"Have I painted that poor a picture of my actions? I'm deeply sorry that we did not have more time together so that we could get to know one another better. I regret leaving you with such a vision of non-caring. Perhaps I should have made contact with one such as you."

She finished dressing and left the tent. Lydia followed. Azure turned to face her.

"And to answer your last question, if I fail to make peace, I will be put to death by my people."

She then motioned for Coryla to lead Lydia back towards the cave. Lydia tried to talk to Azure but she was held back and forced to move towards some brush. As they moved the branches the cave was exposed. The one called Alera struck two stones together as they created a spark onto a thick branch covered with moss that was held by Coryla. Lydia's archeologist side kicked in. She wanted to get a closer look at the flint she was using. She also wanted to talk more with the mysterious traveler and was sorry that she got angry and left a bad impression. She continued along the path she was led until the cave narrowed. The group stopped.

The amulet that Coryla wore was glowing but the others looked worried.

"What's wrong?" she whispered.

"The Jahude are near. We cannot continue on our present course. We must find another way. "

Lydia placed her hand on Alera's shoulders.

"But this is the way I came isn't it?"

Coryla motioned her to move back.

"True, it is the way you came but if the Jahude find us here they will kill you as well as us and they will have the means to enter your world. Enough talk! Please we must hurry."

They continued along a small crystal corridor which opened up into a medium sized cavern. The warriors placed Lydia against the cavern wall with Coryla and Alera flanking her. They then formed a half circle with swords drawn. They kneeled, extinguished the torch and waited. The amulet glowed dark red in the now darkened room as the warriors rose. Lydia could now hear metal clanging off the walls of the cave they just came from. The sound echoed off the walls and Lydia had a hard time telling how many there were. The sound was almost deafening. She aimed her eyes towards the entrance. She squinted in the red glow as she tried to make out figures heading towards them. Finally, the darkness grew lighter and from this light came the dreaded Jahude. Their flickering torches gave the cave an eerie feeling.

Suddenly she could see what the fear gave way to. There were 10 grisly clad warriors with skulls for helmets, large broadswords and animal fur which barely covered their lower extremities. Each had a beard that was braided and hair that looked like it hadn't been washed in years. The odor is what hit Lydia first. A rank, foul, decaying odor that almost brought tears to her eyes. *No wonder they defeat their enemies*, she thought. They make their eyes tear so that you can't fight them. Finally, the clash of swords came together. Coryla stood by Lydia's side with her sword drawn. Each of her five warriors took on two of the Jahude. Lydia could see that the Jahude were more barbaric fighters. They used whatever means it took to defeat their quarry. She watched as they bit the ears and shoulders of their opponent s in close battle. Lydia was surprised that she felt no fear only disgust for her situation.

"What I wouldn't give for a 357. Magnum right now," She said out loud as Coryla moved in front of her.

The fighting seemed to go on forever as neither side yielded. Finally, one of Coryla's warriors tripped and his sword was split in two by the thunderous blow of the Jahude warrior. His death seemed instant. The warrior now headed for Coryla. His eyes were bloodshot and Lydia could now see his yellowed teeth or at least what he had left of them. He thrust his sword into the ground and took a small dagger out from his belt. He smiled as he lunged for Coryla. She managed to block his blow and insert one of her own. Lydia figured she could use some help and held her breath as she grabbed the disgusting creature from behind. She could feel things crawling on her as she held him with his arms at his sides. Coryla took her sword and swung it at his legs. With a clean blow his legs were instantly parted from his body. Lydia let him go as he fell to the ground. He growled in agony as he crawled for his sword. Coryla screamed for Lydia to look out as a sword came whizzing by her left ear. She ducked and Coryla met it with her sword. Lydia was pushed against a wall as she looked around for a weapon. She looked around to see the Jahude take what was left of their victims and carve them up as though they were pieces of meat. One took his sword and opened the mouth of the already dead warrior and cut out his tongue. Lydia could watch no longer.

She realized now why the Jahude were so feared. She turned as she heard Coryla cry out in pain as one of the Jahude warriors squeezed her tightly in his arms. Two more of Coryla's warriors fell as Lydia now swallowed in fear. The one warrior that was left, Alera, now took on three of the Jahude. Suddenly from the darkness came a blinding blur of light. All Lydia could make out was a flashing gleam of metal swinging furiously in all directions. Lydia ran over to Coryla and pulled her out of the way of the action. She had tears in her eyes and was in great pain. Lydia held her to try and comfort her.

"Take...the. Amulet. Do not...let..them...take it."

She reached around in pain and gave Lydia her sword. When she looked up she could now make out the figure with the swinging sword.

135

The image got clearer as each Jahude met his death. Lydia looked around at the walls of the cavern that were now streaked with blood. Then there was silence. Lydia looked up slowly as Azure and Alera stood before her.

"How is she?"

Azure handed her sword to Alera and knelt to touch Coryla's face.

"I'll need to get a better look at her but I don't think we should do it here.... agreed?"

Azure nodded.

"Can I pick her up?"

"Yes, but gently. I think she has some broken ribs."

As Azure bent down to pick her up Coryla stopped her.

"No! Leave me. I will stay here."

Azure silenced her gently placing a finger over Coryla's lips.

"I will not leave you …especially in a pool of Jahude blood."

And with that she gently lifted her up and carried her back towards the darkened pathway. Lydia had never seen a woman be carried more gently.

Hours passed as the new path wound around stalagmites and stalactites. The light given off by the torches reflected on the rose quartz embedded in the walls of the cave. Finally, a tiny bead of light appeared up ahead. Smooth stone stairs curved upward towards the light.

A brilliant glow of light was now visible. Lydia squinted as she neared the light. Once through it she realized it was sunlight. The warmth bathed her body. It was a welcomed feeling. The dampness of the cave had made her joints ache. Their camp was not far. Azure had been carrying Coryla ever since their battle back in the cavern and not once had she stopped or put her down to rest. She followed Azure to a center tent. Inside, a fire had been prepared to ward off the dampness. Animal skins were laid on the ground and wool cloths were then laid out on top for added softness. As Azure placed Coryla down Lydia was already asking for clean cloths, fresh water and some strong straight sticks. Azure started to remove the woman's clothes. She then threw them in a pile by the flap of the tent. She began to wash the blood off of Coryla's skin. A rag was dipped in a small bowl of mashed up Plantain weed mixed with the Comfrey liquid and Coryla's body was washed. Her hair was draped in a large wooden bowl as Lydia looked on. Two other

136

women dressed in less heavy furs added water to the bowl and began to wash her hair. Aside from some scratches the main injury seemed to be her ribs. Lydia cleaned the area around her ribs and placed strips of cloth around Coryla's lower chest she then adjusted the tension with the straight sticks. The bandages were as tight as she could make them for now. She didn't see any signs of discoloration and prayed that no internal organs had been damaged by the bruised ribs. Lydia mixed the Arnica herb with something that smelled like witch hazel to help the surrounding tissues reabsorb blood.

"She needs to keep still for a while. She'll need someone to stay with her."

Lydia did not turn to look at Azure. She knew she would do as she asked. Lydia's body began to ache. But her main worry was her itching. She knew it was more than nerves. She remembered the foul smell of the barbarian and the things she felt crawling on her when she grabbed him from behind. Azure was watching her. She stood up and motioned to a woman standing at the entrance to the tent. The woman disappeared only to reappear with a small bottle of greenish liquid.

"Here. Dalena will show you where you can bathe. This is the liquid we use after we have encountered the Jahude. It will take care of your body. The clothes on the other hand will have to be burned. I have some clothes that will fit you temporarily."

She handed Lydia the green liquid and left her with the woman named Dalena. She showed Lydia to a waterfall and showed her where the animal skins were to wear on her way to Azure's tent. The woman made a small fire and held out a stick for Lydia to place her clothes on. Lydia reluctantly removed her lab coat, jeans, and shirt. She jumped into the water not caring whether it was cold or not. It felt refreshing. She poured a small amount of the liquid into the palm of her hand and began to rub it over her hair and the rest of her body. It seemed to work on contact. The itch was all but a distasteful memory. She floated for a while and then came to the shore line. Animal skins had been placed on a tree branch. They were soft and had a flowery type of odor. She thought they would smell but was relieved when they didn't. As she put the sinks on she saw how revealing the outfit was.

"Wonderful......Rachael Welch in One Million Years B.C. if the gang could only see me now. How the hell did they ever keep clean? I feel like I'm wearing a thong!"

She looked around as she continued to mumble out loud.

She walked barefoot back to the area of tents continuing to pull down on the bottom half of her clothing. Definitely not one size fits all, she thought. Dalena saw her and waved. She walked over to her to ask which of the tents were Azure's. She was surprised to hear that it was the one she had just come from. As she parted the flap of the tent she saw Coryla resting quietly. Azure was beside her reading a book.

"What are you reading?" she whispered.

"It is a book of poems written in French."

Azure got up and handed her a stack of neatly folded clothes. Lydia unfolded them to find that they were jeans, a blue cotton shirt and some undergarments.

"Where did you get these?"

Azure pointed to a small area where she might change.

"My dimensional travel sometimes requires me to blend in with the surroundings. Je..Jeans as you call them seem to blend in the best."

There were some boots to choose from so she left them by the area. Azure sat back down on a feathered cushion and continued her reading. Lydia changed quickly feeling as though Azure had eyes in the back of her head and was watching her now naked body. Later Dalena brought in several bowls of stew and spoons made of shells. Azure motioned for Lydia to have a seat in front of the fire. Without looking at Lydia she spoke.

"I'm sorry your return was not completed. I will escort you back myself. Until then please accept our apologies and our hospitality. We will try to make you as comfortable as possible."

Lydia watched her host as she ate. It seemed some other apologies were in order. Lydia stood up and moved to Azure.

"I behaved badly before and I wish to apologize for responding to a situation I did not fully understand."

She then sat down next to Azure. Now it was she who was making Azure uncomfortable. She could sense it. Lydia checked Coryla's pulse and her bandages. She noticed a slight fever.

"Has she been sleeping okay?" Lydia decided to break the silence and the tension and switch the subject to Coryla.

"Not really. I think she has a fever. The bandages seem to make her more comfortable but I'm worried about the fever."

"Will she heal as quickly as you did?" Lydia said without looking up at Azure.

"Once she is rested.... yes."

Azure poured her some water in stone cups and handed one to her. Their eyes met. Lydia was curious about Azure but at the same time was a bit frightened of her. The intensity with which she stared at Lydia made her uncomfortable. But still there was something that made Lydia want to be near her and learn more about her. For now, she would be content to share a meal with her. She remembered her mom's remedy described the herb Barberry. She knew if they could find it that the Berberine would reduce the fever. The closest they came to a fever reducing herb was Peppermint. She ground the leaves and came up with a fragrant oil that she gave to Azure.

"Here.....help me rub this over her body."

Azure obeyed and rubbed Coryla's body with the fragrant oil. Lydia noticed the care and gentleness Azure showed towards Coryla's body. It was almost too sensuous to watch.

The evening was filled with pleasant conversation and good food. Lydia tried asking Azure's place of origin but would get a pleasant smile and a different subject. So, Lydia learned to ask questions of how these people developed. She figured a discussion on history was always a safe subject. But as she soon realized they did not resemble any one particular people and that they seemed to be a combination of several different cultures she gave up her line of questioning. Coryla's fever had gone down as the evening wore on. Azure never once seemed to look at Lydia. But seemed interested in her knowledge of herbs and would ask her questions periodically on the different uses and how she would prepare them. Lydia soon grew weary and laid back against the soft furs and woven cloths. Eventually she drifted off to sleep as Azure watched over her. Quietly Azure ordered the tent cleared. She reached over and pulled one of the furs over Lydia's body.

Lydia awakened to an empty tent. She bolted upright and had a sudden fear that she had been left behind. She pulled the furs back and stood up rubbing her face as if to ward off the sleep that engulfed her. As she peered out of the tent she saw the camp gathered in front of a tree stump listening to Azure who stood on top of the stump. The sunlight caught the edge of Azure's tunic and drew Lydia's attention to the shiny object now highlighted. *Where have I seen that before?* she asked herself as she walked closer towards the object. The discussion must have been concluded as the people broke up and headed in different directions. By now Lydia stood in front of Azure. The blue coloring of the metal along with the pinkish striations suddenly gave Lydia the hint she needed. The striations appeared to form a triangular pattern. The metal that first tipped her assistant off to the skeleton on the side of the road was what she was now looking at.

"Is something wrong doctor?"

Azure stepped down towards Lydia.

"I was wondering where that beautiful amulet came from."

She reached up to touch it as if she had seen a mirage. The oval amulet measured approx. three inches in diameter and the peculiar colored metal surrounded a smooth topaz colored stone. It was fastened around her neck with two leather straps that were braided at the ends.

"The amulet has been in my family for many generations. It is the symbol of a traveler."

Lydia continued to feel the amulet.

"Do travelers ever die?" Lydia said this without realizing how it may have sounded.

She released the amulet and stood looking towards the ground.

"Quite a strange question, doctor."

Almost sensing what Lydia was thinking she spoke.

"Have you seen this amulet before?"

Lydia looked up.

"No....not the stone, just the metallic piece."

Lydia suddenly became nervous. She turned and started walking towards the tent she had just come from. Azure blocked her path. Lydia stopped, suddenly feeling frightened. She looked at her as if asking a question but spoke not a word. Lydia decided that she had already let the cat out of the bag so to speak. She might as well continue.

"One of my assistants found a skeleton and the metal was halfway around its neck."

Azure's demeanor suddenly changed. She placed her right hand on her dagger as though one would put their thumbs through their belt loop.

"And the stone?" Azure asked anxiously.

"We excavated the sight but no such stone was found. Could this skeleton be a traveler?"

Azure fell silent as she leaned against a boulder taking in what Lydia just said.

"I must take you back. Can you take me to see this skeleton?"

Lydia's heart felt as though it skipped a beat.

"Yes, of course I can."

Azure stood up and called out commands in a language resembling no other that Lydia had ever heard of.

"We will leave immediately!"

Lydia looked around as the camp was a flurry of people gathering, loading, sharpening weapons. Azure looked at them and spoke again. The people seemed to object to what she was saying.

Dalena stood before Azure and spoke what seemed like angry words. Coryla came out of her tent cradling her side and brushed past the crowd and stood next to Dalena. Coryla turned and spoke to her people. Lydia wished she had a translation but was not about to interrupt. When Coryla finished her people put down their weapons. Azure turned to face Lydia.

"It is settled. I will escort you back to your people. Coryla will wait here for my return. Dalena will travel with us to the halfway point."

Azure headed toward her tent. Coryla brought a small animal skinned backpack and handed it to Lydia.

"Just some extra things you might need for your trip."

Coryla paused and brushed something away from her eyes. Lydia realized that it was a tear. Lydia leaned over and hugged Coryla gently remembering her still healing ribs. Coryla stiffened slightly as though she was not use to being hugged. Lydia realized that in their culture hugs might not be a welcomed expectation. As she straightened back up Azure was by her side with a slightly smaller backpack. The three women headed back down towards the caves. Lydia could no longer keep her curiosity at bay.

"Azure......what was the problem back there?"

Azure continued to move swiftly and sure of foot.

"I could not endanger the Maihab people as well as yours by integrating two groups from a different time into one. They wished to protect me and were prepared to accompany us. It is not necessary for if my thoughts are correct the Jahude are already in your world and have been for quite some time."

Lydia stopped in her tracks.

"What! How do you know?"

Azure gently took her arm and coaxed her to continue walking. The cave was now damp and moss ridden. The combination gave the air a peculiar scent like that of fresh, moist dirt. Torches had been lit and continued to light the way.

"I will explain after I have seen your skeleton."

Lydia fell silent. She thought about her encounter with the Jahude and wondered how they could possibly integrate into her world. She chuckled to her self-envisioning the Jahude on motorcycles. A comic book came to mind as she walked. No further words were spoken until they had reached the familiar boulder. Azure spoke to Dalena and bid her farewell as she put out the torch. The amulet around Azure's neck glowed a brilliant blue. Lydia thought when she looked at it up closely that it was Amber colored but the light it cast against the boulder was a brilliant pale almost neon blue. The boulder moved as the amulet got closer. Lydia could make out a faint spot of light coming from the ground.

"My flashlight. It's still on!"

Azure picked up the flashlight and handed it to Lydia.

"Sorry."

Lydia wasn't sure what Azure was apologizing for.... the way in which she was taken or her abduction.

"Time is crucial, doctor."

Lydia took the flashlight and looked up at the glow around Azure.

"Okay, but first you'll need to call me Lydia and second we're going to have to change into some different clothes."

The night time air was crisp and cool as it surrounded the exposed areas of her body. Lydia remembered her parked car just over the ridge in front of them. She knew they would have to have different clothes if they were going into the tent where the pictures of the skeleton were kept. Once near the car she could see the lights of the night crew down below the hill. Luckily, she left her keys in the car so she opened her trunk and took out a pair of clothes that hadn't quite made it to the cleaners. She handed them to Azure and took the spare lab coat for herself. Lydia cleared the papers from the front seat. Azure backed up slightly out of the car's interior light and changed. Lydia looked in the rear-view mirror hoping to catch a glimpse of Azure's body. Once back in the light the amulet was hidden beneath her tightly fitted shirt. It was now that Lydia noticed her muscles that naturally bulged forth from the short sleeves of the shirt.

Azure looked at Lydia.

"Okay now let's take a look at those photos."

Lydia barely managed to finish speaking as Azure got in. As Lydia started the car and drove down towards the camp she looked at the clock in the car. At 10:30 at night there would be only a couple of dedicated college students still working on logs and packing of the days discoveries. Lydia turned to Azure and spoke softly.

"I'll introduce you as a friend of mine if anyone is still here okay?"

Azure looked at Lydia with those brilliant blue eyes that almost seemed to glow in the dark like the amulet and smiled in agreement.

Karla looked up as the two women entered the tent.

"Aren't you afraid to be here after dark?" Lydia asked casually as she brushed past the computer.

"Oh! I wondered where you were. I just figured you forgot to check in for messages. Where did you go yesterday? Everyone was looking for you. And I'm not here alone. David is collecting some tools and organizing for tomorrow's dig."

Lydia realized that the passage of time must not be the same between the two worlds.

"I had some business in town. I left a message but I guess it got misplaced. Oh! A... this is a friend of mine who came to see Tim's great discovery. Are those photos still around here?"

143

Lydia motioned for Azure to take a seat.

"Does your friend have a name?"

Karla handed Lydia a 11x14 envelope marked 'PHOTOS DO NOT BEND'. Azure turned to face Karla.

"Most people call me......Azure."

Lydia took out the photos and handed them to Azure. Karla looked at Lydia.

"That's a beautiful name."

She saw the two women look at the photos intently. She shrugged her shoulders and continued on with her work. Azure looked at the photos then turned to Lydia and whispered softly.

"These photos will not do. I will need to see the actual piece of metal and the skeleton. If the stone was separated from the metal I will have to find it."

Lydia was about to say something when she realized that Karla might get suspicious with their whispering.

"Well, I guess it's time I took you back to your hotel. See you tomorrow, Karla. I'll probably be in late."

Karla looked up partially preoccupied.

"Sure....Okay."

Once outside Lydia faced Azure.

"What do you mean the skeleton? You don't understand. That skeleton was put on a plane to Washington State and is undergoing radiation tests for carbon dating. As for the metal, it's at Cal Tech undergoing metallurgy tests. These two areas are quite a distance apart."

Lydia turned from Azure in frustration. The frustration she was feeling was confusing to her. *Did she actually believe these things that had happened to her? What was she helping this woman do and why?* As if Azure was hearing her thoughts she walked over to Lydia and gently touched her arm.

"Please......sit."

Lydia looked around and leaned against the hood of her car. Azure stood in front of her.

"I know you are confused and I know that you do not fully understand the forces at work. I will try to explain as best as I can the danger that your people will face if the skeleton is that of a Guardian."

Azure turned to face the horizon.

"Each of us is entrusted with an energy stone that we begin our lives with. If we die the stone returns to its place of origin. Each traveler can feel the passing of another and its stone."

Azure stepped back and looked up at the stars.

"I felt the passing of a traveler but not her stone."

She looked back at Lydia.

"That indicates that someone has it.... the stone.... and like the Jahude can use it for evil."

Lydia stood up.

"But both the skeleton and the fragment of metal were found around here. The skeleton was there for quite a long time! The way you're talking ....a catastrophe is going to take place soon. But I can tell you from the news reports everything is as it was in the past. Presidents talk, people go to war, the rich stay rich and the poor still struggle."

Azure placed her hand to her head as if she was listening to something she had heard many times before.

"Your ozone layer is damaged, murders have increased in this state since four of your years. I think I can figure out when the stone was taken."

Azure's voice was slightly on edge. Lydia was surprised at her tone.

"As for the dating of the skeleton.....(she smiled) Ralyea was about 200 of your years older than I was at the time. And I am sure her bones will reflect that in your...tests."

Lydia starred at the ground before her. She felt the anguish and frustration that Azure now felt. Not being able to function as you want in a world that is unaccustomed to you can cause this she thought jokingly to herself.

"Alright.....let's assume for the moment what you are saying is indeed true. What do we do now? "

"We return to the area and see if it was the sight of the stone and look through what you call 'news reports'. A common name should be evident in the area of these disturbances."

Lydia walked around to the driver's side of her car.

"Tomorrow I can access the computers and have them do some

of that work for us. They can compile names and locations and cross reference them."

Lydia noticed Azure rubbing her eyes.

"Until then we need to get some rest for there is nothing we can do tonight. You can stay with me at my home since I see you having some difficulty checking in at the local Holiday Inn."

Azure turned, "What?"

Lydia laughed.

"Never mind... just get in."

CHAPTER 4

As Lydia drove up her driveway she wondered how Oscar would feel about her new visitor. Both women stepped out of the car and gazed up into the clear night sky. Lydia's home was nestled on top of a heavily wooded mountain plateau. It overlooked the Denver town below and at night all that was visible were the tiny twinkling of street lights. The air was always crisp and clear.

"Beautiful night isn't it?" Lydia said as she picked up her extra clothes from the trunk of her car.

"Yes....beautiful." Azure said softly as Max sniffed at her feet suspiciously.

"Don't mind Max. She just dislikes men not women."

Azure smiled at Lydia and then down at Max. Azure walked up to the front door slowly."

Max sounds like the name for a male yet she is a female?"

Lydia opened the door to her softly lit home.

"It's short for Maxine."

Once inside Azure was overwhelmed by the sights and sounds of this new environment.

"The...music.... where does it come from?"

Lydia put her keys down and pointed to the entertainment center that stretched out on the wall in front of them.

"It's called a stereo. It plays different music and has pictures to go along with it."

She picked up the remote and switched to a different album and turned on the television. Classical Mozart seemed more appropriate than Jazz and the video was that of a rainforest in the wet season. Mary had left fresh cut flowers on the table with a note reminding Lydia of the mini-vacation she had promised her.

"Perfect timing," Lydia said under her breath.

She showed Azure around and placed her in the room that had a large balcony, high ceilings and large picture windows on the second floor. She thought Azure would be more comfortable in an open room with access to lots of moonlight and stars. Lydia gave Azure a change of clothes and showed her where to wash up.

"Just lift the lever and turn the knob to adjust the temperature and flow."

Azure looked puzzled as she studied the knob for the shower. As much as Lydia wanted to watch she left Azure to her experiences. Azure sniffed the soap and tasted the toothpaste as she showered. Lydia went into the kitchen to make some hot tea. As she put the kettle on she looked back on the last few days events and wondered if those things had actually happened. A storm was building out in the western sky. She walked to her bedroom and removed her shirt and bra.

"Ah.....that's much better."

She grabbed a freshly laundered shirt and splashed on some perfume. Lydia watched out her bedroom window, fascinated by the fluid movement of the clouds. She walked back out to the study. She looked once again at the strange cloud formation. Huge rainstorm she thought to herself. She closed the necessary windows and lit a fire in the fireplace. She softened the lights in the house which seemed to lessen the appearance of the storm clouds outside. The glow of the fireplace highlighted the wood bookcases and gilded edges of the books. Lydia looked around the room and smiled at the calm almost romantic aura that surrounded the room. A sound came from behind her and startled she knocked over a carved wooden bookend.

"Sorry, I didn't mean to frighten you."

Lydia looked Azure over as she stepped into the light of the room. Azure's raven hair was no longer in a braid. It cascaded down the sides of her face and over onto her shoulders. The face was softened by the warm orange tones of the flames. The jeans fit perfectly especially around Azure's hips and the flannel shirt had been buttoned only up to Azures chest revealing a very well-endowed upper torso.

Shit! I wish I looked that good in flannel, Lydia said to herself. She picked up the wooden bookend as she spoke.

"It's okay. That storm was just giving me the jitters."

Lydia knew she could lie effectively. Azure looked in the direction of the storm.

"It has begun."

Azure stood motionless as she watched the clouds. Lydia moved closer to her and stood behind her.

"What do you mean; it has begun?"

Azure reached up and held the amulet that rested between her breasts. Lydia noticed the strange bluish-purple glow surrounding the charm.

"The gateway has been opened. Soon the Jahude will come."

Azure's voice was even toned, soft and calm. Lydia placed her hand on Azures shoulder.

"We'll find that other amulet tomorrow. You can count on it."

Azure turned towards the fire and sat down on a large pillow next to the armchair at the front of the fireplace. Lydia couldn't help but chuckle when she watched Azure. Anyone else would have chosen the chair not the floor. But then what does one expect from a Barbarian. Lydia continued to watch as Oscar stretched out next to Azure as though she were a she-wolf protecting her mistress. Lydia wondered where her camera was when she needed it. The whole scenario seemed like a dream but the sudden clap of thunder and flash of lightening brought her swiftly back to reality. Both women stared into the fire and tried to relax. Once asleep both recounted the past day's events through a series of dreams and nightmares.

Visions of clashing swords, mist and armored warriors were her entry into sleep. Lydia tossed and turned while Azure remained motionless. Lydia awoke in a cold sweat and breathing heavily as though she had just finished a strenuous workout. She glanced over at Azure who slept peacefully through the storm. The thunder seemed to get louder as Lydia stood up. She felt dizzy and held on to the arm chair to steady herself. Something was wrong and Lydia knew it. At the risk of feeling light headed again she kneeled down next to Azure and shook her gently from her sleep.

"What's wrong?" Azure spoke softly as she looked at Lydia.

"I'm not sure. Something is wrong but I don't know what. I...."

Azure could see the fear and confusion on Lydia's face. She stood up and looked around the room. Lydia stood up to join her and felt nausea well up her body. Azure noticed this and had Lydia sit in the chair next to her. She poured her a glass of water.

"Here.....take some water. The nausea will pass. The Jahude are close by and now I am not the only one who feels it; for you now are linked to their existence as well."

Lydia took a sip of water as though it were a strong drink.

"Well that's certainly comforting. What am I supposed to do when I meet them? Throw up on them?"

Lydia took another sip. A crash of thunder brought with it a crashing window at the end of the hallway. Lydia jumped up and ran behind Azure towards the broken window. Wind and rain blew into the hallway. As both women looked out of the window a sickly-sweet smell drifted down the hallway. Azure turned and looked. Suddenly she moved Lydia behind her and withdrew a small dagger from the jeans she wore. A thick mist moved down the hallway towards them. Lydia placed her hands-on Azure's back and breathed deeply. The mist enveloped the two. Azure moved and placed her hand around Lydia's waist as she felt the ground shake.

"I....I... can't move!" Lydia shouted against the din of the storm.

"It is the Jahude! Hold on to me. The amulet will provide temporary protection until we have transported."

"Transported! Transported where? What the hell is going on?"

As she spoke she lowered her hands to Azure's waist and held her tightly to her. She tried to look around but could see only rain. She then realized that it was raining all around them yet she was not wet.

"I'm not sure I can stand much more of this! It's like being in the middle of a tornado. The sound is maddening."

Just as Lydia shouted the last line the rain stopped and all was quiet. Azure turned around quickly and looked around with the dagger still in her hand.

"Come....we must find shelter."

Lydia chuckled a nervous chuckle.

"Find shelter? How can we find shelter when we don't even know where we are?"

Azure let go of Lydia.

"You may not know where we are but I know. Come!"

Lydia followed quickly as Azure ran to what appeared to be a forest line. Once within the forest Azure knelt down and held the glowing amulet. Pointed east it glowed a cool blue, west it glowed a brilliant red, north a cool blue, south a cool blue. Lydia knew which direction they'd be traveling.

Both women walked on foot to a small tree at the end of the forest. There, tied to a branch, were two saddled horses.

"How did these get here? " Lydia asked as she walked towards the horses.

She realized that these were not ordinary horses. They stood 12 hands high and were incredibly muscular. They were bred for something but it certainly wasn't for speed. The saddles were made of leather and ornate carvings. Gold thread seemed to be woven through the saddle and caught the light as the horses moved. As Lydia looked cautiously at the horse nearest her she realized that Azure had already mounted one.

"We must leave quickly before we are spotted."

Azure held the reins of the second horse out to Lydia. As Lydia took the reins she spoke nervously.

"Won't the owners miss these horses?"

Azure smiled slightly.

"No....for the owner is right here."

"Wait a minute! These are your horses?"

"Please......come.....I'll explain as we go."

Lydia mounted her horse. She thought her legs were going to split from the width of the horse. The two women galloped towards the west.

"This is where I left when I entered your dimension. In my time they haven't moved since then."

As Lydia bounced along she remembered why she stopped her riding lessons. Something to do with sitting down afterwards. As they rode Lydia noticed the strange flora and fauna that they were traveling through. Belladonna, Pulsatilla, Chamomile, and Gingko all grew wild and unattended. Plants that she had seen only in textbooks were now growing before her eyes. If only she could stop and study them for a while. The horses pace slowed as they came to the edge of a misty forest. Azure turned her horse slightly to look back at the horizon.

"We go on foot from here."

She dismounted and helped Lydia from her horse. Once Lydia was down on the ground she saw the vines and lichens that grew around her. The mist formed droplets that clung to the leaves like tiny pearls of tears. Azure walked into the forest and Lydia followed. Lydia realized halfway in that there was very little light and she began to wonder how Azure could see where she was going. Suddenly Azure parted a thick branch and an ocean appeared before them. The sea breeze drifted across Lydia's nostrils. She took in a slow long breath and moved towards the shore.

"We will rest here till dawn."

Lydia looked around at Azure.

"Well I'm glad you know what time it is because I haven't got the foggiest clue."

She looked down at the bleached white sand and wondered how many people had walked on it. It smelled salty yet fresh and clean. Lydia rubbed her back as she moved to free stiff muscles.

"Here......maybe this will help."

Azure picked up a small purple flower from behind a huge tree stump. She pressed the flowers petals together in the palm of her hand to form a clear oil.

"I know that flower! It's called St. John's wort."

Azure studied it.

"I know not what you call it simply that it works on muscle pains. Here....lift your shirt."

Lydia did as she was told. The oil was cool to the touch but as Azure worked it into her sore muscles it gave off a mild heating effect much to Lydia's surprise. Lydia closed her eyes and felt Azure's strong fingers message deeper into her muscles. Lydia began to relax and leaned with each movement closer to Azure. As she now leaned against Azure's breasts she could feel her pulse increase.

"Perhaps you would feel more comfortable resting now." Azure spoke as she used the last bit of oil on her fingers.

"Actually, I'm quite comfortable right here."

Suddenly Azure stopped rubbing. Her breathing became very shallow. Lydia looked around at Azure.

"Are you okay? Azure...."

Azure pushed Lydia forward as a bolt of light appeared out of the western sky. The bolt found its mark. As Lydia got up she turned to see Azure's chest smoking as her body lay still.

"G-d.... no!"

Lydia crawled over to Azure as she looked in the direction of the bolt of light. Looking around she saw no cover. Lydia cradled Azure as she tried in vain to tear the burnt clothing from her body. As she grabbed she felt the amulet beneath and held it wishing desperately to be back in the cave with Alera, Coryla and Dalena. A mist formed as she closed her eyes. Darkness was upon her. She could feel Azures body against her but could barely make out anything else. She felt around her flannel coat pockets and took out a tiny flashlight she'd remembered pulling from her backpack back at the house. As the light shown on cave walls the unlit torches could be seen. She laid Azure down carefully and lit the torches with the waterproof matchbox she carried for her campfires. She could hear droplets of water and stopped to audibly locate their direction. She aimed the flashlight in the direction of a tiny pool of water that was collecting on the side of the cave wall. It almost appeared as though the rock were carved there for such a purpose. *Well, whatever the purpose,* Lydia thought, *it's what I need right now.*

Lydia tried to tear a piece of clothing from her shirt tail. She then looked at Azure's dagger. She pulled it carefully out of the sheath and cut off a swatch of cloth. She then dipped it into the small pool of water and placed it over Azure's chest. She used the dagger to cut away bits and pieces of the burnt clothing until Azure's chest was exposed. The burns seemed minor compared to the intensity of the bolt. Lydia surmised that it was the stone that somehow deflected the energy. She could feel Azures pulse all while she held her so she knew she was still okay. She looked down to see Azure's breasts firm and rising with Azures every breath. She rinsed out the cloth, dipped it into the water once more and then pulled Azure to one corner of the cave.

Lydia pulled her flannel jacket off. She then sat down and gently lifted Azure's head and placed it on her lap. She then spread out the cloth over her chest, covered her with her flannel coat and let her left arm drape over Azure's waist. The cave was damp but warm. Lydia unbuttoned her shirt to let whatever air was present against her. The torches continued to flicker as she watched Azure. Suddenly, she noticed movement in Azures fingers. Azure awoke startled and bolted upright as if the moment of impact had occurred again.

"Shhh...it's alright."

Lydia reached over to hold Azure. "

I think I moved us from ocean shore to this cave.

"Azure's panic now subsided. Lydia could feel Azure's breasts harden against her skin.

"Just relax."

As Azure started to follow Lydia's suggestion she shook herself.

"There is no time to relax. The Jahude have proven that. We must transport back to the origin of the energy bolt.

"Lydia stood up realizing that Azure was right. Suddenly Azure looked at her.

"But......how did we get here?"

Lydia stood up.

"Well, I'm not real sure on that one. You see I was holding you and touching the amulet and wishing we were back in the place we were before."

Azure looked slightly puzzled at Lydia's explanation.

"We must go back!"

"Yes, but how are you going to fight them. Better still what are you going to wear?"

Lydia looked as Azure looked down at her exposed breasts. Azure looked back up at Lydia. Lydia was suddenly taken aback by the imagery of Azure against the cave wall highlighted by the torches. Azure walked over to Lydia and took her face in her hands. Gently she kissed Lydia then whispered.

"We do not have time for such things for the Jahude must be stopped."

She then waited for Lydia's response. Lydia felt like a hot bowl of jello. She blinked several times and then reached for Azure's dagger. She was about to object to Azures implication but thought about her pounding heart. With two swift cuts she placed her flannel coat over Azure's clothes, tied the coat at her waist, and buttoned the rest of the two buttons.

"Well....it's a hell of a fashion statement. Looks like a feminine version of a western duster but it should provide adequate coverage."

Azure took back her dagger.

"Thank you."

And with that the two women transported back to the energy bolts origin.

CHAPTER 5

The building was that of a university complete with a Washington State pennant hanging from one of the walls. The lights seemed brighter and Lydia noticed the sun going down through one of the windows.

"We must be at the university where the skeleton was taken. But I don't understand where the people are. This place should be crawling with them even at this time of day."

Azure gripped her dagger but did not remove it from her sheath.

"Which way would they have taken the skeleton?"

Lydia looked around and found a directory.

"Science section in one of the labs I would presume. It's this way."

Azure followed Lydia through the corridors to two swinging doors. Above were the signs: Science and Technology department. As Lydia swung the doors open she saw several bodies of students lying on the floor. Their clothing looked like that of Azure's after she got hit with the energy bolt. The corridor was filled with a light putrid smoke and scorched marks could be seen along the walls. The glass that once covered the fire safety equipment was shattered and lay atop the body of one young woman. Lydia knelt down to the first body of a young man. His face was severely burned along with his upper torso. She felt for a pulse.... there was none. She rushed over to the second, third and fourth.

"They.......there all...dead."

Azure removed her dagger with one hand and grasped the amulet with the other. The burns were still smoldering on the bodies.

"I cannot permit you to continue." Azure spoke as she moved towards the only door left in the corridor.

"Bullshit! I haven't come this far to put up with this mess again."

And with that Lydia grabbed the fire safety axe from beneath the broken glass. She then hesitated and realized that she didn't want to get that close again to the Jahude and opted for the fire extinguisher instead. The distance was not that great but would be a hell of a lot better, she reasoned, in this situation.

Both women headed for the last door. Cautiously, Azure entered first. The same putrid smoke that filled the corridor was now present in the lab. Behind a black table top desk was a man in a lab coat similar to Lydia's. He was holding a stone in his left hand and holding out his right as if to keep someone from approaching. Lydia saw what he was trying to hold back: a single Jahude warrior who seemed to be just standing there, sword in hand. Neither one seemed to notice the two women.

"Hand over the stone you worthless creature!"

The lab technician spoke very slowly.

"I don't know what you want."

Lydia stepped towards the technician.

"He doesn't understand you. He only understands one thing and that is your death."

The technician turned slightly to acknowledge Lydia.

"He seems to understand how to use this.....this stone!"

Lydia wasn't sure who had killed the students in the hall but she knew she'd feel safer if it were in Azure's hands.

"Give me the stone and this can all end right here."

Lydia moved towards the technician and as she did so did the Jahude warrior. Azure blocked his path. As he raised his sword she kicked it out of his hand and sent it clattering to the floor.

"No!....Don't kill him he can be useful," the technician shouted as he watched the warrior.

As the two engaged in hand-to-hand combat Lydia inched closer and spoke.

"He is a Jahude. They are useful to no one except themselves. They are a warrior clan, a primitive people. Get the picture?"

The technician was now focused on the battle.

"Don't you realize the publicity I would get? The research I could fund with a subject such as him. This could be great....the break I'm looking for."

Lydia turned slightly.

"What about those poor people in the hall?"

He turned to face Lydia.

"They were necessary sacrifices. I had to test it and we have no lab animals here since those bleeding-heart radicals came here last month protesting with their sit-ins. Serves them right.... now they've given their names for science. Fitting isn't it?"

Lydia turned to see the Jahude on top of Azure with the dagger pointed towards her throat. Lydia turned the nozzle of the extinguisher towards the warrior. Azure turned slightly as not to get sprayed. Lydia covered the warrior with white foam as she emptied the fire extinguisher on the warrior. He fell forward motionless onto Azure. Azure pushed him off as quickly as she could and stood up facing the technician.

"Good......good... He'll make a great specimen to....."

Lydia cut him off by throwing the fire extinguisher at him. But she missed.

"You fool! You just don't get it do you!"

He pointed the stone towards her and Azure stepped in front of Lydia with her hand on the amulet. The two stones released beams of energy and clashed halfway between the rooms. The lab took on an eerie glow as everything electrical began to overheat. Glass shattered, wires burned yet the beams still held their ground. Lydia moved close to Azure as though to touch her.

Suddenly Azures' beam pushed closer to the technicians. Lydia moved closer still. The beam from Azure's amulet was inches from the stone the technician held. Finally, Lydia understood the power of the stone. She reached out and held her hand over Azures as if she were helping her hold the amulet. Once the touch was complete Azures amulet over took the stone and proceeded to burn the technicians whole upper torso. Azure released her grip but Lydia still held it up. Azure turned and spoke softly to Lydia.

"It is over. He is dead. The further burning of his body will not bring back the others.... Lydia......Lydia."

The soft mentioning of her name slowly brought Lydia out of the hypnotic trance she seemed to find herself in. Azure walked back to the Jahude warrior.

"He must return with me lest he causes a rift in our dimensions."
Azure placed her hand on the amulet but before Lydia could shout stop. The two had vanished!

"Wonderful! How in the hell am I going to explain this one?"

Lydia walked around surveying the destruction. She saw a small shimmering object from behind the technician's body. It was the lost stone that Azure sought. Lydia pulled a cloth out of one of the desk drawers, gently picked up the stone, wrapped it up and placed it in her pocket. She could hear ambulances off in the distance. She knew she had to cover as much of the incident as possible so she turned on the gas jets and lit a wad of paper in the wastebasket. She ran towards the stairs and managed to make it through the doors as the gas reached the wastebasket. The explosion rocked the building and blew the doors outward along with Lydia. She was thrown against the wall with enough force to kill her instantly yet she was conscious when the firefighters came running up the stairwell. She felt herself being lifted up and taken down stairs to an awaiting ambulance.

After some preliminary the police and firemen closed their investigation and Lydia was released and flown back home. She was told by her boss to either submit voluntarily to a two-week vacation or be fired. She naturally opted for the two-week vacation. She had placed the stone under a glass case she used for one of her quartz crystals. She knew that one day Azure would return to claim the stone and say a proper goodbye.

Several days had passed after her plane trip from Washington as she enjoyed the fresh air and sunlight Denver had to offer when she noticed Oscar barking furiously at the broken window that was covered with plywood near her upstairs bedrooms. She walked hurriedly up the stairs. She peered out one of the side windows and noticed a familiar cloud formation heading her way.

"Oh no! Not the Jahude again." She spoke out loud to Max as if he understood her.

But as she looked around the room for something to defend herself with when Oscar and Max became very calm and knelt down in front of the plywood window. Lydia turned and starred strangely at Oscar.

Suddenly a familiar mist was seen down the hallway. Before her stood a hooded figure. Lydia stood motionless.

The hooded figure advanced towards Lydia. She backed up in fear and clutched the fireplace poker she had picked up. The hooded figure stopped and folded down their hood. It was a familiar face......that of Azure. She was dressed is a flowing lavender gown with gold trim and ornate stitching. It was the most feminine clothing she remembered seeing on Azure. Lydia dropped the poker and smiled. She thought she knew what Azure had come for.

"I've kept your stone safe. It's down...."

But before Lydia could finish her sentence Azure handed her a small jeweled box.

"The Navox humbly thank you for your help and wish to give you a token of their thanks and friendship."

Lydia took the box and sat down on the sofa.

"How are the Navox?"

Lydia looked down admiring the box as she spoke. Azure moved closer to Lydia trying to make eye contact.

"The peace will be a lasting one thanks to you. The Navox are even sharing some newly learned healing techniques with the Jahude."

She smiled up at Azure as a warm feeling came over her. As she opened the box a faint scent of earth and tree bark filled the air. She felt as though she were in the woods once more. In the box lay a tiny red stone set in an intricately carved wooden base. As she held it up to the light it refracted all the light in the room and bathed the ceiling in a kaleidoscope of colors.

"It's beautiful!"

Lydia could not pull her eyes away from the dancing colors that were appearing on her ceiling. Finally, Azure bent down and gently kissed her. Lydia was engulfed by a pure soft blue halo. Azure pulled back momentarily to look at Lydia. Lydia opened her eyes.

"I thought I would take you up on your original offer," Azure spoke softly as not to startle Lydia.

Lydia blinked and said, "What offer was that?"

Azure chuckled. It was the first time since Lydia had known Azure that she ever saw her laugh.

"The offer to teach me about your people. Or more to the point...you."
Lydia returned Azure's kiss.

"Gee....I guess you'll have to spend the night since your first lesson doesn't start until the morning."

Azure moved her into the bedroom.

"Well, we could begin a bit early."

And with that she gently pushed Max out, turned down the lights, turned on the sounds of the rain forest and began her next adventure.

The End

Relic

"The earth loveth the shower," and
"the holy ether knoweth what love is."
The universe, too, loves to create
Whatsoever is destined to be made.

Marcus Aurelius Antoninus

The wind howled fiercely as the hooded figure stood below the crest of the moonscape. The two moons illuminated by the reflection of the twin suns created a magnetic force that damaged most planetary ships sensors. The relic that was sought by so many now lies only days away from this barren location. Its discovery would be a gift to some and to others a curse. This hooded figure would determine which course.

"Where the hell is the commander?"

The burly man bellowed as he scratched his beard and sucked on his synthetic stogie. The busy cargo hold seemed to continue its furious pace seeming to ignore the man's urgent question. Barrels and containers moved about as aliens and crew members readied their departure onto the planet's surface. The airlock filled as the vacuum chamber hissed its objection to the change in atmosphere. Everyone paused to watch as the chamber slowly opened. A tall dark hooded figure cloaked in a flowing dark burgundy robe stepped forward onto a metal sensor grate. The figure turned and tapped the button to their left. The grate then formed steps which the figure stepped quietly down upon.

"Commander!"

The hooded figure reached up and grabbed both sides of the hood and slid it down on their shoulders. Hands reached up to pull up a visor and dislodge a helmet. Raven hair cascaded down around the woman's shoulders and over the hood and cloak. She turned to face several crew members.

"Ready Team 1 Lieutenant. They'll begin their assent at 0200. Oh! And tell Barnes to crank up the heat. It's as cold as an iceberg in here!"

The lieutenant nodded in agreement even though he wasn't exactly sure what an iceberg was. Most of the crew was born on Altar 7 and knew of forests, lakes and clouds…. but no icebergs. He figured he'd look it up on the computer later. The commander noticed a tall cloaked figure waiting by the exit ramp. They briefly made eye contact as a small front loader went by stacked to the ceiling with supplies. The commander turned and headed for Engineering. Crates and barrels continued to move towards loaders as the hustle and bustle of unloading aliens and supplies continued.

"Move out of the way you over grown slugs. Alright…. where is she?"

The lieutenant turned to face the boisterous sound.

"Sergeant Barnes, the commander has requested that you adjust the thermal modules to maximum. She states it is a bit cold in here."

He removed his stogie and pointed it as he spoke.

"Look! You poor excuse for an android…. I've been on missions longer than your body coil so keep your diplomacy chip out of my way and let me speak with the illustrious commander."

The lieutenant backed up slightly to elevate his wrist sensor.

"Commander Avir….A Sergeant Barnes needs and urgent word with you."

The rest of the crew resumed their duties and busied themselves with cargo, food containers and sensor equipment.

"Tell the old fool I'll meet him on the Command Deck in 5."

Barnes was already grumbling as he backed up and headed in the direction of the Command Deck.

The lieutenant simply shook his head and muttered *"you're welcome, you asshole"* under his breath. So much for his diplomacy chip. He didn't mind the commander it was just crew members like Barnes that were from the old school of protocol that irked him. He was still human but his spinal cord had been reinforced for combat and every so often his coil and vertebrae had to be adjusted.

The Command Deck was a quiet array of sound and light which was quite a contrast from the chaos and sounds of the cargo bay. The commander sat quietly still contemplating the moonscape this time through the window screen of her spaceship as the planet Tulvos rotated in the distance.

"Beautiful isn't it?"

The voice, with its delicate trace of French origin, very gently broke the silence. The commander smiled but didn't turn to face the familiar voice.

"Yes...*it's strangely hypnotic. Too bad in a few days it will be just another moon to a dust cloud."*

The commander referred to the dust storms and sand particles that were already rising from the surface due to the recent settlers attempting to colonize the planet. These storms were already becoming a navigation hazard for her ship. The search for the ancient relic had brought hunters from far and wide. No matter what nationality or planet her living cargo came from they all had one goal: to reach Planet Tulvos, the sacred planet. Depending upon who one talked to the relic possessed "the wisdom of the ages", "the key to life as we know it" or "wealth beyond your imagination." All the commander knew was that it was the destroyer of planets. In searching for the relic people and aliens used any means possible to tear, rip, dig, uproot and more frequently destroy the land where the relic supposedly lay. The commander's thoughts broke as a friendly hand touched her shoulder. This time the commander turned and smiled.

"And how is our beautiful Science Officer this evening?"

She sat down at the console and swiveled the chair next to the commander.

"Getting offers from all the wrong people. It's a zoo down there in the cargo bay. Thank the moons most of it is leaving along with its owners. I've been pinched, poked and just now ...slimed by one of our guests."

She could see that the commander was preoccupied. It was so quiet up in this area of the command deck that she didn't want to leave. The quiet hum of the instruments and the large viewing screens gave the space an almost tranquil feeling. But Science Officer Christine Almonte had known Commander Avir for several Earth years and had served with her through several campaigns and was respectful of her quiet time. She figured it was because the commander during wartime conflicts and alien battles was surprisingly brutal but effective and that had to take its toll over the years. She witnessed what an expert killer she was when hand to hand combat was all that was left. Quiet time was necessary for the commander to rejoin the human race and reconnect with her gentle side.

"I'm going to check in with Engineering and Flight Control. See you later commander."

The commander nodded as she walked out.

"Alright! What is it? Your time of the month or something? The only way its gonna get warmer is if you start settin stuff on fire!"

The commander rose as the voice bellowed.

"Sergeant Barnes ......if you'd take that sorry excuse for a breast out of your mouth long enough to check your ships sensors you'd find a 5* degree temperature flux in the lower decks. Now... I'm not sure if one of our guests is trying to recreate their habitat the hard way or one of the coils is down but I expect you to be on top of it!"

She towered over him as she placed her hand solidly on his shoulder and squeezed firmly almost making him wince.

"Do I make myself clear?"

His tone changed instantly as she finished and released her fearsome grip.

"Yes...mame...ah.... Commander."

He removed the stogie as he saluted her and stormed out the door. She was willing to cut his some slack but not when it came to maintaining the ship. It was time to check and make sure that the cargo bay was moving along and to see the rest of her ship. As she stood up her communicator badge went off.

"Commander Avir.... there is a coded message for you in Communications. I can route it to the Command Deck if you prefer?"

The commander rubbed her weary eyes as if anticipating trouble.

"No.... Have it routed to my quarters? I'll pick it up there."

The voice pressed on.

"But Commander.....it's marked urgent!"

She headed towards the door.

"It's okay Tavel. I'll be there by the time you transfer its route."

She quickly took the freight transport used for droids because she knew it was faster. She simply had to remember to duck. As she entered her quarters the message light flashed. She sat down at her desk and pressed the appropriate buttons. The message was encoded twice as she shook her head in disgust.

"I love it! They say it's an urgent message yet they put a security code on it that takes you 15 friggin minutes to decode," she spoke out loud as if to vent her frustrations to the computer in front of her.

Finally, the message was decoded.

Commander Avir I do not think we need to express the
Importance of this mission. It is imperative that you
Dust off immediately once you have the relic in
your possession. The council is looking forward
to honoring you with a new ship and commission.
And one more thing Commander.....................
The Keevos have expressed their extreme displeasure
With our presence on this planet and have warned
That they will do whatever is necessary to rid their
Planet of this presence.
We will await your success Commander Avir.

She slammed the button that ended the message. Nothing like a little pressure to add to her already mounting list. She needed to snap out of this mood of complacency and start preparations for the expedition of the planet. The various alien settlers that had disembarked earlier would be protected by a temporary domed energy shield. She checked the computer. Team 1 had just begun their descent into one of the planets many caverns to the east. She walked through the ships corridors checking temperature coils and sensors. Most of the crew were given down time once the cargo was off the ship. They were working the equivalent of 7 straight shifts. If an emergency were to arise she would be working with a stressed tired crew prone to mistakes. In her 40 years of command she had learned that a restful crew was a happy crew and a happy crew usually made very few mistakes. She checked in with the Medical Deck to make sure all was under control. Once the crew retires to their quarters the sensors within the bed monitor their life functions. All the non-essential personnel were following Commander Avir's orders....... they were sleeping.

"Everything seems fine Commander."

The Medical Officer Sandy Kylo spoke as she walked over to the Commander. She had been Commander Avir's current Medical Officer for 5 Earth years and use to see her at the Space Station Alpha when she was in between missions.

"But you look like you could use some rest," she spoke as she gently touched the circles under the Commanders eyes. *"Jenna.... you've got to get some rest even if it's only a few solar hours. You know you're 1-day shy of my ordering you into a sleep chamber."*

Hyperbaric chambers were now combined with sleep chambers and were standard issue on deep space flights.

"Doctor! Please .... this is stressful enough without having medical pressure. Please don't make me argue about this."

She looked at the commander and remembered when she first met her and how she was in awe of her stature and general presence. It was rare to see someone so beautiful as a seasoned soldier who had survived several war campaigns. She watched her now with great interest and had caught herself feeling an attraction towards her. As with the years and past battles she had grown to respect the commander but wondered why she kept an invisible distance. Her regular crew of Navigation, Science, and Engineering and Communications officers had all signed on with a permanent classification under this commander. That translated to anywhere the commander went the crew also went. She kept them safe and a strong trust bond was formed.

"Doctor! Are you alright?" Jenna spoke softly as she gently touched her arm.

"Sandy!"

The calling of her name seemed to snap her out of her dream state.

"Yes...I'm here."

She watched as Commander Avir.... Jenna looked at the crew monitors.

"I'm sorry doctor but I'm going to need a security team shortly. So,

you're going to have to awaken Beta Team since Alpha Team just phased into sleep mode."

Sandy stood next to her and realized this was not the time to force a personal conversation.

"I've been informed by the Council that the Keevos aren't pleased at our presence and I've got an exploration crew out there right now."

Sandy punched several codes into the panel underneath the monitor in front of her.

"I'll take care of it. Where do you want them to report?"

"Airlock 7. I'll be in the Scan room and then Operations."

Sandy turned to use her communicator.

"Okay.... I'm on it."

The Scan room was a small security station on the main deck. It housed several computer systems, several monitors and control cameras that were placed outside the ship. Separate systems monitored the airlocks and engine rooms and could notify the Commander at a moment's notice.

"Alistair.... have our guests disembarked?"

The tall thin young man of 20 checked his screens as he spoke.

"Yes Commander. Only non-essential crews have been approved for down time."

"Fine ...issue a level 3 alert."

"Commander?"

Jenna turned to face the young technician.

"We may have a potential problem with these planets inhabitants and I'm checking on Team 1 as we speak."

Alistair stood up and went to a different monitor and entered a code. The helmet cams were static and fading in and out of Team 1's descent into the western cavern.

"I'm on my way to Operations. See if you can boost that signal. I know those sand storms aren't helping but try...okay?"

"Yes Commander."

Jenna was already getting a bad feeling about her team. She knew they couldn't sense what she was sensing. She knew where the relic was but knew she had to proceed with caution and perform this mission by the book. Her empathetic powers were what enabled her to keep her crew safe all these years and what permitted her to see the location of the relic in the Keevos mind shortly before she left the council on Theta 12. Jenna use to hate her gift until she learned not to fight it but to use it. Hostility and danger seemed to engage it and Jenna learned to use it in war time conditions. She entered Operations in time to hear a frantic call for help coming from one of the aliens whose cargo had been stolen. The Lieutenant informed him that he was not under the protection of the ship and therefore was subject to whatever happened on the surface of the planet. Normally this would not be so but since 175 of the ships 185 passengers were aliens who said they would pay anything to hitch a ride to planet Tulvos they were given only one condition: There would be no protection once they set foot on Tulvos soil.

"*Commander Avir on deck!*" *a* stout female officer announced.

Jenna turned to face the nervous officer.

"*At ease Flight Lieutenant Merritt.*"

Jenna walked to the center of the room.

"*Lieutenant Peters...recall Team 1 to the surface and send in Beta Team.*"

Her orders were followed quickly and to the letter. Two large monitors showed Team 1's confusion and disapproval among the static. But as they began to ascend the team leader's voice monitor picked up a frantic cry to move and "move now."

"*Boost that signal NOW!*"

The camera showed the edges of a huge cavern with some shadowed movement towards them. The helmet cameras bounced around as it showed the other team members frantically scurrying upward towards the opening.

"*Beta Team is standing by at the opening Commander.*"

Jenna smiled as she thought of Sandy and how she never argued about her requests for a fit crew.

"*Send Beta Team Now!*"

The command was given as Team 1 reached the surface. Beta Team attached lines to Team 1's pins and repelled downward in a blaze of power torches and laser fire. As Jenna watched the melee she knew her fears were about to become reality.

"*Commander! Whatever is down there is returning fire!*"

She watched as Team 1 ran for the safety of the transport. Jenna grabbed a headset from the young Lieutenant.

"Beta Team lay down a field of suppressing fire and return to the transport. Notify when clear. Do you copy?"

The laser fire continued in short bursts. Finally, a response.

"Copy that Commander."

She then turned and ordered a Level 1 alert. Sleep chambers were deactivated and all personnel were responding to a red alert.

"I need a scan of the atmosphere at the opening of the crater. Ready weapons and prepare to launch warning beacon. Notify the aliens on the surface of their safety. Tell them we cannot provide safety unless they are within the perimeter of the dome."

Shortly after Jenna's ship landed a protective shielded dome was constructed to protect the alien settlers. The dome was only as good as the field generator that powered it so it was kept running round the clock and in an emergency could be reinforced with the ships shields. Anything outside the perimeter would not be protected.

"Commander......the magnetic storms are returning."

"Where is the transport?"

"All teams are reporting in Commander. Beta Team reporting. They are at the airlock now."

Jenna stood up and returned the headset to the lieutenant.

"Have the doctor meet....."

"She's already at the airlock commander."

"Very well.....engage shields and send in the robot and have that crater gassed."

"As you wish commander."

Jenna walked quickly to the lift that would take her down to the airlock from the surface. As she arrived the doctor was scanning bruises and cuts on Onyx Patterson, one of the soldiers.

"Beta Team?"

"Over here commander."

A roughly scarred man in his 40's raised his hand as he maneuvered his gear off of his shoulders.

"Onyx Patterson? I thought you were in sleep chamber 1ˢᵗ rotation?"

The rest of his armor scraped as he moved.

"Yes, *mame but the doc here thought you needed more seasoned personnel for this one.*"

She looked around at Team 1's frightened faces. Seem she was right.

"*So, what the hell is in that crater?*"

He handed her a disk.

"*We don't know. Never got a clear glimpse or shot at it. Our sensors showed we weren't hitting them yet we aimed right for the movement. Maybe the Science Officer can make something of it.*"

She fingered the disk. She contacted Operations as she turned towards the lift.

"*Everything's quiet commander. It's as if nothing happened.*" "*Keep me informed of any changes. I'll be in the lab.*"

"*What do you make of it?*" Jenna spoke softly as she watched the image from the disk that Onyx gave her.

"*I'll have to clean it up some but it's gonna take me some time.*"

She looked disappointed but understood. Sam Skylar, short for Samantha Skylar, was a small bookworm who loved her computers as well as her old musty books. Each one of her computers had a name and a distinct personality according to her. To most she was just another geek but to Jenna she was a valued member of her team. She could make computers do things that the planetary technicians could only dream of. She was surprised when she first signed on with Jenna 4 years ago. She was quiet, shy and definitely not what she would consider space material. But she endeared herself to Jenna and the crew when she hacked into the government main payroll computer and freed the crew's payroll which was being held up by the usual red tape. She knew if there was an image on that disk Sam would find it. In the meantime, Jenna needed to clear her head and think. She checked in with the doctor once again to make sure there were no serious injuries and then headed towards the viewing area on the Observation Deck. Each member had to file a report on what happened and turn it in within 1 hour of returning to the ship so she had time, providing the planet was stable, the force generator was operational and no crisis erupted. No one was on the Observation Deck which wasn't surprising. You were either manning a station, heading for a sleep chamber or on security watch. She wanted off this mission. She was tired of fighting aliens and tired of fighting with Central Command.

In her 40 years of duty she had seen very little change with respect to the military. Their general philosophy seemed to be grab it, kill it and ask questions about how it was living later. Everything seemed to be a fight: a fight to keep the aliens in a contained area, a fight to keep the government from establishing planetary outposts on peaceful planets, a fight simply to remain in a research capacity with her crew. She even fought to get her crew some sleep time. She knew in her heart she would have to retrieve the relic herself. No other way seemed possible without a major conflict. She believed the relic should remain with its original owners. The problem was ….no one knew who that was. The DNA scans were fairly reliable but had so far yielded no true owners. She looked at the moons of Tulvos as if for some clarity but found none. She sighed and headed for her quarters. Once there she sat in front of her computer.

"*Bio code entered. Awaiting retinal scan.*"

Jenna sat quietly as the computer went through its routine.

"*Commander Genevieve Alexandra Avir entering the Twelfth protocol. Please proceed commander.*"

Jenna knew this was the only way to end this situation. She would go and retrieve the relic from the planet's surface. She also knew she would have to plan for the event of her not returning. She had not remained alive for so long without thinking of all the possibilities including death. So, she was executing the 12th protocol that would, in the event of her death, take over and route the ship form the planet safely back to the nearest space station. Her bio-code was linked to the ships main computer and would monitor her vital signs from now on. Due to the magnetic storms on the planet she gave the system a 72-hour safety check. If the computer lost her bio sign it would not start lift off procedures until 72 hours from the last signal. She also put other matters in order. Her crew had been loyal to her for 35 Earth years and she knew without them she would have died a long time ago. Each commander was paid in accordance with their mission and Jenna had acquired wealth beyond most. Since she had no family to speak of she ordered her monies to be equally distributed among her crew. The longer they served the more they would be entitled to after her death. Finally, the disk was sealed within the computer. She looked around and decided to get some rest. She called Operations and checked in. Everything was quiet or stable. Med Lab reported no serious injuries and the last report of the cavern incident was coming in.

"Would you like me to send up the report commander?"

Jenna yawned as she answered.

"No doctor. I'll look at them later.......thanks."

And with that, she lay down, set the timer on her wrist unit, checked the bio code and went to sleep. But her sleep was not to be a peaceful one. Her dreams appeared as a series of snapshots, vivid in their color and disturbing in their subject. Bodies of dead and dying aliens lay before her on the surface of the planet. A Keevos warrior proudly displayed the relic above the hilltop near the entrance to the caverns. The next snapshot was of Sandy, Dr. Kylo and her in a gentle embrace on the surface of the planet. Jenna smiled at her and turned to see her crew running from the cavern. She turned back to face Sandy and saw her face horribly scarred. Sweat poured down her face as she tossed and turned. The next and most clear snap shot was that of a woman sitting cross legged on the floor of the cargo bay. As Jenna moved closer and peered over the woman's shoulder she saw a crystal amulet and next to it lay the sought-after relic. As Jenna now stood in front of the woman she could now see her flight suit and the name boldly imprinted above the left breast: Commander Avir. The woman then looked up and starred at Jenna. It was as if she were looking at a mirror image of herself. Tears were streaming down the woman's face as she held out her hands with palms facing upward. Blood dripped from them as she whispered one word: Why? Jenna awoke with a gasping sound as she rolled out of bed in a sweat. She checked her screens but everything seemed fine. Most of the time one doesn't remember every dream but Jenna did. Jenna poured some ice water from a thermos she had prepared earlier. She drank the water as though it were a stiff drink. She drew in a deep breath and looked at the time. She had managed to get in a whole 3 hours of disturbing sleep. She thought about taking a dry shower but realized she'd only be hot and sweaty in a few hours when she went to check the hull of the ship as was the routine. She zipped up her flight suit, adjusted her wrist unit, grabbed her weapon and walked out into the corridor of the ship. Flight Lieutenant Merritt met Jenna as she rounded the corner.

"Commander! I thought you were......"

Jenna raised her hand to silence the young lieutenants concern.

"I was but I seem to have some difficulty sleeping. I'm going to the Observation Deck. Maybe I can relax up there."

The Lieutenant saluted and continued down the corridor. She would use the safety ladder as a form of exercise during her normal routine since the lifts were crowded so it made sense to use it now. She entered her code to the Observation Deck. The doors opened onto an expanse of ornately carved wood and large oversized chairs that gave the occupant the feeling of sinking into a large feather pillow. Not at all what one would expect on a space ship. The large floor to ceiling viewing windows opened onto the twin moons of Tulvos and the surrounding stars. The body chairs could secure an occupant should the need arise and the windows could be shut upon a red alert. But all in all, it was a room of warmth that the crew found soothing. As Jenna looked out upon the moons she wondered if anyone took the time to be in awe of the things most took for granted. She wondered how many people and aliens looked upon these two moons as one looks upon a hallway or door. It's there, we use it, but we never really look at it. One more mission and one more planet was how most viewed their existence here. Jenna had been with the majority of her crew long enough to know that this thought process was beginning to take over. Yes, they would do their job to the best of their ability and follow orders to the letter but their thoughts and feelings were as clear as the acrylic window she was gazing through. They needed to go home and reconnect with their families. Even those that were enlisted that had no families needed time to be, as Dr. Kylo put it, human again. Would turning over the relic really do all that?

"Such deep thoughts for one so young."

Jenna turned to see a hooded figure standing in the corner shadow. Jenna faced the figure yet said nothing. As the figure reached up Jenna moved her right hand to rest upon her weapon. Sensing the commander's alertness, the figure moved slowly as it removed her hood. Jenna held her breath as she tensed. She breathed a sigh of relief as she recognized the figure before her. The PaQua were an ancient nomadic people who were known to travel great distances in search of religious artifacts for study. Their original genetic makeup gave them large opaline eyes to take in reflected light in space, ears with a super fine membrane for acute hearing and special vocal cords that were capable of most forms of alien vocalization. Some cross breeding had narrowed the eyes to where they resembled the Asians of Earth centuries ago. But this PaQua was from the original order.

"Your breathing is labored and you are grinding your teeth. Surely your thoughts are not that serious commander?"

Her voice was deep yet soft in its inflection. Jenna moved closer to the shadows as if to verify the figure.

"Forgive me but you seem to have the advantage. You know who I am yet I have not yet had the pleasure."

The figure moved out from the shadows and into the light cast by the Tulvos moons. The PaQua bowed slightly in respect as she spoke.

"I am Adrianna of the 3ʳᵈ Order of PaQua. I have come with a message that I fear you are not yet ready to hear."

Jenna closed her eyes as she thought to herself: Here we go again. Another warning, prophecy, vision or biblical passage telling her what to do with the relic. Adrianna walked towards the window as she looked out at the planet. Jenna walked over and sat down in one of the chairs facing the woman.

"Okay...what's you're pitch?"

The woman turned and faced Jenna but didn't speak. Jenna was tired both mentally and physically. She reached up and rubbed the back of her neck to try and alleviate some of the pain that was now slowly creeping its way up her back. The woman removed her cape which seemed to account for most of the woman's mystical the woman removed her cape which seemed to account for most of the woman's mystical persona. Once her cape was shed she resembled any number of her female brunette crew members, except for those eyes. They were extremely expressive and passionate in their vision. She kneeled down in front of Jenna.

"Permit me Commander Avir to be a bit forward in my actions."

As she said this she raised her slender fingers and placed them gently on Jenna's temples. A warm heat seemed to radiate from the tips of her fingers. It felt pleasurable and relaxing as a circular movement was felt. The heat seemed to travel down her jaw to the back of her neck and down to the nap of her neck.

176

"Relax commander please do not be afraid."

As the PaQua spoke her voice was almost hypnotic in its whisper soft cadence.

"As I said...I am of the 3rd Order of the PaQua and have reached the 7th level of meditation. I am only here as an observer. I am not here to sit in judgment of your actions. Your decision affects many but ultimately it is you who will have to live with that decision. Let your heart and mind work as one commander."

Jenna felt herself slipping into a warm, comfortable, relaxed state. She bolted upright as her breathing was heavy and her mind spinning. Jenna didn't trust what was happening. The familiar sound of her com badge welcomed her back to reality.

"Commander I......are you alright?"

Sandy's concern was evident.

"I thought you were going to your sleep chamber?"

Jenna felt like she was just caught with her hand in a cookie jar.

"No...I mean ...yes. I'm fine doc."

"I can come up there and..."

"No! That's fine .... I mean its fine. Everything's okay. I'm heading back to my quarters."

"Very well commander but if you need anything..."

"Yes...I know where to find it. Thank you, Sandy."

Jenna turned to face the PaQua.

"I'm sorry...I...need to get some sleep. Perhaps we can continue this at a later date."

The PaQua turned and faced the window.

"Then I bid you goodnight Commander Genevieve Alexandra Avir."

And with that said Jenna walked back down the corridors to her quarters leaving the PaQua to gaze at the moons. Jenna was slightly surprised that the woman knew her full name. It was on her medical records but not on the ships records or manifest. Most of the drew knew her as Jenna Avir Commander of the 94th squadron. Jenna was tired and running on overload. She was acutely aware of her condition. She entered her quarters and immediately poured herself a glass of Artesian aromatic tea and readied herself for a date with her sleep chamber. As she changed clothes she couldn't help but wonder how the PaQua knew her information. Jenna had to admit that she was intrigued by her presence on the loading bay before the ships departure on Talos 7. An attractively curved woman rarely went unnoticed by many of her crew. But this woman's presence was extremely noticeable. Perhaps it was her bluish hue or to the more discerning observer it was the scent of fragrant pacific flowers that seemed to be present whenever she was close. Jenna drank the last drop of tea and wearily crawled into her sleep chamber. She notified Dr. Sandy Kylo and dozed off.

CHAPTER 1

"What makes you think this will work?"

Lieutenant Merritt's voice grew to a whisper as other crew members filed into the room that was known as the Conference hall. Flight Control Lieutenant Alanna Peters crouched in between Dr. Kylo and Lieutenant Merritt.

"She needs to know! You've seen her since we started this mission."

Suddenly the din of the room silenced. Everyone stood at attention as the commander walked in.

"Commander on deck!" Kyle announced.

Jenna saluted and then stood in front of the large window as she took a deep breath.

"Permission to speak commander?"

Jenna turned to see Lieutenant Kyle Merritt standing. Jenna looked at Dr. Kylo who gave her a look of puzzlement.

"Permission granted Flight Lieutenant."

"Commander......the majority of us have been with you through 4 campaigns, 2 universal wars and countless adventures in deep space. We've been with you and fought beside you never questioning your orders. We've trusted you with our lives and have never been willing to serve with anyone else. You've always kept us safe and ......Well......your crew thought it was about time we let you know."

Jenna looked into the faces of her crew and for the first time saw a connection she never before had realized.

"We have all sensed the pressure you have been under with this mission. We have doubled the sentries around the domed perimeter,

increased the frequency of the shield and have, with Sergeant Barnes help, made some necessary repairs and services to the weapons array."

Sergeant Barnes grumbled in acknowledgement as he held his short, wet, slightly tinged cigar between his two stubby fingers. The Lieutenant handed Jenna two small disks of the crew's activities. The Lieutenant sat down as he took a quick glance from side to side. Jenna smiled as she looked at the faces of her crew again. It was as if she finally noticed how truly old they had become. She never seemed to realize how young they were when they signed on with her.

"I appreciate those words Lieutenant. We have .... I have been so consumed with mission after mission that I forgot how long we have known one another. You have been my family and as such I will do whatever is in my power to do to keep you alive. This mission is taking turns that I myself am not comfortable with. So many times, the battles have been cut and dry. Right versus wrong, good versus evil. But this mission is different. The relic belongs to no one or so it seems."

Jenna moved to the observation window and looked at the two moons as she spoke.

"This relic is supposed to represent peace yet all it will cause is war. I know that I grow weary of the battles as do most of you. Some of you even see your family in the eyes of those refugees we just left on Tulvos."

Suddenly Jenna gripped the ledge of the window bulkhead. Her senses were picking up danger.

"Lieutenant! Check the protection field of the dome."

"Something's wrong."

Jenna whispered under her breath.

"Commander?"

Dr. Kylo moved in behind her.

"Are you okay?"

Jenna shook her head no. She could sense something wasn't quite right but she couldn't pin point what it was. The crackle of the communicator broke the silence.

"Commander! Sam has something here you might want to see."

Jenna keyed in her eyes to the monitor.

"I'm on my way Skylar."

Jenna turned to face her crew.

180

"This meeting is postponed until 0:900."

She hurried down the corridor. She still could not shake the uneasiness she felt. Her senses were never wrong. She entered the code and walked through the archway to Sam Skylar's' monitor. Sam was pushing buttons in an attempt to line up an image as Onyx Patterson stood over his left shoulder.

"I've cleaned it up some but the computer couldn't determine a match based on the visual resonance signals. So, I linked the databanks to Earth Dome under mythology and we got this image."

There in front of Jenna was a three-headed creature that looked like something out of old earth magazines kids called Comic books. Based on the height of the walls in the cavern the creature was about 6'5" with a leathered armor tunic and pants. The weapons were not visible due to the electrical energy flares that burned into the images.

"That's it! That's what I saw."

Jenna suddenly stopped the image and replayed it.

"Can you enlarge that section right there?"

She pointed to a small section that was a reflection in Onyx helmet visor. As the image was cleared and enlarged they saw the image of the Keevos clearly behind the creature. If it was uncertain who the enemy was in the beginning the fuzzy image on the screen was beginning to make it very clear. Just as the ID was made the red alert sounded. Crew ran though the corridors to their stations as Jenna made her way to the Command Deck.

"Okay.... what's going on?"

Flight Lieutenant Merritt responded.

"It seems the Keevos have fired on the dome Commander. The energy field is holding but we're not sure for how long."

The Communications officer broke in.

"Commander.... the refugees are demanding to be brought back on board."

Jenna rubbed her face and eyes as she sighed.

"Shall we deploy soldier's commander?"

She watched the monitors as she answered.

"No! No act of aggression or retaliation must be shown from us yet."

Jenna moved to the sensor array.

"Let's see how many Keevos are really out there. Scramble fighters 2 and 5. Have the pilots do a flyby only."

"Commander! Someone is overriding the cargo bay doors."

Jenna looked at the screen but could see only the ships lined up next to the cargo bay.

"Change the code and notify security."

"The Code is not being recognized Commander."

"Keep trying!"

As Jenna said that she was out the door heading for the cargo bay. As she neared the corridor to the cargo bay she saw the results of weapons fire on the walls and bulkhead. As she turned the corner the body of a young soldier lay face down in a pool of blood. She felt for a pulse...... there was none. Jenna cautiously withdrew her weapon from its holster and motioned for the two soldiers that had followed her to remain where they were. She checked to see where the intruder was but could see no one. She glanced at the stairwell that led to the upper level of the cargo bay. She stealthily moved towards the stairs and proceeded to climb up to get a better vantage point. She then jumped across the beam connected to the bulkhead to the ledge below the launch window that connected the flight bay with the cargo bay. She could see the ladder lowered from one of the silver tactical fighters in front of her. She moved in closer to see who this intruder was. As she focused on the movement at the end of the ladder the hairs on the back of her neck stood on end. She slowly turned to see the PaQua being held hostage by one of the aliens she remembered seeing in the cargo bay during the beginning of their trip. The alien was from the Morrow District; an area of space that was off limits to all ships and freighters due to its lack of reflective light and intense magnetic field. It was a black hole to all who ventured near. As a result, the aliens had large almost bug like eyes and very pale skin. Their ears were unusually large in addition to their head. Due to their 7' tall frame most Earthers referred to them as Yeti's named after the famous Big-Foot of Earth legend. But no official name existed on the planetary registry. Some were known to be for hire but Jenna had never encountered them in battle.

"What do you want?"

Jenna moved slightly forward.

"Throw your weapon down Commander or the nomad will join the spirits of this galaxy!"

After looking around and seeing no other option Jenna lowered her weapon and threw it slightly past the alien.

"Very good commander.... now move!"

The alien motioned for Jenna to climb the ladder of the tactical fighter. As she hesitated the alien held the PaQua tighter causing her pain. Jenna climbed the ladder. Other soldiers started to fill the flight bay as Jenna sat down to the controls. The tactical fighters allowed space for a pilot, navigator and weapons operator. They were small yet very maneuverable in fight situations plus they had the ability to hover. The PaQua climbed the ladder with the alien close behind. Due to the formation of the fighters interior Jenna could not see the alien or the PaQua once she sat down.

"Go ahead commander. You should know how to pilot this ship."

Jenna placed a helmet on and started the fighter's instrument systems and pressed the appropriate code to start the engines. The roar and vibration could be felt throughout the ship. The cushioned and reinforced seats gave little protection from the engine vibration.

"You should know where to go by now commander."

Jenna sighed.

"I'm not a mind reader so why don't you give me a hint."

She heard a slight shuffle and then a weapon firing. She stood up and turned around just in time to see the helmeted PaQua fall forward in her seat. Jenna moved towards her but the alien motioned for her to sit back down.

"She's just stunned and unless you wish to receive the same fate you will head towards the south side of planet Tulvos."

Jenna sat back down and gave the signal to clear the flight deck. Yellow warning lights flashed as the flight bay doors opened. Once the area was depressurized red lights flashed and Jenna hit the launch button. The fighter emerged from the ship like a shooting star, too fast for the human eye to track but slow enough for the ships computer to log on.

"Why don't you tell me what you hope to achieve with this little stunt?"

"Here are your coordinates. That is all you need to know."

She keyed in the numbers which would place the ship on the other side of the planet. The ship vibrated and shook as it entered Tulvos atmosphere. The landscape was made up of huge stone monoliths and cascading waterfalls. What shades of color that could be seen were far out on the horizon? The ship sped across the surface and through the ships window Jenna could see a large outcropping of rocks. As the ship neared this formation Jenna could see that the rocks formed a pyramid like structure. The solar winds and magnetic storms had begun their assault on the planet's surface. The ship lurched to the left and then to the rights as Jenna tried to keep it steady.

"Land it.... now Commander!"

The alien shouted but Jenna could hear only the howling wind as the ship slid onto the rocks. It sat at an angle as the alien motioned for Jenna to pick up the stunned nomad. Jenna lifted her up and placed an arm around her to support her tall frame. The PaQua came to and looked around.

"You can remove your helmets commander."

Tulvos contained a rich Ozone atmosphere and on clear days would smell like fresh rain. Each helmet had a locator beacon attached to the underside. As Jenna removed her helmet she pressed the locator hoping that the storms now building would not interfere with the signal. The alien placed a small re-breather on as they made their way down the ladder. The Keevos were the only inhabitants registered on Tulvos. Jenna wondered how this alien got here. The atmosphere was obviously affecting it as it frantically adjusted the re-breather. The dense underground caves had flowing icy water left over from when the surface underwent its ice age. This also meant that the caves were rich in Oxygen and Ozone. Between the wind and the fine sand, it was stirring Jenna could barely see the terrain in front of her. The PaQua stumbled as she held on to Jenna. Suddenly, Jenna and the PaQua were bathed in a pale orange light from above. Jenna tightened her grip around the woman as she felt herself being pulled upward.

"What is happening?"

It was the first time she had heard the woman's voice tremble.

"I don't know. It seems our friend here has a ship of his own."

Jenna looked up to see the underside of a small freighter. Scored and pitted with weapons fire. Jenna didn't recognize the markings. Since it was docked on the far side of the planet she wondered if her ships main sensors even knew it was here. By now her crew would have scanners out searching the planet and keying in on the beacon. Once up on the ship Jenna could make out faint markings carved into the walls of the ship. The light, although dim, seemed to come from the floor of the ship. It seemed they were in a central hub of the ship with corridors that radiated outward to the other parts of the ship. Controls, if they could be called that, were illuminated within one small section as were made up of various rocker type switches. Commands seemed to come out of now where as the language resembled an ancient Farcie dialect. Out of the shadows came armed soldiers. Their gear was a hodgepodge of dented and scored armor, sensor plates and old transmitter disks. It was as if the scavenged dead soldier's armor since there seemed to be dried blood on some of them. They motioned the two women towards the mid-deck. These aliens were not ones she was familiar with. Their 'skin' had a brownish hue to it and looked like it was in layers about their bodies. When they moved quickly it seemed to flake off around them. Their faces were pot marked and resembled a bad case of acne. No sex could be determined from their features and their armor hid any other clues one might see. One of the aliens barked out what seemed to be orders as the rag tag crew responded. Both captives were bound around their hand and sensor collars were placed around their necks. These collars were only used in penal colonies and Jenna reasoned that since the armor was scavenged so were the collars. This was not a good sign since it use to take very little to set the old collars off. They were modified over the years and eventually all prisoners had implants within their skulls. Jenna felt the PaQua tap her gently. As she faced her she motioned to the grid screen in front of her. They're to the left of the screen was Tulvos two moons. The ship seemed to be heading towards the one to the right of the screen. The ship lurched and weaved as it made its descent. Between the gravitational pull and the storms, the ship felt as though it were flying through a hail storm. The ship careened to the lefts and then back towards the right. Jenna fell on top of the PaQua as she tried to stay upright.

"Look…. if you don't take these ancient artifacts off from around our necks your piloting skills are going to have us putting a sizable hole in your ship."

The alien powered up the ship using the joystick like device that was in the middle of the rocker switches and leveled off in the upper atmosphere of Tulvos far moon. The alien reached for Jenna's neck and released the control collar. Jenna rubbed the area where the collar once rested. She turned to face the PaQua but the alien grabbed Jenna and moved her towards one of the corridors.

"The PaQua stays on. If you resist…the PaQua will be terminated."

Jenna turned to face him.

"Don't you understand? You may not have as much control over these outdated collars as you think you have. Due to their age they are extremely unstable and ……"

Jenna never got to finish her sentence as the alien slammed his hand against the side of her face causing her to see stars. She felt herself being dragged towards a circular hole in the floor.

"Come!"

'Come' Jenna thought. 'Come' where? There is no other transport visible. Just as Jenna finished her sentence a bright light bathed the ship and Jenna felt as though she were falling. She closed her eyes and when she opened them her the vision before her was one of beautifully lit caverns and thunderous waterfalls. She was shoved from the rear.

"Move!"

As she looked up she realized that the light was coming from the natural phosphorus and algae from the rocks above. They seemed to line the pathway they were walking past. Suddenly the rocks gave way to a great hall. The intricate designs seemed to be carved into the rock itself with large alien statuary on either side. The rock paintings and carvings were like those of the ancient Navajo cliff dwellers she read about on Earth. In the center of the hall were 4 statuesque chairs carved into a central monolith. Several Tulvos walked towards the chairs and sat down. They seemed almost dwarfed by the size of the stone chairs.

"Release them!" came a command from somewhere behind Jenna.

Instantly the collar was released from the PaQua. Jenna breathed a sigh of relief.

"*Commander Avir...please step forward.*"

The voice seemed to come from every direction that Jenna turned. As she looked up at the ceiling she could see why the sound was omni directional. The ceiling was round like that of a dome yet the panels were transparent. She could see the stars shining through as she stepped forward.

"*Commander Genevieve Alexander Avir you have been brought before this tribunal to answer for placement of the ancient Tulvakian relic.*"

Jenna knew that some translations might have a different meaning for relic but for most it seemed to be anything from very old to being religious. Clarity was something she needed at the moment.

"*I'm not sure I understand your reference to the relic. You talk of the placement yet I have not received such an item.*"

The figures before her looked at one another and then back towards Jenna.

"*Commander! Please do not insult us so. We know you possess the Tulvakian relic so why continue this deception?*"

Jenna attempted to move closer but the guards at either side moved their weapons forward as she moved.

"*I am speaking the truth. I do not have the relic you speak of. If you wish you may have my permission to scan me. This will show you proof.... proof that I do not have it and proof that I am not lying.*"

Jenna stepped forward again this time with no escort. She knelt down and held her hands in a crossed fashion in front of her chest in the customary surrendering posture. Suddenly the PaQua moved towards Jenna but she motioned for the woman to remain where she was.

"*It's alright.... they will not hurt me.*"

As the words left her lips a bright yellow light moved from the center of the dome to above Jenna. She remained perfectly still as the scan continued. Jenna felt a slight tingling sensation as the beam intensified. Just as it turned painful the beam stopped. She looked up as the figures moved closer. She now could see that two of the figures were female and the other two were male. All were dresses in Tulvos uniforms with robes denoting their position or rank.

"Please *rise Commander Avir.*"

Jenna noticed the change in their tone and stood up to face them.

"We the Council of Tulvos regret the treatment of you and the PaQua. The Keevos have reported certain events to us that seem to be false."

Jenna noticed that the woman spoke slowly as if translating or thinking of what she was saying.

"During your scan it was noted that these events were not initiated by you but by the Keevos. We have remained at peace with these inhabitants for ...100 of your Earth years. Your actions on this planet were not investigated as fully as they should have been. The Tulvakian relic was created from this planet and therefore must not be removed from this planet."

The woman stepped back and motioned for the guards to escort Jenna out. So many deceptions and so many lies it almost seemed the order of the day. Jenna was growing weary of the misinformation she was given. Who were these Tulvakian people? Obviously, they resided on the planet too yet why was Jenna and her crew only told of the Keevos? And who was the Morrovian alien and what was its connection to the Tulvos council? As Jenna walked past the PaQua the guards restrained the woman. They were allowing Jenna to pass but not her friend.

"I will not leave without the PaQua!"

The guards instinctively raised their weapons.

"The PaQua remains!"

Jenna stayed motionless as she spoke.

"I came with the PaQua against our will. I do not intend on leaving without her. We have shown you patience and understanding and in return you have shown us deception and hostility. Is this what your Tulvakian council represents?"

The guards seemed to be commanded telepathically since they motioned for the PaQua to step forward. Upon doing so Jenna noticed the group of soldiers' step back leaving the second soldier to step forward facing the PaQua. Jenna could see that they were communicating on a different level by the way their eyes met. She waited quietly by the PaQua's side. Jenna's com link beeped indicating that a search party was nearing her location. The PaQua turned to face Jenna.

"It is alright commander."

Jenna clenched her fists and was read to fight.

"Adriana! I...."

She turned and placed her hand gently on Jenna's arm.

"Genevieve.... I will be alright. They wish to talk of other things. Things that do not concern the relic. I am in no danger. It is.... okay."

Jenna reluctantly turned and walked down the pathway made by the Tulvos guards. She walked back towards the fighter. She looked up to see the transport overhead. She placed her helmet on and let her crew know that she was fine. A familiar voice sounded as she looked out the window down at the planet surface.

"Commander...please state your security code."

Jenna smiled briefly, silently congratulating her crew on their training.

"Alpha 7143"

"Thank you, commander. Glad you're back. The flight bay is awaiting your arrival."

Jenna was glad to get back on board her ship even with the current crisis. It was the only home she knew since her enlistment some 60 years ago. With the advent of stasis pods the average human now ages 1 year for every 5. But even with this Jenna was still feeling old. Dr. Kylo and Lieutenant Peters were the first to greet her as she stepped from the fighter's ladder.

"Commander .....are you alright? What happened down there?"

Jenna raised her hand as if to protect herself from the array of questions. She was tiered of questions and desperately wanted some answers. Dr. Kylo's voice was firm yet understanding and diplomatic.

"I believe protocol demands that you be examined Commander before you can return to your duties."

Jenna didn't argue for she knew that the medical bay would provide some temporary solitude. The security alert indicators flashed on every deck as Jenna passed crews racing to their designated positions.

"Lieutenant...I want a meeting with Operations crew at....."

She looked back at Sandy and determined that the doc was serious about her examination.

"Say at 12:00."

A nurse met both women as they rounded the corner of the med bay.

"Dr. Kylo? We were...."

Sandy looked over at the empty medical bays.

"*It's alright nurse. I'm simply going to check out the commander as regulations dictate after her abduction. I'll be back on line for the equipment check in an hour.*"

As the nurse walked out Sandy turned to Jenna.

"*You and these damned drills. Your crew follows them so religiously that I can't even get any work accomplished.*"

As the medical bay doors closed the din of the ship was temporarily silenced.

"*Right! Privacy mode engaged.*"

Dark tinted shields lowered around the room.

"*Okay Jenna...you know the routine.*"

She sat up on the table as monitoring cuffs were placed on her wrist.

"*Commander Genevieve Alexandra Avir reporting for medical check Stage 2*"

As Jenna recited the standard protocol dialog Sandy switched buttons and monitors and placed entries on several charts. She then picked up her stethoscope and walked over to Jenna.

"*With all this high-tech equipment and scans yet you still insist on using that archaic device. I'll never understand you doc.*"

She chuckled as she slowly unzipped Jenna's flight suit to expose smooth round breasts. As Sandy touched Jenna's flesh with her stethoscope she could see Jenna's tanned nipples harden. Jenna looked away as if embarrassed. Sandy thought Jenna always maintained an air of coldness and distance. Her examination was revealing otherwise. After 10 minutes of probing, prodding and pressing Sandy switched on the recorder.

"*This is Doctor Sandra Kylo reference Med Check Stage 2. Commander Genevieve Alexandra Avis is clear for reactivation of duties as Commanding officer of the Argos Embassy 1.*"

She reached up and flicked off the recorder.

"*Alright Jenna.... what happened? And where is the PaQua?*"

Jenna leaned back against the clear headboard and sighed. Sandy noticed the dark circles around Jenna eyes but said nothing.

"*I'm not quite sure Sandy.*"

Jenna closed her eyes as she spoke.

"*Evidentially there are two inhabitants on this planet, the Keevos and the Tulvakians. The Keevos lied to the Tulvakian Council and said I had possession of the relic.*"

Sandy pulled a chair over and sat next to Jenna.

"*Tulvakian Council?*"

Jenna rubbed the back of her neck.

"*Yes...something our records failed to indicate. Makes you wonder what else is lacking from our information. Their technology seems comparable to ours at least with regards to our scanning techniques.*"

"*They scanned you?*"

Jenna hopped off the table and poured herself a glass of water.

"*Yes, I was scanned but by the Tulvakians.*"

Jenna rubbed her weary eyes.

"*The Keevos armor and weapons are made up of Black Market and scavenged items.*"

Jenna swallowed the water as if it were a stimulant.

"*Since we don't know much about these people we have no way of knowing what kind of further hostility I or my crew will face.*"

"*What did they want with Adrianna?*"

Jenna sat back down on the table.

"*I don't think the Tulvakians will harm her. She seemed to be communicating with them on a different level which didn't seem to involve the relic.*"

Jenna closed her eyes and sighed. As Sandy moved towards her Jenna's eyes opened.

"*They said the relic was created from this planet and that there were others.*"

Sandy waited for Jenna to finish but couldn't wait.

"*Others? You mean other relics?*"

"*I don't know. That's what I need to find out. Whether they are all part of one or individual pieces. One way or the other my path seems clear.....I must retrieve the relic.*"

Sandy admired the woman in front of her. It was hard enough making decisions that involved life or death. She knew Jenna's decision would affect nations and planets. Wars were certainly started over less. She wanted to somehow soothe Jenna's troubled thoughts. All she could do was reach out her hand in friendship for Jenna always kept her distance. Jenna stood up, adjusted her uniform and turned towards Sandy.

"I need you to do some tests on the inhabitants of this planet."

Sandy sat back down.

"That's fine ....I would be happy to but unless I missed something within the last hour we are fresh out of Keevos. And since I've just found out about the Tulvakians that will be equally as challenging."

Jenna smiled at Sandy.

"Doc....if it were easy you wouldn't be doing it."

Sandy turned and rubbed her forehead.

"Look....if there were blood residue from Alpha teams skirmish I'd say maybe......but all the soldiers are scanned and cleaned before entering or returning to the ship. So...unless you have a Keevos body stashed somewhere that you aren't telling me about......."

Jenna raised the privacy mode level with a flick of a switch.

"I'm going for the relic. If I'm lucky you'll have a sample shortly."

Sandy stood up.

"I can have a team ready in...."

Jenna raised her hand to silence her.

"Sorry doc but this is something safer done on my own. I'll call if I need help."

And with that said Jenna walked out of Med Lab and back into the busy corridors of the ship. Sandy alerted Lieutenant Peters as to Jenna's plan but before she could notify Jenna, Engineer McMann was alerting Flight Lieutenant Kyle Merritt of Jenna's imminent departure. Jenna needed to get her affairs in order before she left the ship. Her crew had given her loyal and devoted service for some 35 years. She was not about to forget them so upon her death, her account would be divided amongst key personnel. Next was the safety of the ship. She keyed in her Bio-code and entered the code for activation. If for any reason her Bio-code signal was lost for a duration of 4 hours the ship would initiate dust-off within 72 hours of the lost signal. She felt no note was necessary since instructions for her will were already on disk. It was mandatory for all military and deep space service personnel. She changed into her flight suit and headed for the flight deck.

Lt. Peters stormed in front of the monitors.

"What do you mean she took a tactical fighter? Why didn't you stop her?"

Alanna was visibly irritated.

"With all due respect Lt. Peters what exactly would you have me do? Say excuse me Commander but you can't take one of your own ships! I'm not programmed to disobey a Commander."

Onyx Patterson was behind the Flight Lieutenant directing a group of soldiers when suddenly the Communications Officer interrupted.

"Communication from the commander on Frequency Delta."

Alanna turned to respond.

"Patch it through on a secure channel."

The room turned quiet as they all listened for the familiar voice.

"Didn't wish any discussion on this matter. I'm heading for the relic. Have all troops placed on standby. I've contacted the Keevos and Tulvakians for a meeting. Hopefully I can get them to come aboard the ship. If they agree please have our guests remanded to Doctor Kylo. I'll send my coordinates as soon as I have located the relic."

A Red Alert sounded throughout the ship. All crews were at their posts. Static was now heard on all channels.

"Doctor.... there is an emergency signal for you coming in on a low frequency. I can try to boost it."

Sandy walked up the console and reached for the ear piece. Once placing it securely within her ear she could hear the voice of Adrianna the PaQua.

"Yes... this is Dr. Sandra Kylo."

"The Tulvakian representative has agreed to meet on board your ship within 1 solar hour. The Keevos, however will not be attending due to certain private negotiations with Commander Avir."

Sandy reached over and checked the signal.

"Affirmative. Will you be joining our guests?"

There was a long static pause.

"No......I will be assisting the commander."

With that the power to the refugee dome powered down. Screams could be heard through the sensors.

"Get that shield back up!"

The crew frantically tried their controls but nothing seemed to work.

"There is a power drain detected at surface level."

"Pinpoint its location and restore it immediately."

Alanna looked around as the monitors flashed images of different locations within the dome. She watched the images as the readings still read '0'.

"It's starting," Sandy muttered under her breath.

"Talk to me people."

The Engineer read out storage levels of energy cells. The Flight Lieutenant launched 2 pilots in recon ships to monitor the domes inhabitants while the doctor placed a message through the translator beacon to the refugees on the planet's surface. Just as she was about to issue another order, power to the dome was restored.

"Well done! What was the problem?"

Silence once again fell on the command deck.

"Sorry lieutenant but we don't know. We have no explanation as of yet."

Alanna turned away from the crew slamming her fists against the protective railing of the command chair.

"Great! An important delegation is to meet on this ship in 1 hour and I can't guarantee safety due to an unknown glitch in the domes energy field."

The crew frantically searched their monitors and instrumentation for answers.

"Any word on the commanders' location?"

"According to our sensors she is on the far side of the planet. It seems to be stationary for the moment."

The Lieutenant sighed as she watched the vacant monitors.

"What about the recon team?"

The Communications Officer signaled the Lieutenant to connect her ear piece.

"Delta Wing 2 to Delta Wing 6.....all clear in quadrant V7."

"Delta Wing 6 to command: The Keevos appear to be erecting a stone wall on the west side of the dome. It looks like there are approximately 3 groups of about 5 to 7 Keevos. Any closer and we risk being detected command."

194

Alanna removed her ear piece.

"Recall recon Delta Wings and ready the surface probe."

Onyx Patterson was nearby when he heard Alanna order the surface probe.

"Lieutenant Peters......a probe won't be able to navigate those rocks and boulders. My team can get you much better observations and be ready for protection if the need arises."

Alanna looked at Onyx bearded face. The beard did little to hide the battle scars and age of this worn soldier. But Alanna knew that he didn't last this long by being stupid or foolish.

"Alright Mr. Patterson position your team within striking distance of that wall and report in every ½ hour. If we don't hear from you we'll assume the worst."

He smiled at winked at Alanna.

"Just pray those solar storms don't interfere with our COMM badges or we'll be starting another Universal War."

CHAPTER 2

The planets howling wind masked the helmeted figure on the Tulvos landscape. Its breathing increased as it scaled the abrasive walls of the cavern entrance. The figure stopped and watched momentarily as the combination of wind and sand created a tiny vortex whirling feverishly across the surface of the cave. As the figure perched atop a boulder its heavy leather coat billowed in the wind like that of a comic book hero. It provided the necessary protection against the wind and sand of this inhospitable planet. It watched as the Tulvakians were shackled in electronic cuffs and herded into the cave. The helmeted figure raised its sun visor. It followed the guards and their prisoners as they went deeper into the cavern. Soon the light grew dim. Any closer and its presence would be detected. It switched to night vision as the shadows were illuminated. The phosphorus within the cavern walls provided the intensity that the night vision needed. One Tulvakian male fell behind. A Keevos guard scolded him once then shot him at point blank range. The other 6 Tulvakians cowered in fear as their captors once again led them deeper within the cavern. The helmeted figure scanned the area and focused in on a waterfall several yards from the prisoners. It checked the Ozone present in the air along with the Oxygen levels. A green light appeared on the inner glass of the helmet. The hiss of air as the helmet unlocked was masked by the thunderous roar of the waterfall. Raven hair cascaded about the figures shoulders. Jenna looked at her reflection in the helmet.

"*Let's get this over with,*" she whispered to herself.

Slowly and quietly she made her way past the prisoners and their guards. She headed towards the waterfall. She waited till two Keevos guards moved across the cavern floor to another passage way as she positioned herself at the back end of the waterfall. The breeze created by the thundering water was cool as it blew in her face. She removed the long leather jacket to reveal a black skin-tight flight suit. Like an Olympic diver she entered the water without a splash. The water was crystal clear and cool as she headed for a small red rock beneath the water. Warm currents were detected as she swam further down. She grasped the rock, twisted and turned as her air was running out. Finally, it gave way and a shell-like object was removed from its watery grave. Jenna swam upward towards the surface releasing the air that was left in her lungs. She finally emerged behind the splashing waterfall. She breathed heavily as she wiped the water from her eyes and nose and squeezed the water from her hair. She partially unzipped her flight suit and wedged the shell-like object underneath her left breast knowing that her ample size would keep the object totally secure. As Jenna looked up, the Keevos brought out a familiar figure from the other passage way. Jenna caught her breath as she watched the Keevos lead Adrianna, the PaQua, to the other Tulvakians who were now chained to one another. Jenna looked around but had lost sight of the 10 other Keevos that entered this cave with the Tulvakians. They chained Adrianna to the first Tulvakian then motioned for them to sit. They then lit torches that now lined the cavern. Jenna pressed the locator beacon on her comm. Badge in silent mode. She shivered a little as the cold, damp air now raced through the cavern fueled by the storms at the entrance. She quietly put on her leather coat back on over her flight suit. Her weapon was useless at this distance since it would create more damage bouncing off the walls of the cavern. Suddenly, the Keevos seemed to stand at attention as another hooded figure entered the area where the Keevos sat. The figure was tall and seemed to point at the various Keevos that were near. Without a listening device it was impossible to hear what was going on due to the waterfall and the domed structure of the cavern. She could only read their lips and make out a few commands such as position, shoot and locate. She knew they were looking for her but she didn't know what they were saying about Tulvos. Jenna also knew that the minute she moved from the protection of the waterfall her presence would be noticed. Any action on her part could endanger Adrianna not to mention the Tulvakians. What Jenna saw next was confusing to say the least. The Keevos took off their armor and forced the Tulvakians to wear it. The helmets barely fit the Tulvakians and their ears had to be tucked underneath the visors before they would sit properly on their head. Adrianna was unchained and moved to a metal bar where she was rechained to a bar that was hammered to the wall. One of the taller Keevos walked over to Adrianna and ripped a portion of her cloak off revealing a metallic like body suit. She struggled with her chained hands as he grabbed for her zipper. She managed to kick him but it only succeeded in making him more angry and determined. He hit her in the stomach and again in the face. Jenna felt helpless. The relic beneath her suit was hardly worth a death. Yet many more would suffer and die if she turned it over now. Jenna needed help but how and from where? As if someone was listening weapons fire could be heard above the din of the waterfall. The Keevos then shifted their attention to the cavern they just came from. One by one they seemed to vanish down the corridor leaving only 2 visibly nervous soldiers to guard the prisoners. Jenna waited till their attention was drawn to the entrance to the cavern. She emerged slowly from behind the waterfall. The mist fell on her jacket like beads of glistening sweat. A Tulvakian prisoner noticed her first. She motioned for him to keep quiet. Adrianna looked up to notice movement. She turned to face the corridor. Jenna somehow knew she would be her lookout. The 2 nervous soldiers moved further down the corridor in an attempt to see what was going on. Jenna moved quickly towards the Tulvakian prisoners who were not sure of her intentions. She released them one by one and motioned for them to scatter about the cavern. As Jenna looked around she noticed several different tunnels that seemed wider than the one she had come from. She wondered if one of them led to the chamber where she met the council. If she could determine that she would know her position more precisely. The bar that Adrianna was attached to was partially rusted and worn closed with ages of use. She looked around for a small angular rock that she could use for digging. She picked up a perfectly pointed crystal from beneath her feet and wondered if it would be strong enough. She started carving around the edges where the rust seemed to overlap onto the rocks. Slowly she began to wear away at the rock, grinding it slowly to fine sand. Jenna gave her a thumb up sign and continued closer to the tunnel on her left. She saw movement and hid behind a boulder. She looked around and saw no trace of the prisoners. Two poorly armored soldiers looked around in disbelief. One was short and slightly balding with one worn metal glove on his weapon. The other was tall almost gaunt looking with several dented and damaged weapons hanging from his shoulder. \

"Where are they?" The taller of the two shouted at Adrianna but got no response.

The shorter soldier raised his weapon and pointed it at Adrianna's chest. Jenna looked down and saw a shield that one of the soldiers must have left behind when they pulled the clothing switch. At that moment she lifted it up and ran towards the two soldiers. Suddenly, weapons fire streaked the cavern walls hitting the taller Keevos. Jenna raised the shield and took a swing at the smaller soldier with the gun. The shield hit its mark. The small soldiers weapon flew up into the air with the impact of the blow. Jenna jumped for it, grabbed it and aimed it at the rusty bar Adrianna was attached to. The bar shattered as she slid her handcuffs down the opened end. Adrianna turned towards the gunfire coming from the cave to her left. A familiar face appeared from the smoke-filled cave.

"Sorry we were a bit late Commander!"

Onyx Patterson's face was almost radiant as she smiled at his eye contact. A sound shuffled from behind them as all weapons faced the direction of the sound. One of the Tulvos dressed as a Keevos emerged from behind a clump of boulders.

"No!" Jenna shouted to the weapons she saw in front of her. *"They're not Keevos. They were forced to wear the clothing of their enemy. Hopefully, the trick backfired."*

Jenna reached for her com badge.

"This is Commander Avir to Station One."

Jenna surveyed the damage as she waited for a response.

"This is Flight Lieutenant Merritt commander. Are you okay?"

The young lieutenant sounded relieved at the sound of her voice.

"Nothing a cooling shower won't take care of! I need a Document Team down here ASAP."

"On their way commander."

Jenna spoke briefly with Onyx and then headed for the transport. Adrianna, the PaQua, watched her as she walked past briefly making eye contact. She continued to translate directions to the Keevos prisoners while the Tulvos gathered up the strays.

Sandy was the first one at the docking bay awaiting the injured and her commander. As Onyx team stepped out she directed her medical crew to the more severe injuries, of which there were relatively few. Sandy continued to wait. Suddenly, the air lock opened and there stood the Pa Qua with Lieutenant Peters.

"Where's the commander?"

Both women looked at one another.

"What do you mean where is she!"

Adrianna stepped forward.

"She left in a transport over and hour ago. It was right after she ordered the Document Team."

Sandy opened a frequency on her com badge.

"Alanna.....check and see if the Document Team has seen her."

Sandy's Com Badge crackled with static as a faint signal came through.

"Commander Avir is entering the transport grate now. If you wish to contact her you'll need to do that now since she has requested another transport to take her to the far side of the planet."

Alister McMann continued to report.

"She had trouble with her Com badge so she took it off. She said it go a little damp."

Sandy moved forward and adjusted her headset.

"Commander? Are you all right?"

The static seemed worse as Jenna spoke.

"Yes...I'm fine Sandy. I just have to take care of one last issue and then we can dust off."

As the second transport docked Jenna ordered the Flight Lieutenant and Co-pilot to leave and took the transport up by herself.

"What do you suppose she is doing? I mean...I thought everything was taken care of?"

The PaQua moved in quietly behind them.

"Everything except the relic."

Alistair spoke first sounding puzzled.

"She *went back for it?*"

"*Yeah! I thought she knew where the relic was.*"

Sandy turned to face Alistair. The PaQua stepped towards the large view screen and leaned against the bulkhead.

"*She already has the relic.*"

Several voices spoke at once.

"*Then what's she doing with the transport?*"

"*Returning the relic,*" Adriana spoke as she gazed out the window of the ship.

Jenna touched down just outside the mouth of the cavern on the North side of the planet. Her calculations placed her as close to the original coordinates of the council chambers as possible. She was greeted by the same Tulvakian guards that were in the council chamber.

"*I must speak with the council. The matter is urgent!*"

The young guard conferred with the small communications unit within his helmet and motioned Jenna to proceed within the cavern. AQ cloaked woman suddenly appeared in front of her.

"*Forgive me Commander but he council has disbanded. What is it you seek?*" Jenna spoke softly, "*May I know your name?*"

The woman surveyed Jenna very carefully before she spoke.

"*My name is Vashara.*"

Jenna reached into her pocket when a guard carefully studied the action at gun point. The woman placed her hand on the weapon.

"*It's alright,*" she said as she forced the soldier to holster his weapon.

"*I believe that this belongs to your people Vashara.*"

And with that she handed her a leather-bound object. Vashara held out her hand, Jenna placed the object in it and unwrapped it slowly. The light from the flaming torches glistened within its center.

Vashara whispered, "*The relic! but why? How?*"

Jenna smiled, turned and walked away.

"*The relic was not ours to take. Its alloy is from this planet and as such was meant to stay on this planet. I'm starting to understand why the creators broke it apart.*"

Jenna turned to face Vashara.

"*If you will permit the settlers to remain within the dome and to*" *live peacefully on your planet, our Federation will offer no further interference."*

"*You have my word as a Tulvakian Commander Genevieve Alexandra Avir.*"

Jenna climbed up onto the transport and lifted off as suddenly as she had landed. Back on the ship her crew anxiously awaited word from the command center.

"*I have the Commander's transport on screen. Tracking her onto Flight Deck 7.*"

Sandy left the command center along with Alanna and Adriana. All headed for Flight Deck 7.

Dr. Kylo rubbed her weary eyes as she walked through the deserted hallways of the ship. Things wound down once the commander returned. The Tulvos had their relic, the aliens were settling in under the dome, the Keevos were undergoing rehabilitation Tulvos style and the crew of the Isis I could finally get the rest their bodies and minds needed. The hum of the ship seemed almost hypnotic as the doctor made her way to the Observation Deck. The ship had lifted off shortly after the Commanders transport arrived and was orbiting Tulvos second moon when the doctor made her rounds. Her body was exhausted but her mind was racing. She was mentally checking off all the regulations and protocols following a planetary skirmish, altercation or war. She read charts, made notes and double checked those who were wounded. She needed to check on one last thing before she settled in and gave in to her exhaustion. She entered the Observation Deck via the stairs. There in the corner of the large picture window beneath the bulkhead sat a figure in the moonlight.

"*Peaceful isn't it?*" She spoke softly so as not to disturb the serenity of the view.

"*Yes...quite peaceful yet at the same time deceiving.*"

Sandy moved in closer and sat next to her.

"*Why deceiving?*"

Jenna sighed as she spoke.

"*It hides the turmoil and chaos that went on beneath the surface. It's moon light gave us the illusion we saw. A planet with no known inhabitants, I mean.... According to Federation law we supposedly had*

202

the right to take whatever even though it was not really ours to take. The sad thing is…. we've learned nothing from this."

Jenna stood up and placed both hands gently on the window as if to touch the moons.

"Pretty soon we will hear of another relic or part of one and the whole chaotic mess will start all over again."

Sandy stood up and put her hand gently on Jenna's back rubbing her as she spoke.

"The hope for change remains in some people. Those that don't give up, those that speak the truth and those that still have compassion for other beings will effect change."

Both women sighed as they turned to face one another.

"Rome wasn't built in a day. Do you remember that saying?"

"Yes! But it wasn't destroyed in one either. You need to stop thinking about things you cannot change and work on those that you can change. But the way…. you're certainly not going to do any good if your too tired to command your ship."

Sandy placed her hand in hers and gently led her away from the mesmerizing Command Deck and to her quarters. Once there she turned the ambient light control to Rainforest. The lights dimmed to a warm blue green glow and the sounds of a gentle rain could be heard softly in the background.

"There! Now your mind can shift to a more relaxing mode."

She unbuttoned Jenna's jacket and removed it as she stood in the middle of the room.

"Come on…...sit down on the bed."

Sandy went to the replicator and ordered 2 glasses of warm milk.

"Here…drink this doctors' orders. It's an old Earth remedy."

Jenna looked up at her Medical Officer and smiled.

"Why my dear doctor, if I didn't know better I'd swear you were trying to seduce me."

Sandy smiled and kneeled down in front of Jenna. She wondered if that would be so bad.

"Hey, wait till I get out the chocolate chip cookies…then you'll be all mine."

Jenna reached down and gently kissed Sandy. It seemed like an eternity but lasted only seconds. Sandy realized that at that moment she wanted this to continue. She stood up slowly not wanting to appear startled. Jenna took off her shirt to reveal tan, beautifully rounded inviting breasts. She took off her pants and climbed into bed.

"Thank you doctor; once again I am powerless to your charms."

What was said in friendly humor made Sandy warm all over. She knew she had better leave before saying or doing something stupid or foolish.

"I don't want to see you up for at least 8 hours. Is that understood?"

Jenna rolled over causing the sheets to follow the perfect curvature of her back. Sandy tried not to focus on that picture but it was very hard.

"I'll a....(cough) I'll see you in 8 hours."

Sandy walked towards the door.

"Sandy....."

Dr. Kylo stopped in her tracks.

"Yes Jenna....a... Commander?"

"Thank you for being a..... friend."

Sandy walked out and engaged the privacy mode on the Commanders quarters. She then leaned against the wall of the ship as she held back a single tear. It was as if the past day's events were crashing through her mind to create a wall of confusion. She had completed 2 tours of duty with Jenna and opted for this mission when she found out that Jenna would be heading it. She enjoyed Jenna's company but always longed for some quiet time to know the other side of her. It seemed that she just never got the time. Between ships duties, cargo inspections, passengers and emergencies there just never seemed to be enough time to get to know her. She shook her head as she walked along the corridor. Was she experiencing a hormonal imbalance? She smiled briefly. Wondering if she was missing a "normal" life could hardly be called a hormonal imbalance. She was glad that there were no registered Telepaths on the ship or she would be feeling more confused than she already did. She realized that the crew and Jenna were the only friends she had. Sandy had been in space for so long that her bonds and attachments from earth were long gone. Through all of that this was the first time that Jenna had called her by her first name. Sandy would patch her up after battles and knew almost every scar on Jenna's body. She wondered if Jenna even knew what color her eyes were. Her thoughts were interrupted by a slap on her shoulder.

"Hey doc! Though you'd be with Mr. Sandman by now?"

Sargent Barnes shifted his stogie to the other side of his mouth.

"I'm on my way to join him…. how about you?"

He pushed several buttons on the panel next to Sandy.

"Yeah….I opted to be the odd man out. I'm on call till Engineering comes off sleep mode in about 24 hours."

The two walked to the air lift. Sargent Barnes checked the panel as he spoke.

"Well….see ya in 24 hours."

And with that Sandy headed to her quarters for some much-needed rest.

CHAPTER 3

Jenna awoke to her Com screen flashing. The message had arrived ½ an hour ago. It was as she expected. The council on earth and the Universal Federation were not pleased with Jenna's decision to leave the relic in its current resting place. She had no doubt that they would find a way to take it by force or by stealth. There had to be another way. As she dressed she thought how relieved her crew should feel knowing that they would be going home soon. As she exited her room she noticed the halls busy with robots and droids checking and tending to minor repairs. Dr. Kylo came around the corner nearly colliding with Jenna.

"*Doctor! Aren't you up rather early? Your patients should all be resting comfortably.*"

Sandy smiled as she watched a droid skirt up a wall to a bulkhead.

"*I could say the same for you Jenna or should I go back to calling you Commander Avir?*"

Jenna was a bit taken back by Sandy's tone.

"*Is everything alright?*" she asked cautiously.

"*Sorry….I don't know. I can't really put my finger on it. It just doesn't feel right. I have nothing scientific or medical to base it on but…*"

Jenna placed a hand on Sandy's shoulder and motioned for her to follow. Once back in Jenna's quarters she had her sit down in a wide non-regulation easy chair and poured her a cup of hot tea she had made before she got dressed.

"*If it's any consolation I'm feeling the same way. I know that technically the mission is over but somehow I feel responsible for what is about to happen to these inhabitants.*"

She stood by the bulkhead as she spoke.

"I'm tired of the lies I'm bound to enforce. I'm tired of not being able to relax, have pleasant conversation or even relate on a sexual level with anyone. The Federation cut me lose 2 years ago yet every time there is a 'situation' they reinstate me. Since all of this is supposedly research funded my crew gets minimum pay for putting their asses on the line with me every time we have one of these government missions."

Jenna leaned against a window port and closed her eyes.

"You and I both know what will happen to this planet now that the relic has been found. They will take the relic by force and a bloodbath will ensue. Aliens, Keevos and Tulvos will die....and for what! A 31st century Holy war?"

Sandy took a sip of tea, placed her cup down and walked over to Jenna.

"Why can't we give them the relic?"

Jenna gave her an incredulous look.

"Because it is not ours to take or give."

Sandy turned away from Jenna and sighed. Jenna reached out for her and held her against her body.

"I'm sorry...I"

Sandy turned and looked at Jenna. She reached up and placed her fingers gently over Jenna's lips.

"Maybe there is a way out of this. Maybe there is a way to give both parties what they want."

Jenna looked into Sandy's eyes and was momentarily lost in their warmth. She reached down, softly and passionately kissed Sandy's lips. Sandy felt faint as she melted in Jenna's arms. A feeling of passion came over her that she had not felt in years. She was a bit frightened by it and pulled away. At that moment Jenna turned around.

"That's it! Sandy contact the Federation and stall for time. I'll be back."

Sandy tried to regain her composure.

"Yes...yeah.... sure!"

"Keep your private channel open that way they can't listen in."

And with that Jenna hurried out the door.

CHAPTER 4

A hooded figure stepped on to the planet's surface. The wind picked up small pockets of the planets dust and sand and whirled them around like tiny tornadoes searching for a place to land. Every once in a while, small pebbles bounced off the hooded figures visor as it moved closer to the entrance. Every footstep taken left no trail due to the severity of the wind. The opening to the Tulvakian chamber was straight ahead.

Meanwhile, back on the ship the crew were manning their posts.

"I have unauthorized field movement 5 clicks from the shield."

Lieutenant Baily moved towards the sensor screen.

"I need to know who is out there. Switch to photo sensors."

"Object is moving past the shield to the Tulvakian chamber."

The lieutenant rubbed his eyes as he spoke.

"Notify the commander and have Teams 1 and 2 go on standby alert."

The lieutenant's orders were interrupted by a voice from behind.

"The commander has been notified and is well aware of the situation."

Everyone turned to see Dr. Kylo at the side of the commanders' empty chair.

"Dr. Kylo...I'm simply following my orders. The commander....."

Sandy placed a hand on his shoulder.

"The commander already knows."

She nodded towards the view screen. She then flicked a switch on her Com badge.

"Commander Avir your crew is quite concerned about your safety. Can you please verify your status?"

A familiar voice with the occasional static came through the speakers.

"I need to finalize some things with the Keevos and Tulvakian people. Prepare for immediate dust off on my orders."

The lieutenant was about to object when he looked at Sandy. If there was something going on it seemed to have the approval of the Medical Officer and the Commander so he swallowed and followed the commanders' orders. The crew obeyed as they silently watched the storm from both sensors and cameras inside the dome. The commander headed for the cave where yesterday's battle had ensued. Onyx Patterson stood behind Science Officer Christine Almonte as they too watched the screen.

"I should have gone with her. Things still aren't quiet down there. There could be trouble."

Onyx voice was measured yet concerned. The Communications Officer Tavel asked for silence as he boosted the signal from the commanders' microphone.

"I'm getting a faint signal from the commander. She is requesting Flight Lieutenant Merritt to fly escort when she leaves the cave. She is also requesting a drone be sent to her location."

He tried to boost the signal again but the magnetic storms were back to their usual fury.

"I can't gain verification."

His voice trembled slightly as he spoke. Combat Captain Alana Peters tapped Onyx on his back.

"Did she tell you what she was going to do?"

Onyx shook his head no.

"Notify Merritt to escort the commander as soon as she emerges from the chamber."

"He is off loading the drone as we speak. The command shuttle is in route to this ship. ETA 5 minutes."

Dr. Kylo whispered to the lieutenant who then issued an order to Onyx and Alana. They hurried to the flight deck.

Flight Lieutenant Merritt hovered as he awaited the commander's shuttle.

"Argos I I have the commanders ship on sensors. I am also reading several ships now exiting Tulvos atmosphere."

The lieutenant adjusted several buttons on his ships console and then looked out his ships window.

"Argos I there are 5....I repeat ....5 Tulvos ships on a straight vector for the commander's shuttle."

As the lieutenant turned his ship in the direction of the shuttle his ship suddenly vibrated and pitched briefly from side to side. Three Keevos fighters now flew past Lieutenant Kyle Merritt's ship. Their large wingspan, omni directional engines and unusual flight signature made them quite formidable looking ships. A coded signal was coming in across his headset. He verified it several times and then broke contact with the warships and headed back to the planet's surface.

"Lieutenant Baily this is Onyx Patterson requesting permission to launch."

Combat Captain Alana Peters took over since this had now become her jurisdiction.

"Negative Onyx maintain tracking distance via the Flight Deck."

She adjusted her headset and watched her screen.

"What the hell is that?"

All eyes were drawn to the screen. A ship twice the size of Argos I now appeared above planet Tulvos. The commanders shuttle maneuvered above the planet's atmosphere as the Keevos fighters surrounded it. The Tulvos fighters took up flanking positions.

"Lieutenant Baily I have a message from the commander ...but..."

"But what Tavel?"

"Well...its coming through on an unsecured channel."

Everyone had a puzzled look on their face.

"Put it through."

Sandy closed her eyes as she listened.

"I repeat...this is Commander Genevieve Alexandra Avir. I have possession of the relic and am requesting full military escort to Argos I."

Suddenly the ships lights flickered.

"Now what...did we forget to pay the light bill?"

Onyx said as he stepped over to another console in the Flight deck. Onyx went to his communications pad to his left.

"This is Onyx Patterson. What just happened?"

Alanna's voice answered.

"We are being scanned by the Tulvos and Keevos."
Suddenly red lights flashed and alarms went off throughout the ship.

ALL COMMAND PERSONNEL REPORT
TO THE COMMAND DECK ON THE DOUBLE.

All the corridors were filled with support crew scurrying for their posts. Onyx, Alanna and Christine Almonte met in the corridor.
"What the hell is going on Christine?"
"They've attacked the commanders ship it was docking with that command ship!"
"Let's go people!"
As the three turned the corner they came crashing into a tall cloaked figure. Onyx reached for his weapon as did Alanna. The cloaked figure removed its hood to reveal a black Arkanoid helmet. The hiss of the helmet release made the two women stand to the side of Onyx.
"Just the three people I wanted to see."
Sandy came running from around the corner as she crashed into Christine.
"Commander!"
All of them shouted at once.
"What's going on?"
She handed Sandy her helmet and Christine her cloak.
"Come with me."
Onyx sheathed his weapon. All four followed Jenna to her quarters.
"Computer.... Secure chamber level 6."
The door was automatically locked and a pale blue light scanned the room as she motioned for everyone to sit.
"Quarters secure Code engaged," a computer voice, sounding almost human, confirmed.
"I'm sorry for the deception but I had to solve a problem quickly. Have we already been scanned?"
"Yes," Alanna spoke as she shifted in her chair.
"Why did you take back the relic?"
Jenna poured each of them a drink and sat down on the edge of her bed to face them.

"We all knew of the council politics. I knew they would never be happy with the Keevos or the Tulvos keeping the relic. I knew that there would be more bloodshed if the council didn't own it."

An imprinted message came across the computer screen at her desk.

"I think you'd better take a look at this. According to the crew you are.....dead. Your ship has been blown to pieces and your Second in Command Baily is buckling."

Christine spoke shaking her head.

"Who the hell put him in charge?"

"Captain Peters.... looks like you'll have to give the order to stand down."

Jenna said as she calmly sipped her drink.

"But why can't you tell him? Your crew is incensed over your attack and.... death"

Christine said as she herself looked confused. Captain Peters sent a coded message to the command deck stating for the Argos I to 'stand down'. Any time a ship is engaged in a hostile action the commander relinquishes command to the combat captain. Lieutenant Baily may not like the order but he had to follow it. Christine looked at Onyx puzzled.

"Do you understand any of this?"

He looked as though he were trying to think it through as Christine asked the question.

"May I commander?"

Sandy stood up and placed her drink down on the desk next to Onyx. Jenna smiled and nodded the okay.

"The council can't pursue the relic if it is destroyed. So, the commander went back to the planet and 'publicly' took it knowing they would come after her. She publicly gave it to the Keevos and had the Tulvos blow them up with the relic aboard. Only the command ship was a decoy. The pilot came with Lieutenant Merritt then he went pack to pick up the commander. Thanks to the encoded signal the Universal Federation knows as well. You can't start a war if the object doesn't exist."

Onyx stood up and spoke.

"But the retaliation over the commanders' death.....the Keevos attacking the Tulvos ...the war will start and be even more fueled."

Jenna sat down at the desk.

"*The universal Federation didn't like me because they couldn't control me. They won't risk manpower and ships for my honor. As for the Tulvos and the Keevos they still have the relic.*"

"*What?*"

Onyx, Alanna and Christine all said quite puzzled.

"*The Tulvos cooperated with this little ruse because they wanted to protect the relic. It belongs to them not us. They will say and do whatever is necessary to protect it.*"

"*This can't possibly work...it's too simple.*"

Onyx voiced as he finished his drink.

"*Besides....the Tulvos loved the charade. You should have seen the pilot trying to fly that command ship.*"

"*That's why you needed a drone!*"

"*Yes.... since they are certainly easier to replace than a human or alien.*"

All were silent as they pondered the facts placed before them.

"*Okay...wait a minute. What about you...your...dead. How are you going to function?*"

Onyx acted as though he had just swallowed the canary.

"*Well Onyx...you're going to discover and escape pod in the debris and you're going to save me. I'll take some heat with the Federation but it's nothing I can't live with.*"

Jenna typed in a verbal command for Lieutenant Baily that would originate from the debris field. She lifted the lock on her quarters. She then turned and spoke to the thinking faces.

"*I'm hoping that all of you will help perpetuate the rumor in each of your departments.*"

Onyx poured himself another drink.

"*It might just work.*"

Sandy looked at Jenna.

"*I'll go through the motions in Med Lab. Time to check on my other patients. I'll see you later?*"

Jenna nodded in agreement. Onyx swallowed his drink and walked over to Jenna.

"*I'll make sure the right tidbits go into the right ears. Guess I should also prep for my rescue mission.*"

Alanna finished her drink and stood next to Onyx.

"I'll help you prep. We can dust off the Tekken 4. It's a little bit more maneuverable."

Both he and Alanna left the room discussing procedure. Christine stayed and stood beside Jenna.

"They are a bit confused but they'll work through it eventually."

Jenna looked into her eyes as they sparkled in the available pale blue security light.

"If I saw another way I would have done it but there wasn't enough time to confide in you. I hope that isn't an issue."

Christine stood behind Jenna and began to message her shoulders.

"They trust you or they wouldn't have come this far. You sometimes forget how long we all have been together. Remember Onyx as a green recruit wanting to take on the world. And what about Alanna wanting to make a name for herself and buzzing the Flight Deck in that Delknoian flier. Remember when she almost clipped the Observation Deck. I thought you'd have her in the brig before she even came aboard. But you saw her no fear temperament and knew you could mold it into a fine Combat pilot. Half this crew won't question any thing you've done so far. And the other half will be quelled by the loyal portion of your crew."

Christine pulled her up and moved her over to the bed.

"I think you need to relax Commander. Perhaps Dr. Kylo can give you something to help you sleep."

Jenna turned to face her long-time crew member. She wondered how observant she truly was.

"Thanks Chris. I'll take it under advisement."

Christine walked out of the commander's room and down the hall.

Sandy checked the computers and saw that all appeared to be well with the exception of the somber crew over the apparent 'death' of their commander. Onyx was given permission to launch to recover what he could. She went over her inventory list and added a few things she had forgotten. She looked around at the empty beds and emergency chambers. The silence would have been deafening if it weren't for the occasional clicking of the air recyclers. Jenna was going to replace them but now that Sandy noticed it she welcomed the noise. Sandy began to scold herself for not appreciating the silence. She could concentrate

214

and get things done like write her logs, catch up on her experiments do some past due medical articles. But the events of the past several days left her mind racing. She had difficulty keeping her mind on track. She would find it wandering back to Jenna on the loading dock and then on the command deck. How beautiful her profile was even in the dimly lit section of the deck. She remembered how fearful she was when Jenna went to the caves on her own to locate the relic. She remembered when Jenna was wounded and how her concern for her crew was all she wanted to address. She admired Jenna's noble traits and her always proper behavior around her. As she continued to search within her mind a familiar voice brought her back to reality.

"*Why doc! I do believe you were zoning.*"

Sandy turned to see Jenna in her long black coat that resembled a robe and her black helmet with the visor up.

"*What? No...I was ...a...just collecting...my thoughts. Ah.... For my notes. What are you doing here?*"

Jenna hopped up on an examining table.

"*I have to get ready for Onyx to bring me to you so you can save me.*"

Sandy was focused in on Jenna's lips.

"*Doc...are you okay?*"

Jenna's voice was concerned.

"*I'm fine I..*"

"*Onyx will be bringing in the entire pod so the crew will see the pod but nothing else. You had better seal off Med lab.*"

Sandy readied a tray of tools and entered the security code for quarantine of the lab.

"*Okay...you'd better lay back.*"

The doors to the Med Lab flew open as several crew members surrounded the charred pod. Onyx and several crew members lifted the coffin sized pod and placed it on one of the beds in the lab. Sandy sprang into action as she pulled the curtain all around the pod then ushered out all non-essential crew which wound up leaving Onyx and Alanna. They then opened the pod for effect and helped Jenna off with her helmet. The then rolled her bed in place of the pod and called several soldiers to remove the pod and in doing so would see the commander. Word then would be spread about the ship that the commander was alive.

Everything worked as planned and 3 hours later the crew was informed that the commander was doing well and was expected to return to duty in three days. Until then the ship would remain on its present course for Arkania, Commander Avir's home. Slowly the ships activities began to return to normal. The hallways once again were breathable and the crew were settling in for some well needed rest.

Sandy walked back into her office and finished up her notes on the Commanders miraculous recovery. She logged in the time she had moved her back to her quarters, 6 hours ago. Sandy starred at the bed where Jenna was placed.

"You're zoning again doc."

"What?"

She turned to face Jenna.

"What are you doing here? I take it you need something from Med Lab?"

Agitated Sandy stood up and stacked her notes. Jenna backed up slightly to watch Sandy.

"Well...since there was some quiet time I thought..."

Jenna hesitated in finishing her sentence. She turned away from Sandy. This wasn't the right time or place she thought. Of all the times Sandy had been in her quarters talking and now when she wanted to be a bit personal she could hardly speak. Sandy realized she was being a bit curt to Jenna so she turned and placed a hand on her shoulder.

"You were thinking?"

Jenna sighed heavily.

"I was thinking .....this was a mistake."

Jenna walked towards the Med Lab exit. Sandy blocked her way.

"I'm sorry....I didn't mean to bother you. I don't know what I was thinking. I guess I was .....having a hard time coming down after all the constant excitement."

"Yeah...I know what you mean."

"Kinda wish Adrianna was here so that she could show me some of her relaxation techniques."

"Yeah....how is she?"

Jenna seemed to loosen up slightly.

"She's fine. She is studying our events and finishing her observations on Tulvos moon."

Jenna moved away from the exit.

"That sounds positively boring!"

Jenna laughed

"Yeah …it does…..doesn't it?"

Sandy turned briefly away to turn off some of the Med Lab machines.

"So! What was it you were going to ask me?"

Sandy figured if she'd busy herself Jenna would feel less self-conscious.

"Well…I was …a … going to ask you if….a… you'd like to finish that tea we had earlier?"

Sandy smiled as she turned off the last data machine.

"I'd love to! Just give me a half an hour to get some of this grime off me. Shall I meet you in your quarters?"

Startled by the response all she could say was, "Yes."

Jenna quickly walked back to her quarters and decided that a shower was a great idea. She laughed at herself when she went to the closet to pick out something appropriate to wear. Uniform number one, tow, or three or for something with a little snazzy she could choose several Flight suits.

"Well that's pathetic!"

She looked once more in the closet, groaned and headed for the shower. Sargent Barnes watched as Dr. Kylo went into the Commanders quarters. He adjusted his stogie as he walked past.

"Ahhh….no wonder the temperature is always too hot for her. Temperature coil malfunction my ass."

He continued to grumble as he headed for Engineering.

The End

The Antarian Manuver

$$\boxed{\text{CHAPTER 1}}$$

The AI units hummed and clicked as the sensors on their titanium bodies disengaged the sleep mode on the crews transport chambers. The shiny metallic feet tapped along the corridor to the Flight deck as the awakening crew yawned, coughed and sneezed their way to their uniforms. The Commander was already at the helm checking the flight recorder, sensor arrays, and current flight path of her ship. She watched the monitors as her crew discussed their impending visit to Space Station Orion IV. An inspection ship was already requesting permission to board the Isis I when her crew funneled onto the Command deck. She placed the call on screen and was greeted by a pleasant face and a smoky voice. The woman in front of her had a military hair cut and the standard issue uniform.

"Greetings Commander Stevens! Welcome to the Orion sector. Please transmit your documents for review and prepare for inspection."

Marin and her crew checked the docking links and permission was granted. Inspections were a standard operation in the Orion quadrant and were generally done by drones or robots. Contraband was usually smuggled in by smaller faster ships using Tarsis IX moons as cover. The Isis I was a research vessel of unusual lineage built by the aliens on Space Station Vega. She carried state-of-the-art scientific equipment and was permitted by the Universal Agreement of 3010 to carry certain weapons and defense shields. Marin was privileged to have known several of the alien designers and was one of the few Terrans that could understand the language of the ship. They seemed to accept her as one of their own. Her involvement in several historical war campaigns made her known throughout several galaxies. That may have been why she chose her last 5 years of duty on the refitted Isis I as a research vessel.

The inspection ship docked without incident however, instead of the drones carrying out the normal duties the young woman Marin had seen on the screen appeared before her.

"Commander Stevens?"

The woman was slightly shorter than Marin and was much more attractive in person. She glanced down at her id badge.

"Yes Inspector Yorx, how can I be of assistance?"

The inspector signaled for a single drone to continue on down the corridor of the ship with the manifest.

"I know this is a bit unusual but I just had to meet the idol of my flight academy in person. Back home you are truly larger than life."

Marin smiled politely but was uncomfortable with her young admirer.

"I'm sorry to disappoint you Inspector Yorx but that person has long since retired. Those campaigns were very long and very hard. Some never should have gone as far or lasted as long as they did. I would love nothing better than to be able to tell you some fanciful story of war but it wouldn't be the truth."

The young woman seemed to cling to Marin's every word. Finally, the drone reappeared with several PDA charts to sign off on.

"Well then, looks like you're all clear. Perhaps I'll see you at the space dock. I know of several places to eat when you've had time to acclimate."

Marin smiled and bid the young inspector farewell. She went back up to the command deck and watched as the crew maneuvered the large ship past the two planets and on towards the Space Station Orion.

The cargo bay opened slowly like huge cathedral doors as the crew prepared their exit from the steel and titanium shell they called home for the past year and a half. The captain looked wearily through the huge landscape sized windows at the activities below and sighed as she filled in the miles once again on the chart. The crew looked up from the Space Station Orion IV and motioned for her to join them. She smiled and waved them on. For fifteen years she had been an officer and captain for the Research Vessel Isis I. She had seen this space station inside and out. It was the prototype for most of the space stations in this galaxy and with the exception of some new security sensors, was like all the others. The job and people remained the same. Even the sight of aliens was common place. She watched her screen as the planet below was projected. Tarsis IX was a planet that had become invaded early on by large private interest corporations. It now resembled a game board. Areas were divided into a cloned version of Earth I, Altor and N.Z.E. You could visit Earth I with its modern high technology, fantasize in the tall, lush forests of Altor or go to the No Zoned Entry which was sanctioned by the government for war games. Personally she preferred the moons of Tarsis IX with their reflective atmosphere and moon lakes. Time in space with routine activities day in and day out would frequently find the crew wanting to see an adventure behind every mission. Weapons were well maintained and battle gear finely polished but went unused. The captain knew where her crew would be and requested their passes for the N.Z.E. ahead of time. She began to think of all the other planets she had been to. She turned and walked down the busy corridors to her quarters. As she packed her steel regulation luggage she chuckled at how little she had to pack: 2 dress uniforms and 3 standard issue space flight suits, nothing to denote individuality or years of traveling. With the exception of her gold and turquoise medallion and her rank insignia she was no different than anyone else aboard her ship. But she was different. The missions she had undertaken, the aliens she had come in contact with, all left her with unique life experiences. She had watched as wars devastated aliens and biological weapons ruined what was left of formerly fertile planets; she picked up survivors and pieces of starships that were left rotting by pirates; she followed orders and watched crew members die while entering hot zones in uncharted space. She was what one would characterize as a 'good soldier'. She watched her reflection in the steel containers that were being off loaded as she boarded the shuttle which would take her to her quarters on the space station. The ride had to be interrupted due to an unknown security problem. She was too weary to require additional information. She sat back until the shuttle reached the Communications building. Small rooms with monitors were available for private or business calls. She placed her bags on the chair and pulled out her government I.D. She was led into a dimly lit room by an alien Arquesian woman of oriental decent. How beautiful their skin tone was even in this light. It was as if the contact between alien and human had brought out some of the most stunning beauty she had ever come across. Marin entered her code as the woman sealed the door behind her. A flash of light appeared on the screen in front of her and a blonde-haired woman with freckles and fair skin appeared.

"Chris! It's me, Marin. How are you?"

Marin was tired but was beginning to get her second wind as she gazed at the sleepy face before her. The woman apparently had been asleep, for her response was slow and unsure.

"Where are you?" the woman asked.

"I'm at the space station. I just got in. Thought I'd give you a call to see how you were."

Marin's voice was softer than usual.

"How's your brother?"

The woman held back a smile.

"He's fine, still stubborn and possessive."

Marin smiled as her body began to relax.

"I could take the cruiser and be there in a day if you wanted me to."

Chris' smile disappeared as she tensed.

"No, you don't have to do that. I...I couldn't be with you. I'm working a full schedule. It would be a waste of your time."

Marin closed her eyes.

"Marin, we've discussed this before. Why must you process it? It's over. You know I have difficulty being 'just' friends."

Marin sat up in her chair and breathed quietly.

"I didn't mean to upset you. Forgive me."

Marin concluded the conversation and signed off. The communication button was still lit indicating an incoming response but Marin did not respond. She unlocked the room and walked back up to the front. Two and a half years in space and it was as if the pain of the relationship had happened yesterday. She would not process it any further for she was too tired and hungry to waste valuable brain cells.

"Excuse me! Could you possibly tell me where one might get a decent meal for human consumption?"

Marin knew she had to classify human consumption since, as with other stations, humans only represented 47% of the work force.

"You might try the new one on Earth I. It's supposed to have ancient and rare Earth delicacies as well as the standards. But I think a new one just opened on the space station promenade that is supposed to be quite good."

"Thank you," Marin replied, grateful for any different suggestion on places to eat.

The Earth shuttle functioned normally as it whisked its way into the station bay. Marin keyed in the destination and sat back in weary comfort. Thoughts of Chris filled her mind. The forest planet where they first met and the water planets they visited held pleasant memories. Thinking of Chris' brother and his chauvinistic ideas of family life along with her one father with his visions of honor caused Marin's muscles to tense. The time spent away from Chris was more of a detriment than Marin realized. Didn't her brain just agree that she wasn't going to process it any further? She grew wearier as she also thought of the travel reports of new medical drugs her ship had come across that never got published and the cover-ups she was forced to agree with regarding planetary invasions. The lies, greed and ignorance, which were now common place, had taken their toll on Marin's ability to cope. Her job was no longer necessary as younger academy trained officers were indoctrinated with the new "We own it we don't care" policy. But as she looked around she did not feel compelled to make drastic changes at this moment. She was tired and hungry, and as her stomach growled as a reminder to her brain. Addressing this hunger became her main thought. The shuttle reached its destination and rolled to a stop. The guards checked passes and I.D.'s as Marin saw the sign of the restaurant the Arquesian woman had suggested. The prices seemed a bit high but Marin looked down at her stomach and smiled. An Elodian was doing the seating.

"I'm sorry; Captain Stevens, but we don't have any seating available at this time."

Marin placed her bags down, looked at him wearily and said she would wait.

"Do you have seating for two?" said a voice from behind Marin.

"Yes, but....."

Before the Elodian could continue, a formally clad woman dressed in a camel's hair jacket and trousers walked up through the line that was beginning to form.

"Perhaps if the captain doesn't mind a fellow human, we can dine together."

The woman was as tall as Marin but her complexion was somewhat lighter. Marin smiled and motioned for the woman to enter first. The woman had a graceful yet paced walk as Marin did her quick scan. The food looked appealing and the wine list seemed to be non-artificial.

"Well, my name is Helen. What's yours?"

Marin smiled again.

"I'm Marin Stevens. I'm glad you suggested this. Frankly, I was too tired to deal with the logical mind of an Elodian."

Helen noticed the darkened shadows underneath the captain's eyes as she spoke. She also noticed the insignia and honors this woman wore on her uniform. *Funny,* she thought, *she doesn't look that old.*

"Elodians are extremely logical people and if you are a single person they sit you at a single table never assuming you could share a table."

Helen smiled.

"Well..... Shall we choose a wine?"

"Sure, I'm into experimentation!"

They both laughed since they knew that original authentic wine had not been manufactured for ages now and the only available substitute was a synthetic mixture of chemicals which, if you were lucky, tasted somewhat like an alcoholic beverage. Their order was placed and the wine turned out to be very good.

"This is a welcomed sight," Marin said as she took another sip of red wine.

Helen looked at Marin as if she were studying her.

"What do you do that causes you to look at synthetic red wine as if you were in love?"

Marin couldn't help but blush.

"I'm sorry. I've been in deep hibernation for two years."
"So that explains it." Helen looked at her and smiled.
"Explains what?"
"The reason why you're so young with all those accomplishments you wear on your uniform."

Marin looked down at her uniform for what seemed like the first time. She then looked up and smiled.

"Well when you work for the government you sometimes don't have a choice."

The smile on Helen's face quickly disappeared. Marin noticed this and quickly asked her about her profession.

"I'm a government psychiatrist on the research vessel Ventros 6."

The two women suddenly made direct eye contact with one another. The two realized that their ships had been at odds with one another for years. The politics of research and planetary settlements had affected both ships with mixed feelings. The Ventros 6 was a vessel that did deep space research on military personnel, their crew and the effects of long term hibernation. Marin would constantly get reports based on their studies that she would have to implement and found that they were more of a hindrance than beneficial asset. The food came as they were about to speak to defend their views to each other. Both women had been in space for a long time and laughed when they saw each others starving look.

"Truce!" Helen said as she tapped Marin's wine glass.

Although no harsh words had been spoken regarding their explorations, each knew the verbal battle was better left for a more appropriate time.

The two women enjoyed their dinner and wine. Neither one had room for dessert. Both presented their government I.D.'s and charged their dinners. Marin couldn't help feeling that anyone who enjoyed her food as Helen did couldn't be as horrible as the years of silent feuding had indicated.

"Well," Marin said quietly, *"That was fun! I really needed that."*
"Which one? The company or the food?" Helen said calmly.
Marin turned to look at her.
"Both," she said.

What Marin wanted was to talk to this woman some more. She was partly fascinated by her interests and partly curious to find out why the hatred between the two ships existed in the first place. But she did not want to seem overly anxious. Both women stood up and Marin grabbed her bags. Helen looked down at the well worn backpack and attaché case. Marin watched Helen's eyes.

"Would you like to walk off dinner?"

Marin held back her usual quick pace.

"Sure, but what about your luggage?"

Helen reached over to help Marin place the backpack on her shoulders. Marin went to a small callbox and punched in some numbers. As they walked a drone appeared. Marin gave her luggage to the drone and had it scan her government I.D.

"See, nothing to it. They'll be waiting for me at my compartment."

Helen could see that Marin was familiar with this procedure. She imagined that Marin had been through the space stations throughout the galaxy and knew the in's and out's of each one. They continued their walk and spoke of cultures and places they had been. Each woman was enjoying the others company when suddenly, Helen's locator went off.

"Excuse me," she said as she ran to the nearest communications box.

Within a minute of that sound a shuttle appeared. She came around the corner and before entering the shuttle walked over to Marin.

"I'm sorry, but my duty calls. You know how it is. Perhaps we can get in touch after work? We have so many interesting things to talk about."

"Yes," Marin said, a bit puzzled.

"See, it can be done."

Marin looked up to face Helen.

"What?" Marin said.

"We can talk and dine together without killing one another!"

Helen laughed and then reached over and kissed Marin on the cheek. She then entered the shuttle and within moments was out of view. Marin felt a bit saddened by her new friend's departure. Marin was trained to be curious. In most cases, it's what has kept her alive. But she could identify with what Helen was saying about duty. She headed towards the government housing areas not realizing how far she and

Helen had walked. She had to walk through the more seedy parts of the area to reach a shuttle heading in her direction. Marin was surprised to see human prostitutes in this area since cyborgs were basic in this area and a lot safer. Marin thought for a moment as an attractive one passed by but smiled then entered the shuttle. She was too tired for anything other than sleep. She wanted to get some rest and go exploring in the morning. Perhaps she'd do some more research on Helen.

CHAPTER 2

The control panel at the center of her cabin was flashing when she reached her room. *What now?* she thought.

MESSAGE: REPORT TO DOCKING BAY 12.

URGENT.

MUST LEAVE AT ONCE.

SECTOR IV OUTBREAK OF VIOLENCE.

TAYBORS ENDANGERING WILDLIFE.

CLASSIFIED EXPERIMENT ABORTED.

Marin formed her fingers into a fist and punched the message monitor. The Wildlife experiment was her brain child. It was a collection of rare species that were undergoing a mating process which meant life for hundreds of almost extinct species. The Classified Experiment was the government's project. It involved bacteria collected on several planets and the studying of its effects on animals and environmental changes. Marin knew her project was in danger. She had developed a very pessimistic attitude when it came to her employer: the government. She changed clothes and was about to leave a message when a familiar buzz sounded.

"All right, I'm coming!"

She opened the door and was greeted by the familiar government escort.

"Your crew is waiting, Captain Stevens."

"Thank you."

And with that she picked up her backpack and was on her way to the ship.

The docking bay was crowded with ships loading soldiers and supplies. Marin couldn't remember when she had seen it so busy.

"Here you are, Captain Stevens. Your orders and crew list."

Marin looked puzzled at the neatly dressed Lieutenant.

"My crew list?"

She looked at the piece of paper.

"Lieutenant! Why has my crew been changed?"

"Several of your crew are in suspension and the commander felt it better to use more experienced personnel."

Marin knew what that line of bullshit meant. The experienced personnel translated to military soldiers. At the space station there was no crew more experienced than Marin's. They had been together for seven years unlike most crews that rotate after three years. Prior to that, they had been in deep space together for three.

"I don't understand. This isn't a mission of war."

"I'm sorry, Captain. If you have any further questions, you'll have to speak with Commander Drugge."

And with that he walked out onto the platform. The speaker system signaled Marin to her ship and to the bridge.

"Good evening, Captain Stevens."

Marin turned around to find a rather good looking lieutenant in regulation Space Force clothing sitting in the co-pilot's seat. She remembered him from her seminar at the academy graduation 5 years ago. He was a bit gangly then but seemed, from the current looks of things, to have turned into quite a handsome fellow.

"Hello, Lieutenant Tier. And what brings you to this busy place?"

"Orders, same as yours Captain."

The intercom went on.

REQUESTING PERMISSION TO COME ABOARD: DR. BARTOK AND SERGEANT MAITTLAND.

"Permission granted."

She turned to the navigator and read his first name on his flight jacket.

"Skip. You don't mind if I call you by your first name? Do you?"

Skip smiled and knew he had found someone he could work contentedly with.

"No mame Captain."

Marin remembered reading his file on the way over to the ship. She remembered thinking that he had the same training as the rest of her crew but was very young for his accomplishments.

"Who is Dr. Bartok? The name sounds familiar."

"I don't know. He's listed as a doctor of psychiatry."

"This mission gets stranger by the minute."

"Ha! Wait till you see the android we have in engineering...... Captain."

Marin turned around at that point to face Skip.

"What! That does it. I'm going to have a look around."

Skip logged in the rest of the crew and gave Marin a data chip copy.

"Okay, but 1/2 hour to lift off Captain."

"Don't worry Skip, I hear you."

Marin didn't mind Skip. She felt she already knew him. It was the rest of the crew she had to deal with on such short notice that she didn't know. She wasn't on the ship five minutes before she started to feel as though the government was blowing the Sector IV incident way out of proportion. She watched the hallways as men and women in full military gear were loading equipment throughout the ship. She tried to get a look at the cases being loaded but there were too many personnel guarding them. She continued walking through the ship and making her usual checks. As Marin turned the corner she bumped into a familiar figure.

"Well, hello again," Marin said with a smile.

"Marin....I...I mean Captain Stevens!"

"Yes, you remembered."

But of course Helen remembered. She had difficulty thinking of any thing else since they dined..... Their leaving was too abrupt as far as Helen was concerned, especially when she wanted to know this person better.

"What are you doing on this ship?" Helen asked, puzzled.

"I'm the Captain and this is my ship."

As Marin said this she remembered why the name on the crew list and intercom sounded familiar.

"You're a doctor?"

"Yes, I'm here to study the crew's reaction to certain condition's which might arise on this mission."

"Guinea pigs again I see. It only seems fitting that instead of having to follow your ridiculous recommendations you finally observe the real trenches."

Marin paused for a moment not wishing to insult her newly found friend. But she also suspected that observation doctors were privy to certain information that she as a field captain was not.

"If you'll excuse me for asking....is there something you know about this mission that I haven't been informed of yet?"

Helen's smile faded.

"No."

Marin didn't like the sound of that answer but decided to let it go and continue her pre-flight checks.

"Well, I hope your quarters are comfortable. I need to continue checking on some cargo listings."

Helen could sense a sudden coldness about the captain but marked it off as mission jitters. After all, she realized that Marin couldn't have much time if any for sleep since their last meeting. Marin walked back through the corridors and up to the flight deck.

"Clearance has been given, Captain."

"Very well. Inform our...crew that we're taking flight in 20 minutes."

Take off was rougher than usual due to the excessive weight the I.R.I.S. was carrying. All systems were reading fine. Several hours into the flight Marin decided that since there was no immediate crisis she would take this time to grab some well needed rest. She logged off and went to her room. She showered and changed into a fresh uniform and already started to feel better. Marin set her timer, notified the bridge and drifted off to a peaceful sleep.

CHAPTER 3

Marin's timer buzzed as she yawned. At least she had a few hours required rest and could log back on duty. She checked in with Skip.

"Well, since everything seems to be fine I'm going to check on that cargo and make sure it's secure."

"Be careful Captain. G-d only knows what we're transporting."

Skip laughed as Marin fastened her locator to her belt and headed off towards the access way. A beep sounded from her communicator as soon as she reached the access way.

"What is it Skip?"

Skip's voice was urgent.

"Okay, tell her I'm on my way."

Marin had barely gotten aboard and beyond the first solar system and already things were beginning to heat up. She reached the cabin door and keyed in the alert code.

"Dr. Bartok. It's Captain Stevens."

The door opened and Helen motioned for her to enter quietly.

"What's going on?"

Marin was truly puzzled by this behavior. She looked in the direction that Helen was pointing. She saw one of the women officer's in Helen's bed shaking feverishly.

"I didn't have time to take her to the medical deck. She was leaning outside my door when I arrived. "

Helen walked over and showed her the strange marks on the woman's arms. At that moment, the woman bolted upright and took a swing at Marin. The punch hit its mark and Marin reeled backwards. The woman then proceeded to attack Helen. Marin used the table as

232

leverage gripping the edges to hoist herself up from the floor. Marin moved towards the woman and delivered a measured blow to the back of the woman's neck. She fell on top of Helen and remained motionless. Marin placed the woman back on the bed and checked her ID badge. The badge read a rookie officer by the name of Andrea Taylor. This was her first deep space mission. She looked to be about 21 years of age. Marin turned and saw Helen on the floor. She turned and went over to tend to the doctor.

"*I'm fine,*" Helen said as she pushed Marin's hand away from her wound.

Marin got up and walked towards the door. Helen removed a black box from her container.

"*I'll keep her restrained until I can run some tests.*"

Marin turned.

"*You'll run nothing until the medical officer aboard this ship has examined her.*"

Marin's voice was strong and commanding. Helen, recognizing Marin's authority, proceeded.

"*I called you because I found a packet of fluorescent blue powder on her. I don't understand why we are transporting a psychotic drug to a war zone. I mean I haven't analyzed it yet but judging from her actions I'd say that's a pretty safe bet.......Are we entering a war zone?*"

Helen's eyes were penetrating.

"*I don't honestly know, doctor. This is a registered research vessel. It's equipped for protection and defense, not battle. There are no drugs of any kind listed on my manifest except for a sulfur derivative.*"

Marin wanted the mission halted right then and there especially when she started to put all the things she had seen upon loading together. She knew she would never succeed in getting the mission cancelled. Technically, she was outnumbered. She knew even with Helen on her side she would never be able to stop what had already been put into motion...at least not without more conclusive proof. Helen looked at her and began to feel outraged.

"*You're the Captain of this ship and that gives you complete control over....*"

Marin interrupted.

"My dear doctor, everything I do is cleared first by the government. You should know that. My duty is to protect Terrans and all other life-forms who have signed the treaty. I may question the orders I am given but I don't usually get any answers."

Marin walked back towards the door.

"Then why do you stay?"

Marin turned to face her and took a deep breath.

"This is neither the time nor the place to get into this, Dr. Bartok. I'll check on the information you have given me and include it in my report.... Good day, doctor!"

With that, Marin clicked in her communicator and telecommed the bridge and command deck.

"Lieutenant Tier."

"Captain!"

"Hi skip. I want a security officer to meet me in the cargo bay in 5 minutes with a sealed manifest. And get two security personnel down to Dr. Bartok's quarters and have them escort an Officer Tayler to the medical deck at once!"

"Yes Captain Stevens."

Although Skip Tier was young, he was highly efficient and sensed when there was a time for levity and a time for total seriousness. Skip knew where this order fell.

Marin felt angered at herself for treating Helen so abruptly but she knew that if she didn't, Helen would win that particular discussion and realize what Marin's true feelings for the government were at that point. As she moved through the corridors of the ship she felt an eeriness about her as though she were being watched. She looked around but saw no one. Not even surveillance monitors were in this stretch of the corridor. Marin walked quickly towards the elevator. The intercom clicked on and she instantly felt a sign of relief.

"Captain Stevens to the cargo bay seven.....Code 4."

"This is Stevens on deck 3. I'm on my way."

She brushed back her hair and entered the lift. She took a deep breath as the door opened to a scene of total chaos. Smoke quickly filled the lift; bursts of fresh air from the vents were quickly mixed with an odor Marin was quite familiar with. She knelt down on the ground and could feel bits and pieces of debris. She was suddenly grabbed from her left side and flung into an adjacent corridor. She heard a second explosion. As she turned to look she was met with a thundering blow to her jaw. She felt instantly numb and drifted off to the sounds of alarms and computerized emergency voices blaring loudly.

Meanwhile back up at the bridge: *"Mother of G-d what was that?"*

Lieutenant Tier looked down at the scanners and looked towards the Navigator for answers.

"Did we hit something or did something hit us? Why didn't the proximity sensors go off?"

Technicians came running from all over to man additional stations.

"Sensors indicate it was an implosion on Deck 4. Interior walls are holding at 98% and no hull breach is evident at this time."

The young female technician calmly read off additional reports and announced that engineering and medical teams were on route to Deck 4.

"Oh my G-d! The captain! She was on route to deck 4."

Skip said as he turned to face the young female technician.

"Has anyone heard from the captain?"

The crew checked their sensors and monitors as they shook their heads. The then looked to Skip with concern.

"Get a team to Deck 4 ....NOW!"

CHAPTER 4

When she came to, Marin was in the medical lab undergoing the scrutiny of Dr. Renil.

"Hold still, Captain. The scanner is almost finished."

"The cargo bay is...."

"It's been taken care of, Captain."

Dr. Renil examined Marin's eyes.

"Are you experiencing any headaches at the moment?"

"No! But then I'm lying down."

With that she attempted to get up. As she rose slowly she noticed three other beds with the outlines of bodies under the sheets. She turned to Lieutenant Tier whom she noticed standing by her side.

"Full report, Lieutenant!"

He stood at attention and clicked off the past two hours' events. Dr. Renil handed Marin some pills as they listened to the report.

"An implosion was detected in the cargo bay at 1100 hours; cause yet unknown. Damage to the structural walls has been repaired. No decompression was detected. Fourteen barrels of Sodium Trioxide were damaged and several medical containers the contents of which are currently being checked by Commander Drugge. The bodies of Officers Carre, Jaquel and Timmons were found among the debris."

Marin's head felt like a whirling dervish with no sign of slowing down. She took a deep breath and tried to get her brain and its thoughts aligned. Her lungs ached as she took deep breaths.

"You said implosion, not explosion. What imploded?"

Skip looked at his clipboard.

"Unknown at this time, Captain."

236

"Who grabbed me and pulled me into the corridor?"

The look of puzzlement gave Marin an uneasy feeling. Dr. Renil moved closer. She looked up as Dr. Helen Bartok came in. Dr. Renil nodded as she spoke.

"You were found on level 3 in front of the elevator. We thought you went to level 4, saw what happened and made it down to level 3 before passing out!"

"Someone in an emergency atmosphere suit pulled me into a corridor as I was crawling on the floor of the cargo bay."

Skip looked at the papers.

"Maybe it was one of the officers."

Dr. Renil walked over to the body closest to her and removed the sheet part way.

"None of these officers that were brought in had emergency atmosphere suits on; just flight uniforms."

"I want an autopsy done on them as soon as possible."

Dr. Renil looked distressed. She had done several tours of duty with the captain and knew that her methods and requests could sometimes be a bit demanding.

"But Captain...."

"I want to know if the fumes killed them or something else did. By the way, which one had the sealed manifest I requested?"

She looked around and then at Skip.

"None, Captain."

And with that Skip pulled the envelope from under his clipboard.

"I was able to download a copy of what they were going to give you."

Skip handed her the list. Dr. Renil entered her code in the computer and requested two additional medical personnel. Helen moved in closer to the bodies but said nothing.

"I'll start on these autopsies immediately, Captain."

On that note she was off to the other room. Marin sent Skip to check on the rest of the ship while she read the manifest.

SEDATIVES-4 CASES (LIQUID)

BANDAGES-4 CASES

TEMPORARY SHELTERS-6 CASES

HYDRATED NOURISHMENT CONTAINERS

-14 CASES

*SODIUM TRIOXIDE-14 BARRELS

*SEE SECONDARY TRANSPORT MANIFEST....

MILITARY TRANSPORT ADVISORY

Nothing highly explosive nor anything that would be likely to explode. Marin turned the page to the secondary transport manifest. Attached to the manifest was an order of authorization for transport to the ship, Isis IV. This was not unusual since Isis IV was a deep space vessel which received much of its supplies from relays of other neighboring ships. Marin called up the command computer to check and make sure that the rest of the ship was functioning normally. She looked at the medical monitors and saw the faces of Carre and Jacquel. Both women had served with Marin before and she smiled as fond memories came to her of their past adventures. Both women were highly skilled and extremely competent. Carre had a family back on Alto V and was only 1 year from retirement. Jacquel she had dated several times before she earned her command as Captain. But because she was part Elodian, this had caused the relationship to end. The government's laws on the treatment of Elodians were very clear: Maintain a friendly posture--no personal contact after hours is permitted. No one knew why and no one was permitted to ask. Marin's eyes began to water. She turned away from the monitors. She got out of bed carefully. She could still feel the effects of the smoke when she took a deep breath. Her ribs ached and her lungs burned with every breath. She decided to head to her room and some form of sanctuary from the outside activities. Along the corridor she saw Helen leaning against her door for support.

"Doctor, are you alright?"

Helen's eyes met Marin's, and then glanced down at the photo in her hand. Marin reached down and took the photo; a freckled, red-haired boy of 18 dressed in his Space Force blues at the academy. The face was a younger reflection of Officer Timmons.

"Your brother?"

Helen's eyes were full of tears as she nodded a yes in response.

"Martin," she managed to say.

Marin entered her code as the doors to her room opened. She motioned Helen in and locked the door behind her. She thought about calling Dr. Renil for some sedatives but knew that she would be interrupting the autopsy regarding the last orders she gave. She decided against the call. She poured Helen a glass of ice water and reached into one of her drawers. She pulled out a photo album and turned to the middle of the book. She took out a photo of Jacquel, Carre and Marin with Carre's children, and handed it to Helen. Marin's ribs ached and her head was still spinning.

"These are the two other officers your brother died with."

Helen looked up to find Marin's filled with tears, but Marin quickly turned away. Helen walked over and hugged Marin from behind. Marin's first thought was to pull away. She had to remain distant. But the album was partly opened to the other photos of the two officers she called friends. Marin pulled away. She wasn't sure which pain was worse; the one in her body or the one in her heart. She sat down on the edge of the desk. Helen looked down at Marin and noticed the familiar red color seeping through one of her bandages.

"Your bandage needs to be changed."

She went to the area of the cabin where emergency bandages were as in all ship cabins. She withdrew some along with some antiseptic. She walked back as Marin was standing.

"I think it is best for you to return to your cabin now doctor."

Marin steadied herself. Dr. Renil's pills must have been taking affect. She turned to Helen and placed her arms around her.

"I'm sorry......."

As Marin tried to speak Helen placed her fingers gently to Marin's lips hushing and quieting her protests and apologies. The softness of her hair was as Marin had imagined the first time they had met.

"Here.....lift up your shirt and I can take care of that bandage for you. Where's your med kit?"

Marin pointed the direction and did as she was told. She was beginning to feel light headed and didn't have much energy to protest. Helen finished bandaging Marin's wound and seemed to take her mind temporarily off of her sadness over Timmons death. Marin knew she couldn't afford to sleep, not just yet. She wanted answers to her questions. She stood up and walked over to one of the small drawers beneath her view screen. She watched in the reflection Helen putting the excess bandages away. Marin reached in and pulled out a small silver tin. She opened it and found 4 tiny blue pills lying side by side. She picked up two and quickly placed them in her mouth. She knew she needed to take only two since they were known as very powerful black market uppers. Just as Helen came back into the room the bridge com lit up and an emergency signal was sent to Marin.

"Captain to the bridge. Code 4 alert. Captain to the bridge!"

She responded to the call as much as the medication would allow her and signaled she was on her way. Helen followed her out the door. Both women wanted to speak but knew this was not the time. Marin brushed the remaining dust from her uniform and tried to shake off the effects of the sedative the doctor gave her and make room for the uppers to take effect. As she entered the elevator she wondered what the two crew members were doing in the cargo bay just before the blast... One of these moments she needed to shower and change into a decent uniform. But again, now was not the time. Marin appeared at once through the dimly lit bridge.

"Officer on deck," Marin stated with authority.

She needed to find out what was going on as quickly as possible.

"Captain! We are being tracked by an unidentified starship. While scanning we experienced loss of power to both starboard solar panels. Thruster banks 1,2,3 and 7 are off line. Engineering is attempting to supply temporary power in banks 4,5, and 6."

Marin scanned the bridge through the flurry of technicians.

"Do we still have defense power and engine mobility?"

"Yes, Captain. Ion drive initiated and laser banks 1, 2, 3, 4, 5, 6, and 7 are at half resonance."

"Lieutenant?"

"Yes, Captain?"

"Any relationship between our unknown observer and our temporary loss of power?"

Skip punched several buttons.

"Unknown at this time, however, our observer is still closing in."

"Speed?"

"Sub-light."

Marin confirmed the distance of the ship below the enlarged view screen at the center of the bridge.

"Go to sub-light speed and raise all defense systems that are operational. Commence communication contact with unidentified ship. Try the intergalactic communication code."

Marin thought to herself....*why now did you choose to show yourself?*

Since she had a feeling this ship had been with her all along. She looked at the star maps to her left. This zone was known for some pirate activity but was reported relatively secure by the recent military patrols. The order was given and the ship came about...still. The ship was barely moving when the sensors began to flash blue. This meant that whoever the observer was had just armed themselves.

"Open communications frequency 5."

Since the year 2000, all peaceful forms of communications throughout the galaxy agreed to use the universal code that went along with it. Marin hoped that the observer would scan her ship before engaging in action. She was right. The lower deck turned pink as the ship's sensors indicated a scanning beam throughout the ship.

"Lieutenant Tier?"

"Yes, Captain?"

"Have the computer give out a full reading on our mysterious observer."

"So ordered, Captain"

With a rush of air Marin turned to find the Terran military commander behind her.

"What the hell is going on?"

Marin looked at the Commander and then at Skip.

"Get this man off my deck. Now!"

Two security officers stood on either side of the commander.

"You've got to be joking. You're going to throw me off? This is an outrage!"

Marin now at frightening boiling point turned to face the commander. She read his name badge: Commander Drugge. She stepped down from her seat and became nose to nose with the Terran.

"What is an outrage dear sir is that you would even consider entering the deck while a possible confrontation was in existence. You know the

rules as well as I. You are in command on planets and stars. I am Captain of this space vessel."

Marin never blinked nor moved from her position. She could smell the Terrans breath.

"Now you have a choice....you can either walk off the deck or back to your quarters or I will have you carried off and into the brig for direct violation of the combat code 783-9. Do you understand me COMMANDER?"

With a silent nod he backed up and entered the elevator. One could have heard a pin drop on deck. Marin turned around and her eyes became transfixed on the sensor screen in front of her. Her senses noticed someone behind and to her side. She glanced down quickly at the hands that were holding onto the arm of the command chair. Dr. Bartok was under regulation order to be present at all mission conflicts. Marin smiled and went back to concentrate on the screen.

"Captain, message from unidentified ship coming on screen."

COMPAQ COMMANDER AKARO OF THE COUNSEL
SHIP ANTARES REQUESTS THE PRESENCE OF THE
COMMANDER OF ISIS I. SIGNAL URGENT.

Marin read the message and relaxed her breathing.

"Communications frequency 2."

"You are clear Captain."

"This is Captain Stevens of the Isis. I will comply with the request of the honored Commander Akaro when her ship is restored to its normal position and friendly status."

Almost immediately the interior of the ship turned pink and all red sensors returned to blue.

"Identified observer has lowered armaments and ship is returning to normal docking speed."

Marin stepped down from the command seat.

"Prepare Explorer I for launch command."

There was a slight pause. Marin turned to meet the eyes of Dr. Bartok. The communications officer realized her hesitancy and responded as normal.

"Yes, Captain."

Helen followed Marin into the transport elevator.

"*You're not serious about meeting with that 'creature' are you? At least take security or one of those military transports with you!*"

Marin faced Helen and laughed.

"*Why, doctor! If I didn't know better I'd swear you were jealous! Besides, bringing security or soldiers could be considered a hostile action to this alien.*"

Helen's face was firm and her eyes fixed.

"*Do you know this alien? You don't have any idea what is on that ship, you don't even....*"

"*I don't even carry a weapon because I don't need one. Commander Akaro is one of the most feared yet respected commanders of the Antarian fleet. She is also a very important political find, if I can talk to her and have her join the federation. Besides, she apparently wants to talk.*"

Helen's face did not change.

"*But she belongs to no galactic government and refuses alliance to all. Most of them, it is said, resemble the vampires of old Earth legends. What makes you so sure of what you're doing?*"

"*The Antarians have a very old code of honor and her signal was urgent.*"

Helen was silent.

"*But your concern, doctor, is duly noted.*"

And with that Marin exited the transport elevator. She then stopped, turned and smiled.

"*Well, doctor, are you coming with me?*"

Helen thought most certainly after that discussion she was not in the best of favor with the captain. She smiled and reached for a space suit. Marin signaled Skip to inform Commander Akaro that she was bringing a Dr. Bartok with her.

CHAPTER 5

The inside of the Antarian ship was huge. The corridors were dimly lit and Marin guessed that it was to try and diminish the size of the ship. Yet what light was available lit the huge cathedral ceilings like those she saw in her ancient history books. The arches and curves gave the appearance of being in a great hall. As Helen gazed up in wonder she bumped into the commander. A shadowy figure stood at the lighted end of the corridor. Helen caught her breath suddenly surprised.

"Welcome, Captain."

The Antarian was tall and well proportioned but had a series of scars to the side of her face. Her suit was black with various small armaments attached.

"My commander is within the engine room. Please follow me."

The series of chambers and hallways were varying degrees of temperatures and the air seemed almost stagnant in some areas.

"Perhaps Dr. Bartok can assist our medical officer in Corridor B."

The voice was deep, yet controlled with a slight foreign accent. Both women turned to see a very tall, attractive woman dressed in a black uniform with silver trim.

"Commander Stevens, I'm sorry for the behavior of my crew or lack of, but we have run into a problem with our life-support systems and we can not seem to repair it."

Marin looked around and saw heat burns and scared wires.

"Did your ship sustain battle damage?"

Commander Akaro walked closer to Marin as if she were trying to determine her response.

"Yes. We lost our engineer and one of our medical officers."

Marin knew that the Antarians were deep space people and were the type, as legend had it, to finish a fight but would rarely ever start it.

"Well, perhaps I can take a look at the problem first."

Commander Akaro motioned for the young officer standing next to her to move next to Helen.

"Thank you Commander Stevens. This way."

The room, which housed the computer systems, was partially burned. Probably a helix beam fired at point blank range. Marin assessed the damage and began to calculate the time for major repairs. Helen went with the young officer and disappeared into a far off corridor. The commander of the Antares watched Marin as she re-directed the ship's command into one main computer bank. Marin started out as a computer programmer in the medical section of the corps. She worked her way up slowly through the ranks and never thought that in the 35 years as a commander she would ever be reprogramming an Alexis Data Computer. But as a captain of her own ship on deep space voyages it was up to her to fix things when the specialists and crew had exhausted their talents. So she was well versed in the operations and repair of a lot of ship systems. Marin used her own ship's computer to issue commands back through the Antarian ship. Marin knew politically she was taking a risk since the Antarians were not known for their friendly nature and Marin's computer held a wealth of information which could be deemed sensitive in nature. But so far they had shown her and Helen courtesies she had not expected. She took a chance that her knowledge of computers would still be up to date and therefore would not cause the computers to fuse which would then cause a transfer of information. Her communication badge went off as she began pulling wires.

"Yes....what is it?" as she reconnected several fused wiring harnesses.

"Sorry for the interruption Captain but a Commander Drugge is demanding you return at once and cease your current action."

Marin stood up.

"Lieutenant! Tell Commander Drugge that is he interferes with the running of my ship one more time I will escort him to the brig personally!"

"Yes Captain"

She kneeled down once again to finish what she had started. Once again her badge went off.

"My apologies Captain but he says that the time table is crucial regarding his mission and......"

Marin interrupted: *"If Commander Drugge would let me finish what I'm doing perhaps he would be at his destination a bit early. Tell the Commander that his time table will be met. Now see to it that he resumes his station."*

Hours passed as Marin worked pulling harnesses and welding wires together. She knew her engineer could have easily done the job but would have had to put up with his complaints for the remained of the trip. Marin gave the final command and replaced several wires she had pulled before.

"Alright, Commander Akaro, all life support systems should be back on line and long range communication is back to 80%."

Commander Akaro's eyes were fixed on Marin's every move. Akaro placed a hand gently on Marin's shoulder.

"Thank you, Commander. I am grateful for your assistance and will escort your ship as far as my code allows. Here is my sub-light command code should you ever need me."

Marin felt a little strange. It almost felt as if the commander was making a pass at her. But she smiled and racked it up to simply being "friendly." To have an Antarian as an ally was extremely desirable since they made excellent, loyal fighters. And since their paths had crossed once before she felt that she had an advantage that no other person had with the

Antarians.......familiarity. Marin always admired their attack systems and weaponry. She even studied their style of warfare in the academy. But since no one really met Antarians the writing were supposedly methods that had been written down through generations and stories from those they had supposedly vanquished. Back to reality, she said to herself quietly. The loyalty of one Antarian was not going to solve her problems of the moment. Helen was still working in Corridor B. She sent requests for additional medical assistance and even though her title was that of psychiatrist she still remembered her training from med school. When the last of the injured Antarians had been secured, Helen signaled the return of the extra personnel. She took one last look at the ship fully lit. It was a magnificent display of craftsmanship. She wondered if their home world shared in the same architecture. She entered the shuttle and found herself wishing she could have stayed longer.

CHAPTER 6

The Antarian ship released its docking umbilical and drifted within a safe monitoring distance. The official envoy who, up until now had remained at a quiet observation distance, came up to Marin and blocked her passage to the elevator.

"Commander, there is not precedent for this. You will have to clear it with counsel."

Marin resisted the urge to slap this little man before her.

"Commissioner Garret, I am about to set a precedent with the Antarians and as for the counsel....they have already been notified. Perhaps my knowledgeable Commissioner would like to offer his assistance with the fact that my original crew has been taken off this mission and I have been placed in charge of soldiers I don't know and who are NOT answerable to me. Why is that Commissioner? What kind of mission are we on?"

Marin's voice was firm, yet tempered. The commissioner backed up and looked at Marin with narrowed eyes.

"I don't know what you're talking about, Captain. However, if you are 'uncomfortable' with your command, then I am sure that the counsel can provide a remedy."

Marin was about to answer when a sudden jolt rocked the ship. Lights began to flash and emergency beacons went into motion.

Marin whispered under her breath, *"What now!"*

She pushed past the commissioner and said, *"We will finish this later Commissioner Garret!"*

Marin raced up to the command center and saw smoke and wires from the entry way.

"*Report Lieutenant!*"

"*We're being fired upon by 2 unidentified ships. The Antarian ship has engaged in battle with the first ship. The engine room has minor structural damage and our galactic communications system is down. Minor injuries of the crew reported.*"

Marin looked around at the crew.

"*Who the hell was monitoring the long range sensors? Didn't anybody pick these guys up on sensors?*"

"*They didn't show up on sensors, Captain.*"

A woman from behind the fallen wires responded.

"*Have we tried to contact the ships?*"

"*Yes, Captain, but no response.*"

"*Get a close up of the shaded area on that ship. How are the armored shields holding?*"

"*Armored Shields are at 80%, Captain.*"

In simple English, that meant that they could sustain two more direct hits before things became critical.

"*Evasive action people. Let's not give them a target.*"

Marin was praying that the Antarians were as good as their war-like reputation and that Commander Akaro would be back to help when she finished off the first ship.

The close-up of the unidentified ship revealed a shadowy outline of a spider with small skull and crossbones painted over the body. Some things throughout the centuries don't seem to change much she thought. Marin's eyes narrowed and her muscles tightened.

"*Pirate ship! Damn it! Get Commissioner Garret up here on the double!*"

"*Yes, Captain.*"

"*Who is near the cargo bay?*"

Her order was calm.

"*Checking.....a. soldier Pruett.*"

"*Tell Pruett to place two of those blue containers in the transport chamber.*"

Skip looked over at Marin.

"*Captain, he states that he cannot do that without the proper code.*"

At that moment Commissioner Garret entered. Marin moved quickly and grabbed Garret's arm and clenched it tightly.

"See that ship, Commissioner Garret? That's a pirate freighter and it's firing at us at point-blank range. We're at 80% shield strength and going fast. Now, he wants something, Commissioner, and I have an idea of what that might be. But I have a soldier down in the cargo bay that needs the code, which I don't have, to release that cargo. Now don't tell me you don't know what I'm talking about because you're going to die along with the rest of us unless you let me do my job!"

The commissioner starred at the view screen at the freighter.

"I cannot give you that code. Millions depend on that cargo and...."

"Perhaps you didn't understand me, Commissioner. "

Another powerful wave hit the ship.

"Armored shields at 70% and weakening Captain!"

Marin reached out and grabbed him by the collar.

"Millions are not going to see one speck of that cargo if we can't remove ourselves from this situation. We will all die if I don't bait that ship!"

Suddenly, another blast rocked the ship.

"Code R-Y17 Authorization Garret."

The open communication between the soldier and the helm was still functional. The soldier released two of the blue containers. Marin figured that the freighter would break their firing to either inspect or blow up the containers. What she didn't expect was their next move.

"Captain, they're...."

"Yes, I can see what they're doing."

Everyone's eyes were on the view screen.

"Captain, they are powering up their weapons again."

"Captain, sensors are picking up another ship behind us. It's the Antarian ship. It's preparing to......."

The screen lit up the entire console. The light was too bright for Marin's eyes and she winced in pain as she shielded her eyes.

"Captain!"

Marin looked at the screen cautiously but saw nothing but space.

"Captain, the Antarian ship just blew up the pirate freighters."

Marin sat back in her chair and stared at the screen before her. Her face tightened once more and she turned to the Commissioner.

"I want to see you in my cabin in five minutes, privately!"

Before the Commissioner could respond, Marin was up and out into the corridor. Marin thought to herself, how could she be so foolishly blind? That pirate freighter beamed those blue containers aboard almost immediately as though they were expecting them. And why didn't the ship's sensors pick the ship up sooner. Marin rushed over to the communications screen.

"Have the Commissioner and Dr. Bartok meets me in the cargo bay at once!"

"Yes, Captain."

She walked down the corridors as men and women picked up bits and pieces of their quarters that flew into the hallway when the attack came. She was tired of playing a guessing game. She was tired of not having all the answers. She could have resigned her commission before this. She could have settled down with Chris and been happy. She had to chuckle at that. Who was she kidding? She was born in space and entered the flight academy at an early age. All she knew was space travel. Sure she had seen some planets that intrigued her but none that gave her that overwhelming sense of home. She shook off the "getting in touch with self" theories and thought about the current problems at hand.

CHAPTER 7

She gave the access code to gain entry into the cargo hold. Almost instantly Commissioner Garrett came flying past Helen towards the Captain.

"Captain, this is an outrage! What is the meaning of this behavior?"

Marin stepped past the commissioner to face Helen. She smiled slightly and then turned towards Garrett.

"Commissioner, I have had it with your political game playing. You may feel that crew members are expendable and that you have some immunity over the laws of our government but...."

"What are you babbling about?"

"Yes, Marin," Helen said, with a bit of concern.

"What are you going on about?"

"It's very simple....drugs. Drugs are what I'm 'Babbling' about."

The Commissioner burst out in laughter.

"Drugs! This is normal cargo on any research vessel, especially one traveling to Sector IV where there are no medical outposts. This ship is expected to be not only a research vessel but a hospital as well."

Marin notices the change in his tone. Marin walked calmly over to one of the blue containers. She removed a welding kit from the large pocket of her uniform. She fired the torch and began to cut a square swatch on the outside of the container. Commissioner Garret moved towards Marin but Helen moved in between the two. Marin extinguished the torch and tapped at the cut out she just made. The metal square fell to the ground and in between the shell of the container was a powdery residue. Marin tilted the container and out came a white powder flowing like fine particles of sand.

"You may be right about the service of this ship, Commissioner; however, we are not permitted to carry a Classified A2 drug. This drug is highly addictive and was supposedly banned from Earth, Terran and Federated planets eight years ago. I wonder why it is so nicely concealed within these containers."

Marin walked over to one of the three security teams that showed up. She removed the envelope from one of them.

"The lead shield prevents anything from showing up on X-ray."

She handed the photo to Garret.

"And the sulfur drug inside the container prevents the dogs from sensing it. Someone's gone through a lot of trouble to make sure this drug gets to its destination with very little trouble. The problem is....seems like everyone knows what's inside this container except you, Commissioner."

Helen was pushed from behind to reveal Commander Drugge.

"Ah, yes, the military escort of this mission. Please come in, Commander. No need for hostilities, Drugge. We're all friendly here."

Drugge's hand moved over to his weapon but didn't remove it.

"Cut the clowning, Stevens. I was right. You should have retired along with that last mission."

The Commissioner moved along side Drugge.

"You could have gone out a wealthy Captain with a clean record. Not it seems your record will be slightly altered. The politics and the will of our people have always been able to come to agreement on things with the slight exception of drug addiction."

Drugge drew his laser and pointed it towards Marin.

"Yes, you see captain; certain members of government did not count on such unanimous agreement of the ban on CV2 and the successful treatment of those addicted. Since they made the treatment free of cost with no threat of prosecution to those who once sold it, the profit margin went down considerably. But now, thanks to your help, we now have a new planet and a new paying customer, Nilos 7."

Marin was puzzled. Helen could see the confused look and turned to face her.

"You see, Nilos 7 is a small mining planet the size of Earth's moon. With miners working at an increased pace the profits would be doubled. Nilos 3 was an independent planet up until a few years ago when a certain

Captain recommended changes. Now it's a planet whose profits are seen as a necessary addition to the council. Nilos 7 and its small moon is the last remaining planet to hold out."

Clarity began to pour onto Marin's face once more.

"Who owns Nilos 7?"

Helen looked up at her and smiled. Drugge spoke as he motioned for Marin and Helen to move to the security team.

"It is owned by the Antarians."

Marin now noticed that only one team was made of her crew. Drugge smiled as he talked.

"Yes, it's where the Antarians get most of their materials for their ships and weaponry. Aside from which it is nestled right in the heart of Sector IV. The Taybors found our hidden supply and ate right through the containers. The harmless little creatures went out of control. Our supply was gone completely so we had to prepare another shipment. We only have seven containers left before the two-year production can begin again. So you see, Stevens, we're not about to let you destroy what we've worked so hard to set in motion."

Marin moved closer to Helen.

"How will you explain my disappearance to the rest of the crew?"

Marin needed time which she knew she didn't have.

"Might I remind you that they are not your crew, but mine? At one time or another we have all worked on that pirate freighter. We were upset when the Antarians blew up some of our friends."

Marin couldn't believe that Commander Akaro was part of this plan but she had no proof otherwise. Drugge aimed the laser at Marin. Helen moved forward.

"No! Let me give her a sedative. Then you can make it look like an accident. Less questions and talks."

Drugge took his eyes off Marin for a moment.

"Not bad, doctor. I knew you had to be with us sooner or later. After all, you are a psyc. Doctor. You can tell the good stuff from the bad, ah, yes."

Marin's eyes grew watery as Helen injected her. She was starting to feel something for Helen but now felt betrayed all the way around.

CHAPTER 8

Marin opened her eyes slowly to reveal her own compartment. She turned her head towards the sound of voices.

"I always knew you were hot. I just didn't know how hot. I remember seeing you with that wimp escort at the last convention. All I could think of was you out of that uniform."

Marin could see Drugge kissing Helen and moving his hands over her body. Marin felt rage and tried to move but her hands were linked together by an electronic beamed restraint. She could move her body but not her hands. They were cuffed in front of her. She glanced once again at Helen. Drugge had his uniform off at the waist and was working on Helens. Marin thought if she could reach a laser she could kill both of them with one shot. She felt a disturbance behind her left ear. She moved her hands up very carefully. She felt the back of her ear and recognized the small pin like projection. She carefully removed it and placed it in her mouth. The dull blue light of the restraints went off as soon as Marin short circuited the lock with the small pin from her mouth. She then remained very still as she saw the two lovers move towards her.

"Come on, Drugge, haven't you ever wanted to do it with two women before?"

"Babe, I have done it with two women before. You think this will be that good?"

Helen moved down his body and lowered herself to his crotch.

"Well she is kind of attractive."

Helen placed a hand firmly over his trousers. Marin couldn't believe this was the same woman she had known on this mission. Drugge was beginning to loose his coolness. He was giving way to his sexual desires as his trousers began to fill out. Helen kept rubbing as she rose up to his nipples and began to bite them. Marin couldn't figure out whether she was getting sick or turned on. She suddenly realized that Helen was watching her. Marin looked at Drugge, who was totally turned on with his eyes at half mast, not concentrating on anything but Helen's hand. She unfastened his trouser uniform and pulled them off. She threw them next to Marin on the bed. Marin searched quickly for Drugge's laser while his back was to her. Suddenly, Drugge stopped Helen's hand. Marin grasped the laser and resumed her prisoner position.

"Alright, doctor, enough foreplay. I have something you can mend."

Drugge's sexual readiness was apparent. He turned Helen around and unzipped her uniformed trousers and then turned around again.

"You should like this, doc."

Marin's line of fire would be awkward; could she hit Drugge first and then Helen? Helen stopped Drugge. Marin gripped the laser tight in her left hand.

"I like it from the front," Helen said.

She placed herself next to Marin on the cot and motioned for him.

"Make sure it goes in smooth."

He held himself with one hand and grabbed her leg with the other. Just as he moved to enter her Marin sprang up. She looked at Drugge and smiled. The quiet zap of the laser was all that could be heard. Helen struggled to get the weight of Drugge pushed off of her.

"I wish you would have hit him sooner. I didn't exactly want him inside."

Suddenly, Helen realized that Marin was pointing the laser at her.

"Marin, I know what you're thinking."

Marin gripped the laser tighter.

"How could you know? I don't even know what I'm thinking, you......
you disgust me."

Marin slapped her across the face.

"I trusted you. I saved your damned life! You......."

Marin lowered the weapon and buttoned her shirt. Helen starred at Marin.

"Did my shot go to your head?"

Marin raised the laser once more.

"Have you lost it totally? Why do you think I insisted on giving you the injection? Why do you think I threw his damned pants over to you? Why do you think I even touched him! I tried to diffuse the situation the best way I could with as little casualties as possible."

Helen's eyes flashed. Marin looked down at the gold chain Helen wore. The necklace held a heart and in black onyx was a small lambda. Marin lowered the weapon. She turned away from Helen. Marin's stomach began to turn.

"Finish dressing doctor. We've got work to do."

CHAPTER 9

Marin had to take a chance on Commander Akaro. Why else would she have destroyed the pirate freighter? If she had been part of Drugge's plan she would have done nothing. Marin hoped the Commander was not too far along in space. Helen would have to detain the Commissioner, hopefully not in the same manner as Commander Drugge. Skip Tier was finishing his rounds when he ran into Marin.

"Captain! The Commissioner said you weren't feeling well."

"No, Skip, I'm fine, but the rest of the ship may be in danger."

"How so?"

"Those military personnel we took on board have a mission of their own, which may involve the destruction of this ship."

Marin explained the events as she showed him the containers. The powder was still on the floor where Marin had emptied it. Skip told Marin of those crew members which were on her original flight who could be trusted. Skip then set about to try and make contact with the Antarians. If any of the military personnel were to ask, Skip would simply say that Drugge had ordered it. Marin had a feeling the Antarians never made a deal with the Commissioner or his people. This whole setup was based on making contact for the first time. Marin was hoping since she was the first that she would be able to explain. Marin's beeper went off. Helen was using inner ship communication to contact Marin.

"Lieutenant Tier, I'll be in Dr. Bartok's quarters till further notice."

Helen looked up suddenly as the doors opened.

"I got here as soon as I could. Drugge will out for several hours. I gave him a powerful sedative."

Helen reached down and pulled up a small electronic screen.

"You were right about the Antarians not knowing. Look at this communiqué."

Marin read the screen that Helen handed to her.

"Any mention of who is on the inside?"

"What do you mean?"

Marin walked over to the table and sat down.

"There has to be someone who can give governmental okay and assign special troops to this mission."

Helen sat in the chair across from Marin.

"Isn't that the Commissioner?"

"No, he hasn't got that power out here. Drugge was contacting someone on a regular basis on the priority channel."

Marin rubbed her face trying to think. Helen got up and poured both of them some juice.

"I've got it! Yates...Sebastian Yates. He was recently elected to the Counsel of Elders due to Bernard Simpson's death."

Helen then set down the glasses and looked for the screen where she had read the information. Marin sipped the juice realizing how the lack of food and a shower made her feel. Helen found the file and handed it to Marin.

"You're right, that could be it. But, what now?"

Helen sat down again.

"Send him into a panic. Contact the other members and send them a voice transcript. Then televise the destruction of the cargo."

The Captain was being hailed.

"Captain Stevens, the Antarian Commander is responding to your message. She will await your presence on her ship."

"Perfect, Skip! Good work."

"Oh! Captain, what about the military personnel?"

"Have them report to the cargo bay. They'll think Drugge or the Commissioner made a deal and they're off to unload the cargo. I'll arrange things with Ali Akaro."

Marin signed off. Helen looked at Marin.

"We are on a first name basis already?"

Marin looked up at Helen.

"Why? Are you jealous?"

Marin smiled and looked at Helen. She was smiling and moved closed to Marin.

"*Why? Should I be?*" Helen said in a low seductive tone.

Marin got up from the table and looked at Helen.

"*We don't have time for this. We'll sit down and talk when this is finished, okay?*"

Helen got up and walked Marin to the door.

"*Okay.*"

CHAPTER 10

Marin's visit was quite different from her last one. She was greeted by two impeccably dressed officers who were very polite. The ship's interior was fully lit revealing a cavern of machinery and crew. A tall figure appeared from the hallway.

"I did not expect that we would meet again so soon, Captain."

Ali was firm yet soft in her approach to Marin.

"Thank you for taking care of that freighter."

The Antarian motioned for Marin to follow. She led her to a room decorated with various weapons of both ancient and modern times. A small table had been prepared with fruits, breads and several pitchers of deliciously smelling nectar.

"Well, after all, I did owe you one, did I not?"

Marin smiled as she looked at the food in front of her.

"I'm afraid I have yet another favor to ask of you."

Commander Akaro smiled back.

"Very well, but first let us eat. I sense it has been a while since you have had nourishment."

Marin wondered what else she could sense but didn't want to get off track.

Time seemed to pass slowly as the stage was being set. Marin knew that only one mistake could ruin the plan and cause the deaths of several people including her own. Every player had to do their part quickly and efficiently when the signal was given. Marin waited in her command chair as she thought over the events of the last five hours. She waited patiently as the instrument panel flashed a familiar governmental message. Marin had sent the visual tape of the Antares encounter with the space pirates shortly after leaving Ali Akaro's ship. She prayed now that the council would do the right thing.

THE COUNSEL OF ELDERS HAS REVOKED
COMMANDER DRUGGE'S MILITARY ORDERS
REGARDING NILOS 7.
REGARDING ALL MILITARY PERSONNEL
UNDER COMMANDER DRUGGE
ARE TO REPORT TO SPACE DOCK 12 FOR
IMMEDIATE INTERROGATION.
AS OF THIS DATE ISIS MISSION HAS BEEN
CANCELLED. ISIS 1 IS TO REPORT TO SPACE
DOCK 5 FOR REFITTING.

Marin closed her eyes with relief as things started to move in her favor. Skip was down in the cargo bay and ordered all weapons handed over. Marin was amazed that no shots were fired. Skip knew better and simply leaned on the twelve crew members holding laser reflectors. No one seemed to argue. Commissioner Garret was brought to the main control beside Marin.

"I hope your quarters weren't too uncomfortable Commissioner Garret! You should like this next vision."

Marin pushed the green pin on her hand held communication device and at once the bay doors opened. Out drifted the remaining seven blue containers. Commissioner Garret's shouts fell on deaf ears as the Antarians destroyed all seven containers in the blink of an eye.

"They do that so well, don't you think, Commissioner?"

He turned towards Marin.

"You're crazy! Do you realize what you have just done?"

Marin leaned down to face him.

"Yes, I think I do. I've destroyed seven containers of deadly drugs, put you and Drugge out of business, found the traitor within the Counsel of Elders and gained a new planet to the Federation!"

262

Helen thought of the other things Marin had done but felt it best not name them now. Marin set a course back home to the space station and proceeded to begin filling out the necessary paper work for this mission. All in all she thought it went well since this was the first time a council sanctioned mission lasted only two solar days.

CHAPTER 11

*COUNSEL ELDER SEBASTIAN YATES STEPS
DOWN DUE TO HEALTH REASONS.*
Marin chuckled at the headlines as she picked up the old fashioned
newspaper before being seated. Given the choice she always chose the
paper over the electronic news pad. She looked forward to enjoying
a good meal after the two days of debriefing and five hours of filling
out forms for three different departments. She looked at her reflection
from the highly polished mirrored windows in the restaurant. Her new
uniform and new position felt good Marin thought. The restaurant was
quiet this evening as Marin began to relax and become part of the mood.
"May I share this table?"
Marin turned around to object when she caught sight of those
familiar eyes.
"Hi, I was...."
"You were going to tell me to take a hike, right?" Helen said as she
started to turn around.
"Yes, well, no. I...."
Finally, exasperated Marin got up and touched Helen's arm gently.
"Would you like to join me for dinner?"
Marin thought it best to switch subjects and control her nervous
thoughts. She was glad to see a friendly face again.
"Perhaps this time we'll have room for dessert," Marin said innocently.
Helen smiled.
"Perhaps this time, Commander, we'll have time to talk."
Marin cleared her throat as the Elodian came to hand them menus.
"Would you ladies prefer candles?"

265

Before Marin could object, Helen answered softly, *"Yes, thank you."* Marin was not sure what the evening would bring, but smiled at the prospect of finding out. The two women became lost in the atmosphere that the candlelight produced.

The End

Printed in the United States
By Bookmasters